WISH HER
SAFE AT HOME

Stephen Benatar

Wish Her Safe at Home

THE BODLEY HEAD
LONDON SYDNEY
TORONTO

British Library Cataloguing
in Publication Data
Benatar, Stephen
Wish her safe at home.
I. Title
823'.914[F]   PR6052.E/
ISBN 0-370-30491-8

© Stephen Benatar 1982
Printed in Great Britain for
The Bodley Head Ltd
9 Bow Street, London WC2E 7AL
by Redwood Burn Ltd, Trowbridge
Set in Linoterm Plantin
by Keyset Composition, Colchester
First published 1982

For my family again
—with love

1

My great-aunt in middle age became almost a recluse and when she died I remembered very little of her, because the last time I'd visited that stuffy basement flat in St. John's Wood had been thirty-seven years before, when I was only ten. So perhaps my most vivid recollection was of hearing her tell us, my mother and me, on at least half a dozen occasions, like a favourite fairy tale, the full unchanging story of a show called *Bitter Sweet*. Afterwards, I couldn't believe it was the only show which she had ever seen, but she almost made it sound like that. This was 1944, some fifteen years after its first London production, yet she spoke of it each time as though she had been present just the previous night. And on those six occasions, too, she entertained us with the same two songs. She would stand up, this rather dumpy woman, and render them so seriously—either with her hands touching her bosom or else with arms thrown wide; her gaze intense and misted; her full voice slightly throaty—that my mother and I had to look down very hard into our laps and I would drive my nails into my palms; it was a strangely companionable time for both of us. And almost forty years later I could still hear, very clearly, my Aunt Alicia as she sang: 'Although when shadows fall I think if only . . .'—there'd be a brief, sacramental hush—

> Somebody splendid really needed me,
> Someone affectionate and dear,
> Cares would be ended if I knew that he
> Wanted to have me near . . .

Somehow just those five lines stayed with me without my making any effort to retain them and one afternoon in the playground I surprised all the other girls at school by

7

suddenly bursting forth with them during break. The most popular songs of the period were 'Swinging on a Star' and 'Don't Fence Me In' and morale-boosting, lump-in-the-throat things like 'The White Cliffs of Dover', but this one became an instant hit, a curiosity, and I was often asked for it: Rachel's 'party piece'. It seemed to bring me both acceptance and renown and I used to do some wicked take-offs of the old lady—she was at that time about fifty—my exaggerations growing coarser and more extravagant with nearly every repetition. I used to have frequent hangovers of guilt about this, naturally, but I would tell myself that it didn't do my great-aunt any harm and that it certainly did me a fair amount of good (of a kind). I could uneasily reconcile it with the knowledge I had even then, that I very much hoped to find, one day, my place in heaven.

Each time my mother and I came away from Neville Court my mother would say something like, 'Poor Alicia. One can only humour her.'

'Is she mad?' I once asked.

'Good heavens, no. At least . . .'

'Yes?'

'Well, if she is, she's perfectly happy. There are many who'd even envy her that type of madness.'

She didn't seem to me to be perfectly happy: stout, downy-cheeked, heavily dusted with powder that was most cloyingly scented, wearing dresses which, as my mother said, were made for women thirty years younger—or anyway had been once: above all, always wistfully searching, as it seemed to me later, for something unattainable in the dark corners of that lush and over-heated room—perhaps, even, for somebody splendid, affectionate and dear, who really needed her; who could say? No. When I was ten years old I certainly didn't regard her as especially enviable.

And my mother said—I suppose it must have been that same occasion—'Actually your father did once mention there being a strain of insanity in his family.' Pause. 'So all naughty little girls had better watch out, hadn't they?'

I knew this last bit was a joke; in any case, I wasn't particularly naughty.

Aunt Alicia was looked after by a large and blustering Irishwoman called Bridget (who perhaps saved my life once, by crying out sharply as I was about to turn on the kitchen light with wet hands—nobody had ever told me) and when my aunt suddenly moved away from St. John's Wood, without appearing to inform anyone of where she was going, or why she was going, Bridget went with her. Even the porter hadn't been left a forwarding address, as we discovered, tealess, on the last occasion that we called; nor could he bring to mind the name of the removal firm. We received no Christmas cards nor birthday cards nor five-pound notes to be shared between us, and gradually, despite the frequent bitter murmurings which this at first gave rise to (though I myself, I think, felt no resentment), I more or less forgot about my aunt: both that snatch of song and the impersonations—if that's what they could ever have been called—soon proved to have had only transitory appeal. Even when my mother died I heard nothing; perhaps Alicia never read the papers. This should have seemed sad (it didn't in the slightest) because by then she was the only relative I had left—always supposing, of course, that I *did* have her left—and to live our lives out in such ignorance of one another appeared a sacrilege of everything the word 'family' should have stood for.

Later I learned that Bridget (who may once have saved my life) committed suicide in Bristol at the age of eighty-six, and that Aunt Alicia, who was two years older, had gone on living in the same house, alone with Bridget's body, for a further six weeks before the situation was discovered. She had then been taken away to the geriatric ward of St. Lawrence's.

'Tragic,' said Mrs Pimm, the almoner, some months afterwards, answering my enquiries as fully as she could. 'Tragic,' she said, her round face shining with health and now, all this time later, even with enjoyment, with a storyteller's relish. 'The old lady only lasted for a short while. And to end like that! Imagine! When you think of the background she'd come from. Well, it was obviously well-to-do. Middle-class, turn-of-the-century. A nanny. Little bottom lovingly powdered with talc . . . A pretty little thing, I'd think, and probably made much of . . .'

9

Mrs Pimm pursed her lips and shook her head and there was silence: an unconvincing moment of requiem. Her small office, white and functional for the most part, had a framed photograph of her family on the desk and two large water-colours on the walls, both depicting gardens. 'Like the woman with the cats,' she said.

'Cats?'

'Oh, yes, didn't you read about it? Nine of them. Pets. But when she died—and she, too, was a ripe old age—poor things, they couldn't get any food, so they started eating her and after that they started eating each other. Well, that's nature, I suppose, but as one of my youngsters said to me, "Mum . . . just suppose they didn't *wait*?" Well, I soon shut her up, of course, but just the same I couldn't stop thinking about it.'

I shuddered.

'I often think of *her* little bottom being powdered too, her rosy little lips being kissed. The flesh had been torn away all round the mouth,' she added, noddingly.

'Horrible.'

'I'm sure,' she said, 'she never thought she'd come to that.'

Her laugh in some way wasn't callous. It was aimed against the irony of life rather than the poor woman with the cats who may or may not have had her bottom lovingly powdered.

'Linda Darnell—such a beautiful actress—dying in a fire,' she said. 'C. B. Cochran slowly scalding to death in his bath. Such glamorous, successful lives as both of them enjoyed. Nearly anybody would have envied them, you know.'

She clearly had a catalogue of such disasters. And yes, too, there *was* almost a relish: a compensatory garment to wrap about herself to make up for the lack of beauty or glamour or success that she felt existed in her own life.

The office had grown increasingly claustrophobic; ceiling moving slowly down on you. You couldn't like her. She told me of a man who had jumped off a high building in New York. Oh, yes, he had meant to kill himself and he'd succeeded. Poor man. He had also killed the gentleman that he'd fallen on top of. 'He must have thought,' she said, 'that things just couldn't possibly get any worse . . .' No, you couldn't like her; and yet I sat and yet I listened.

Why?

I drew her back to the subject of my great-aunt.

She said, 'Of course, you realize she was gaga?'

That came as no surprise.

'How she and that Irish woman ever managed at all for so long: that's what beats me. And how they used to scream at one another, the neighbours said. Even through those thick walls it could be heard. How they used to curse, as though they were quite doing one another in. Pathetic,' said Mrs Pimm. 'You'd expect to have a bit of peace, wouldn't you, when you got to that age? And the filth,' she said, 'the squalor; the mountain of rubbish in one of those nice rooms . . .'

But I had already heard about that, and witnessed the deterioration it had left behind.

When I left, Mrs Pimm accompanied me to the door of the hospital.

'Still, there you are,' she repeated—these were almost her final words to me. 'I suppose none of us ever know what we're going to come to in the end.'

I think that, vaguely, she meant this to be reassuring. While she went back to her coloured photograph of a similarly beaming apple-cheeked husband and three gormless-looking daughters and to her summer gardens filled with roses I went on, alone, to the bus stop; and I remembered Bridget letting me lick out, on my finger, the cake mixture from the bowl and telling me of the pictures she'd seen on her days off and about her two harum-scarum nephews in Donnegal who were both waiting to marry me when I grew up; and I remembered my great-aunt speaking of swirling ball gowns almost entirely in pastel shades and of Lady Shayne, the erstwhile Sarah Millick, defier of convention and runner-off to happiness (and tragedy; yet would she then have sacrificed the one in order to avoid the other?), now old but with an exquisite gown and a still slim figure, finally left alone on stage through the self-absorption of those who had surrounded her, standing quite still and beginning to laugh:

11

a strange, cracked, contemptuous laugh: then suddenly flinging wide her arms—

> Though my world has gone awry,
> Though the end is drawing nigh,
> I shall love you till I die,
> Goodbye!

And I thought of that as I patiently waited for the bus to move off: the one really lovely evening which I knew for sure my aunt must have had in her life: an evening of exhilaration and joy and perhaps too—at thirty-five or thirty-six—of hopes of a romance.

2

'Sylvia! Oh, I don't believe it! Just listen to this,' I said.

It was a Saturday and we were sitting over a late breakfast—she with that morning's paper, myself with the previous day's. I had been reading some of the Personal Ads: 'Love is a red silk parachute. Take care. Swarms of kisses.' 'Divorced? Separated? Single? Then meet new faces at private parties . . .' My eyes had suddenly slipped across to the next column, as though supernaturally drawn there, and I had seen, with both a start and a feeling of humming yet soundproofed distance, my own name.

'Can it be me?'

Sylvia, having lowered her own paper, messily, was now staring with an impatient frown, her eyes screwed up slightly against the smoke from her cigarette. 'Give.'

I read it out loud: 'Would the person born as Rachel Waring, last known to be living in Marylebone in 1944, please contact Messrs Thames & Avery (reference Wymark), Bristol 841981, whereupon she will learn something to her advantage.'

There was a pause.

'Christ!' said Sylvia. We continued to look at one another for several seconds. 'Well, don't just sit there, lovie. Bloody well get on that blower.' She started to cough—almost automatically—yet for once my stomach didn't tighten.

'It must be Aunt Alicia.'

'You've never even mentioned an Aunt Alicia.'

'I didn't realize she was still alive.'

Sylvia spluttered with laughter, and the laughter turned into another of her coughs. 'Let's damned well hope she isn't.'

'Whatever made her go to Bristol?'

Messrs Thames & Avery, it soon transpired, did not practise law upon a Saturday.

During Monday lunchtime Sylvia rang me at the office, too impatient to wait until the evening. 'Well?' she demanded. I could picture her flicking the ash off her jumper as she spoke. You can sometimes come very close to hating people that you live with—however good-natured they may be—for the most shamingly trivial of reasons.

'Yes—Aunt Alicia,' I said, grateful for her interest while irritated by her curiosity.

'And *was* she filthy rich?'

'No, it seems she left a pile of debts.'

But the debts in fact were not really so large and a sale of some of the furniture, Mr Wymark had suggested, would probably cover them quite easily. He was not an expert, of course, but there were some rather good pieces, he thought, underneath the cobwebs and the dust.

'And was *that* the something to your advantage?' Sylvia exclaimed—though underlying her disgust was surely a faint suggestion of relief. 'So you're not a millionairess after all?'

'Not quite.'

'Well, bang goes that present of five thousand quid or so that I was hoping you were going to make me.' So perhaps I had been mistaken—or partially so at any rate—in what I'd just suspected.

Then her common sense reasserted itself.

'But there must have been something.'

'Yes, there was.'

'Well, out with it, then, for God's sake.'

'Her house.'

'Her house? In Bristol?' She gave a whistle. 'Property prices must be pretty high in a place like that. Is it in a good neighbourhood?'

'Apparently. But on the other hand it's in a rather poor condition. It's been totally neglected for years. Just two old women . . . well, you can imagine.'

'Christ. That does sound like a cosy set-up. When are you going down to see it? Next weekend? And that'll give me a valid excuse, too, to miss that do of Sonia's.'

I had planned against this moment; planned against it, even, with an awareness of some pleasure.

'Well . . . actually . . . I was rather thinking of asking . . . whether I could take the day off tomorrow.' I said, after a few seconds: 'Are you still there, Sylvia?'

'Yes, just as you like, my dear. It's your house, of course.' Her tone suggested funeral.

'Saturday, you see, wouldn't be quite so convenient for Mr Wymark.'

Oh, weak, weak!

Yet Mr Danby wasn't much happier about it than Sylvia. Well, congratulations seem to be in order, then, Miss Waring. It just couldn't happen to anybody more deserving. Really. He couldn't be more pleased. But what was the rush? The house would still be standing, wouldn't it, on Saturday? (A slightly awkward laugh—just in case I didn't realize that this was meant to be a joke.) In all the seven years I'd been his second-in-command up in Mail Order I'd not once asked for a day off. All right, Mr Danby, I thought, this is where the worm turns. I went in on Tuesday, Wednesday and Thursday as usual. Then on Friday morning (wily as the fox!) I telephoned just after nine to say that I was ill. And as soon as I'd replaced the receiver I ran out to get a taxi for the station.

Not much difference, you will say, between a Friday and the Saturday. But yes. In the first place it expressed—in a small way—a new-found sense of independence. I was a woman of property. And in the second place—far more importantly—it meant that I could travel alone. It meant that I could read a novel during the journey; go to the type of restaurant that *I* liked the look of; have a silly little feeling of adventure.

And the hitherto timid, though apparently rather staid, middle-aged woman who said to the taxi driver, 'Paddington, please,' felt in some ways more like a girl of seventeen going off to exotic climes, where romance and the unknown awaited her. At seventeen I myself might have gone to Paris with a party of five other girls. It would have been—I was quite sure of it—a truly memorable holiday. It could have led on to so much: so many dazzling things that often followed just from making the right contacts. Of course I had only met the one girl—the one whose parents had placed the advertisement—but she had seemed so nice and so assured that it was nearly impossible not to imagine her friends being equally as charming. Yet I had never been from home before; anywhere more than fifty miles from London seemed to me un-normal, almost to the point of hostility and danger, even though I knew rationally that this couldn't be true; and at the last moment I did what I had sworn this time I wouldn't do—I lost my nerve. I felt so grateful to my mother, as she came away from the telephone; and yet, at the same time, already disappointed and even mildly resentful: grateful she didn't look displeased, despite the inconvenience I had caused; resentful for very nearly the same reason. At seventeen I might have gone to Paris, and it would perhaps have changed my life.

The next morning, over breakfast, I had said, sullenly, 'It's obviously a very moneyed sort of family. I'd have thought, you know, that you'd have really wanted me to make an impression on people like that. Having so much money.' My mother got up and slapped my face, but she didn't suggest my ringing up to see if it was not too late to go. I waited for her to do so, in timorous suspense.

I didn't suggest it either.

Thirty years later, however, embarking on my first real escapade (for such indeed it seemed, despite some quietly exalted periods in the past, never properly channelled), it occurred to me suddenly that I felt now, on my way to Paddington, a little as I ought to have felt then, on my way to Victoria. For a moment, I was seventeen again and off to Paris.

3

The house was beautiful; it was as simple as that. It was terraced, tall, eighteenth-century and elegant. Oh, the stone-work wanted cleaning; the windows were heavily begrimed; their frames required attention; so did the front door and half a dozen other rather minor things. But it was beautiful. I don't know why—I just hadn't expected this.

'Who was Horatio Gavin?' I asked. Philanthropist. Politician. Had lived there from 1785 until his death, in 1797. 'Should I know?' It didn't seem an irrelevance.

Mr Wymark's eyes briefly followed my own towards the buff-coloured, surprisingly clean plaque. He was a young man, small-boned and neatly dark-suited beneath the well-cut overcoat. 'Oh,' he said vaguely, 'he did a lot for the poor. Tried to introduce reforms. That sort of thing.'

'Nice.'

'Yes. I seem to remember, though, he didn't have a great deal of success. He was probably before his time.'

I warmed to him still further, this former resident. There was always something a little touching about failure—especially at a distance.

We went inside.

We walked from room to room, starting at the top of the house. There were only two rooms to each of the three floors. I wondered at first how Aunt Alicia had negotiated the steep stairs; and Bridget, too, of course. The answer was—they hadn't. They must have lived entirely on the ground floor. The topmost rooms might well have been inspired by Dickens: one almost feared to find Miss Havisham sitting solitary in the twilight, forever in her wedding dress, amidst the cobwebs which festooned the bridal feast. It was like a museum, over which the dust of time lay undisturbed by a curator: Neville Court, only more so: cluttered, fascinating, claustrophobic.

But without the plants.

'As I said, there are a few rather good pieces up here.' He pointed. 'For instance—you only have to look at that loom.'

I nodded. The loom was the one thing that I definitely did remember. I thought, though, that I vaguely recalled several of the other items; I tried to place them in that earlier setting.

I was a little girl again.

('Bridget, why must you always cut such very *thick* slices?'

'Ah, do you good, you know it will.'

'Such doorsteps; no refinement. So very *Irish*'—when the door had closed.)

I was sure I recognized that footstool, too.

'Excuse me for what may seem a rather indelicate question—but are you in a position to be able to put the house to rights? The reason I ask . . . this is obviously a most desirable property and I feel that if you were to spend something on getting it back into shape you'd be more than compensated when it came to selling it. As a matter of fact, I even know someone—'

'I don't intend to sell it.'

He was evidently surprised. I myself was probably just as much so. Up till then I had seldom seemed the kind of person who made snap decisions.

'Oh, I'm sorry. I was under the impression that you'd intimated . . .'

And of course I had. Not for one moment before I'd seen the house had it occurred to me to keep it. My roots, my friends (the very few I had), my work, my interests—they were all in London. The familiar might be tedious and un-satisfying, but it was safe.

17

'You mean,' he suggested, 'you see it perhaps as a good letting proposition . . . ?'

'Good heavens, no. I mean, Mr Wymark, that I shall be living here myself.' I suddenly felt the need to make him see; to share my intuition with him. 'There's something about this house—don't you feel it—a warm and very sympathetic atmosphere?'

He answered, 'You haven't seen the ground floor yet.'

'I've never thought of myself as being particularly susceptible to atmospheres. But I think my aunt must have been more welcoming than I remember.' Or perhaps it was Bridget. I recalled Alicia as gentle rather than welcoming. Vaguely melancholy. And nothing that Mrs Pimm was later to tell me of screaming or cursing or feuding would ever alter that, my remembrance of powdered softness. The two old ladies' recriminations when they were close to death, baffled and disillusioned, were mercifully going to leave no greater imprint upon myself than they appeared to have left upon the house. It was a shame it couldn't always be like that; that last impressions were so often the ones which endured. How many of us would want to be remembered for what we finally became, rather than for what we were?

Downstairs, in the room which looked on to the street, the pair had clearly lived and slept and washed and cooked; there was a grease-encrusted Primus stove between the camp-beds, and a ewer set in a basin that was ringed with scum. Long velvet curtains, wine-coloured and faded, hung at the filthy windows. The grey nets were so rotten they would disintegrate upon being taken down.

I noticed that the Primus stove was called 'The Good Companion'.

This was where the plants were, too. They had been large ones. Nearly a dozen of them. They were now more a reflection of decay than they could ever have been of growth.

The other room, in almost startling contrast, was completely bare; here had the refuse of years grown into something to rival the town rubbish tip, I was drily informed, and at some points it had even touched the ceiling. Although the council had fumigated and the rodent inspector had laid his poisons, still the air was fetid, the walls damp, discoloured, and in several places the paper just hung there, like mushroom shreds. I gave a little shudder.

The solicitor smiled at me amiably. 'Does any of this put a different complexion on things?'

'No.'

Perhaps they hadn't cooked in the front room; or not entirely. There was a tiny kitchen-cum-scullery at the back of the house, and in the narrow rectangle of garden—little more than a wasteland, with some concrete by the door—there was a very nasty W.C. (they couldn't have used *that*, surely?) and a couple of coal bunkers.

Mr Wymark was observing my reactions half-pityingly and half-sadistically. It suddenly occurred to me, not only that I didn't like him, but that I didn't seem to like anybody much these days; I suspected them all of ulterior motives. (But *what* ulterior motives, for heaven's sake?) I smiled and gave myself a mental shake. When I was an old lady I should have a terrible persecution complex: I should lock every door, window, drawer and cupboard; I should see double meanings in everything that people said; wonder why so-called friends didn't write to me—or else why they did write to me; watch eagle-eyed the customers ahead of me in the supermarket to make sure they didn't put *my* goods into *their* shopping bags after I had paid for them; check and re-check my slip from the cash machine—had the girl gone haywire or was there just something about me that she didn't like?

I laughed. I looked at him afresh. He was a dark-haired, smoothly shaven, self-possessed young man who meant me and the whole world nothing but good. I said, 'Well, thank you for showing me all this, Mr Wymark. You've been very kind. Now come and let me buy you a cup of coffee at that little place across the road. A cup of coffee and a bun.' In my own ears I sounded just like anybody's favourite aunt.

But he glanced at his watch, spoke abstractedly about another appointment, and said that if I didn't mind he would see me later at the office—that is, unless he could drop me off somewhere for the time being.

I watched him drive away with a feeling a little akin to

sadness: this dark-haired, smoothly shaven, self-possessed young man who so clearly, it seemed, meant the whole world nothing but good.

He didn't return my wave; and for some obscure reason, I thought, he obviously hadn't taken to me.

4

'I think I should rather like to have been,' I said, 'somebody's favourite aunt. I think it would have been a lot of fun.' This was to the woman whose table at the tea-shop I had asked if I might share.

She smiled; hesitated; finally remarked—perhaps a trifle diffidently: 'Well, possibly it's not too late.'

'No brother, no sister, no husband,' I answered with a smile. 'Somehow I get the feeling it's too late.'

'Oh,' she said.

'Did you ever see *Dear Brutus*?'

'Oh, yes. A lovely play.'

'Wouldn't it be fine,' I said, 'if we *could* all have a second chance?'

She nodded—now feeling far more comfortable. 'Oh, I'd have gone to university and got myself an education.' I reflected that she probably needed it. 'But otherwise I don't think that I'd have done things so very differently.' She smiled and started gathering up her shopping. Poor woman, I thought. What a dreadful lack of imagination. (And what a dull, appalling hat.) Yet I knew that I was envying her a little.

'What about you?' she said, as if she felt she had to, while pulling on one of her gloves.

I had a moment's sudden unease upon the question of my own hat. Could others think of that as dull? She presumably would not have considered hers in that light.

'Oh . . . ' I said casually. 'I don't know. I suppose the main thing is—I wouldn't have been so stupidly kind to my poor mother.'

I hadn't meant to embarrass her; it hadn't occurred to me I would. 'Oh, but I daresay she *appreciated* it,' she said. 'Indeed I'm *sure* she did. My bus. So sorry. I must go . . .' She smiled back at me from the doorway, and hurried out into the street.

'No.' I shook my head. 'I think she took it as her due. But it's the old, old story, of course—nothing new under the sun.' I smiled suddenly, as I picked up my bill and totted up the simple figures. This was a happy day; not one for letting in the glooms. 'And after all, I was never really *such* a beauty, I suppose. No reason to believe I'd have been whisked off—just like that—a latter-day Scarlett O'Hara . . .' Or was there? I quickly pulled on my own gloves, with gay determination. It suddenly seemed important, to be gay. In London, strangely, I was seldom so; at work, almost never. I sat at my table and thought about this; and gradually grew quite elated—it was as though I'd just received a revelation. Here, in a tea-room, along with the iced cakes; I wasn't even sure what had led up to it. Of course I *had* discovered the secret of happiness before: courage on one occasion, acceptance on another, awareness on a third: but this time there was a rightness about it all, a simplicity, a certainty, which I couldn't believe had ever been there quite so fully in the past. Gaiety, I told myself; vivacity. Positive thinking. I laughed. Sitting there, I knew I'd made the right decision as regards the house. Bristol, just a name to me until today—how strange—without a true reality, was going to treat me well: provide me with a new start. London in my imagination had now become quite grey; it seemed as though it had always been that. Bristol was in gorgeous Technicolor.

It was the difference, I thought, between Kansas and the Land of Oz.

5

My mother was such a silly person, I explained to that woman from the tea-shop as I strolled around the park a little later on—not that I felt I really needed to explain. She was always so concerned, I said, with what she thought of as good form. There is something I recall particularly; it can still make my stomach clench. When I was a child, she told me I should never accept money without first having tried—gratefully, of course—to decline it. I'm not talking about strangers here but about relatives—and the kind of casual gifts they often make to children upon parting (men especially), digging their hands into their trouser pockets and bringing out half a crown, or a ten-shilling note, or a fifty-pence piece. I can remember saying, 'No, thank you—that's very kind of you, but I really can't accept it,' and then, after a bit of (no doubt slightly disconcerted) coaxing, 'Well, thank you then, very much indeed, it *is* very kind of you,' and later—to my mother—'Well, I tried; I really did.'

Once an elderly uncle of my father's, having offered me something in this way and having received the usual polite refusal, simply put the note back into his pocket, saying, with a shrug and a smile, 'Oh, very well then, if you really don't want it . . .'

My disappointment must have showed, however, because he pulled the money out again and supplied me with another chance. 'It isn't that I don't want it,' I think I remember mumbling, with a burning face and a tremendous feeling of shame . . .

And another time (the two things are connected) my mother was in hospital one Easter—the first after the War—and I was staying with some childless neighbours. On the Easter morning there wasn't an egg by my plate (indeed, I

22

hadn't expected one) but, instead, several sticks of striped candy—Ross's Edinburgh Rock. When I took my place at table I saw them there, of course, and inside I felt pleased and grateful, but I didn't say anything because I had been taught not to assume that something was ever yours until you were actually told so; and after a minute, Mrs Michaels, who'd doubtless been under stress because her husband was crippled and life couldn't have been easy, got up from the table with a small, distressed cry and exclaimed to him as she went:

'It was meant as a surprise. So why isn't she pleased?'

I sat in shocked silence for a moment gazing dully at the gift and then I said quietly, 'But I am. Very.' Yet by then the husband had gone after her and there was nobody to hear.

There was nobody, either (but this I was glad of) to see the silent tears that trickled down my cheeks.

Yes . . . my mother was a very silly woman, I confided to the lady from the tea-shop—misguided, petty-minded; loving initially, yet with no one there to guide her, soften her, point out the error of her ways; nobody strong and under-standing to cling to—for the support, companionship, she always craved.

I laughed. 'Oh, *c'est la vie!*' I fluttered my hand gaily. A duck—rude thing—displayed his bottom. I and the lady from the tea-shop parted company.

6

Sylvia was angry when I telephoned to say that I'd be spending the night in a hotel. She clearly felt that she'd been cheated.

'When the bloody hell did you decide that?'

'Oh—half an hour ago.'

It was as well I'd had the forethought *not* to bring my

toothbrush with me. My hand had hovered over it that morning—'Just in case,' I'd told myself, for it had then been nothing but the merest possibility—yet native cunning had prevailed. I had slipped a clean nightdress into my handbag, and left it at that. Even she would never think of going through my drawers.

But I had bought a weekend-return ticket.

'Is it still drizzling up in town?' I asked; trying hard to leave her in a better mood. 'Here, there's been lovely bright sunshine ever since I arrived.'

'Oh, now my day really is complete,' said Sylvia. 'Thank you so much.' She hung up.

I bought a few toilet necessities at a chemist's shop. 'Not *too* bad a winter so far,' said the grey-haired man behind the counter. We were still in March.

'Oh, what a pessimist!' I exclaimed. 'The winter's over.'

He laughed, too. 'Yes, you're quite right.'

I asked him questions about the town. 'As a matter of fact, I shall shortly be coming to live here,' I said.

'Oh, you won't regret it. It's a good place.'

'I like what I've seen.'

I was glad to be talking of my plans. For one thing it made them more official. Having just spoken to Sylvia—but, naturally, not yet having mentioned to her my decision—I knew that I might falter back in London. I needed to have people down here to whom I had committed myself; as many as possible—though that, again, was merely human weakness. 'Then we'll be seeing you, perhaps,' remarked the chemist.

'Certainly.'

'Hope so, anyway.'

As I walked along the street in pale evening sun I pondered those last words. *Hope so, anyway.* It seemed rather an odd thing for him to say, didn't it, a little unnecessary even, unless he really meant it? There was no doubt about it: this was a most delightful town.

Then I quickened my pace a little and felt even more aware of the approach of spring. A charming red frock caught my eye in the window of an exclusive dress-shop. I stood looking at it, conscious of my own reflection and that of the world which passed me by, for maybe several minutes. After that it felt quite tantalizing to find out that the shop was closed.

At the hotel I ate expensively. Now do be careful, I had to warn myself, but I had a distinct sensation of being on holiday. After dinner I wandered round the centre of the town, cautious to keep only to the main thoroughfares, where there were plenty of lights and still plenty of people about, and came across a small arts cinema where they were showing *A Streetcar Named Desire*, one of my favourite pictures. All my life I had searched for pointers—and nearly every single thing seemed to be conspiring to make me realize that I was unquestionably taking the right step.

As usual (this was my third time of seeing it) I loved the bit where Blanche sings in her bath,

Oh, it's only a paper moon,
Floating over a paper sea,
But it wouldn't be make-believe,
If you believed in me . . .

and I was very much moved again by that pathetically brave declaration: 'I have always depended upon the kindness of strangers.' Somebody had once told me many years before that *I* looked a little like Vivien Leigh—the Vivien Leigh of *Gone with the Wind*, that was—and it was the greatest compliment that anyone had ever paid me: the one I treasured most, hoarded gloatingly to bring out and look at sometimes when in bed; until at length it had gradually turned sour, become a source of dissatisfaction, even of resentment. But that night, in Bristol, the memory of it once again provided me with pleasure.

The following morning I went and bought the dress. It fitted perfectly: a further confirmation I could do no wrong.

'I saw this frock last night. I felt quite scared that someone might have got in here ahead of me. What would I have done then?'

The assistant was middle-aged and *soignée*. 'Yes, madam, it is very lovely, isn't it?'

'I don't imagine anyone could call it dull.' I turned admiringly before the mirror.

'Good heavens, no. I think it's very gay indeed.'

'Yes, isn't it? It's funny you should use that word.'

She seemed to glance at me a little oddly. I was instantly alarmed, but my suspicions were rapidly allayed. 'It really suits you,' she declared.

I told her I couldn't bear to change back into my jumper and skirt, happy though I'd always been with them, and she very sweetly folded *those* for me and put *them*, in tissue, into the smart carrier bag—we had quite a little laugh. Fortunately my elegant black shoes were exactly right for the dress—my hat and handbag, too. I felt almost like a model.

It was another mild morning and with my coat buttons left unfastened I didn't feel a mite cold. I went back to the chemist's shop to purchase a small tablet of soap, but my friend of the previous evening wasn't there: simply a podgy adolescent in a too-tight overall with mild acne and a shiny nose.

It was the first slightly jarring note.

7

In the train I said to the man sitting opposite—he was old enough for me to feel I wasn't being at all forward—'Do you mind if I talk to you a moment? I've just read the most frightful description of a hanging, drawing and quartering, and I just can't get it off my mind.'

'Oh. Yes, of course. Yes, do.' He seemed surprised but not dismayed. He'd only been looking through the window.

I smiled. 'Really, we have no right—ever—any of us—to ever get depressed. Do we? Not about anything.'

'What's that? I'm sorry. I didn't quite catch the last part.'

He cupped his hand apologetically over one ear and pressed it forward a little.

I repeated what I'd said. 'Not about bills or the things that people say to us or even illness. Not even cancer,' I said, 'when you really start to think of it.'

'That's very true, my dear. I—'

'Just *imagine*: waking up in the morning, perhaps from a nice dream, and suddenly *remembering* . . .'

'I'm sorry?' He strained forward a little closer; I raised my voice.

'Not that I can really suppose you'd have got much sleep the night before.'

'I wasn't dozing,' he said, gently.

Poor man; he was obviously much deafer than I'd thought. I raised my voice still more.

'I mean—imagine. Having your . . . thing cut off. Stuffed into your mouth. Being disembowelled. The stomach cut open; the innards taken out . . .'

I suddenly realized just how loudly I was talking, and the relative—indeed, unnatural—quietness of the whole carriage. I glanced about me: heads were craning round and over their seats along the entire length of the compartment. I coloured, and smiled apologetically at the old man, and picked up *Pride and Prejudice* again. I felt an utter fool.

8

'Sunday, bloody Sunday!' declared Sylvia. 'Bloody awful fucking Sunday!'

I hated it when she spoke like that.

'But why? Why are you taking it this way? You'll very easily find someone else to share the flat with.'

'I must say—it's so lovely to be missed,' she said.

'Of course I shall miss you.'

'Oh, pull the other one,' she answered. 'I don't suppose you've ever missed anybody in your life, if you want to hear the truth of it.'

We were meant to be digesting our lunch. I had thought that sitting over coffee with the crossword would be a relaxed and opportune moment in which to bring the subject up.

But, as so often, my Sunday lunch—like so many of my other meals, for one reason or another—was now turning to a lump.

'That isn't true,' I said, outraged and ashamed. I tried to think of all the people I had ever missed, but hardly surprisingly the atmosphere was not conducive to compiling lists. 'And of course I'll miss you, Sylvia. But you speak as though . . . as though we were *married*,' I said.

For the first time I suddenly wondered if she could possibly . . . But no; the thought was too incredible; too remote from anything in my own experience. And yet—now that one came to think of it—she certainly did have some rather mannish ways. It startled me considerably—that is, for the one brief moment before I dismissed it as totally untenable.

'And if it were,' she was saying, 'if it were a God-damned marriage, I know just what kind of marriage it would be. The kind that breaks down the moment the bloody man becomes successful. Which is precisely, as a matter of fact, what happened to my own mother.'

And then—most awfully—she began to cry.

I was appalled, of course. I was the one who cried—cried often, with the quiet grey desperation of it all—not Sylvia. Sylvia didn't cry. I also felt extremely guilty. Blubbering so unrestrainedly; and about what? I had so very little idea, and that seemed terrible.

During those ten or fifteen minutes I came my closest to giving in. Yet she wasn't my responsibility—no one was— and I found an inner rod of strength, of self-preservation, that both surprised and saved me.

I suppose really it shouldn't have surprised me.

Later that afternoon we had further conversation.

contemptuous of my workmates and letting those feelings, very slightly, show. At least half a dozen of my colleagues told me how they envied me. One was a pretty blonde thing of nineteen. Another was the office-boy.

They gave me a book token when I left, for £8.50, and a card on which everyone had signed his name. Though I cried a little when they presented these two envelopes and felt almost sorry to be going—actually *nostalgic* already for my time spent with them, the little things, the little laughs, the silly accidents and birthday cakes—on the bus home I made the mistake (or extremely sensible move) of working out how much, on average, each must have given. It came to 35p per person, with another 10p added. As I myself in recent years had never given less than 50p when someone else was leaving, and usually at least twice that sum, I felt for a moment the tears come to my eyes again, and had to gaze mistily out of the window, blinking hard. But then I shrugged and thought what the heck, I didn't need their liking or appreciation, *I* knew that there were parts of me that meant people well, that I had tried on the whole to lead a fairly decent life, and that I had a value somewhere, in some scheme of things, whether other people recognized it or not.

But surely I was worth more than 35p a head, with 10p to make up, after upwards of eleven years in the same department.

I thought at first I wouldn't spend their book token. I took it from my handbag and looked at it and twice, impetuosity flooding warmly up my body, wanted to tear it through, but my fingers wouldn't let me.

And the card, too, I saved—but purely for the sake of the office boy. If *he* had given even as much as 35p, I thought, it might have been all that he could manage. I kept it, hopefully, for the sake of that one name.

10

All the same I worried lest I might have given too much of myself away and lest, in doing so, I had looked ridiculous. I'd felt a little overcome. After the tea-lady had been up and somebody had handed round the boxes of fancy cakes which I had bought and Mr Danby had presented me with the book token, I had made a little speech.

'I don't know what to say.'

(Cheers. A suggestion of 'Please trot this up to Accounts.' Laughter. I hadn't realized I had got a catch-phrase.)

'I already know what book I'm going to buy with it.'

'The Kamasutra.'

'Shut up, everybody.' That was Mr Danby. 'Let Rachel have her say.'

'Actually it's a book that's just been published—I was reading the reviews. About David.'

I'd forgotten that Mr Danby's name was David. I never called him by it, any more than he usually called me Rachel. There were screams of laughter, and there was much foot-stamping and ribald amusement.

'*King* David,' I said.

'He's been promoted!'

'No. It's just that it's official. He's been calling himself that for years.'

I laughed. I persevered. I always had this urge to share things with those to whom I felt grateful. I said, 'For a long time now King David has been someone very important in my life.'

Nobody quite knew what to make of that. Even those who hadn't been listening sensed that others were intrigued. 'What did she say?'

'Did you know, for instance, that somebody once called him "a man after God's own heart"?'

'*No?*'

I nodded. 'And that was despite the fact he as good as murdered Uriah the Hittite so that he could have Uriah's wife for himself. *Despite* that fact, God still loved him, and God still favoured him.'

And now there was indeed silence. From every side people gazed at me, either standing—as I was—or sitting on chairs or table-tops, their paper cups in one hand, perhaps a cream-horn or a meringue in the other.

'I know what *you*'re going to say, of course. You're going to say that he repented.'

'He repented,' said Una, the pretty little blonde. She gave a giggle.

'But what *I* want to know is—would he have given up Bathsheba? Would he have changed things even if he'd had the chance?'

'Come on, you lot, let's have a show of hands. Now all who think—'

'So that's why you're going to buy the book, is it, Rachel?' Mr Danby seemed to be speaking rather quickly. 'Well—I trust it provides you with a lot of pleasure—indeed I do— and . . . er . . . enlightenment. Thank you for telling us.'

There was quite a lot of clapping. As we all returned to our places in a very relaxed frame of mind there were comments of 'Slayed 'em in the aisles, Rachel!' 'Good for you, Miss Waring.' I was so relieved. I had certainly been a little nervous beforehand, but because I had tried to tell them what was in my heart I did feel that I'd perhaps scored a mild success.

'Want to pack up now, Rachel, and catch an earlier bus?' said Mr Danby.

11
_____

Sylvia came to see me off at Paddington.

'All I bloody well hope,' she said, 'is that some day you won't be regretting all of this.'

I laughed. I hadn't wanted her to come. 'I can assure you—you don't hope it nearly as much as I do.'

'What a dump this station is.'

'I rather like it.'

'Oh, God. You're getting more and more like Pollyanna every day. I'm not surprised they wouldn't take you with the furniture.'

I smiled. 'You think it wasn't the insurance then?' Once I might have worried over that. Now I just said lightly, 'I hope I haven't left the flat too bare.'

In fact I'd only taken very little, and the woman who would soon be moving in had her own things, anyway, which she wanted to bring with her.

I said, after a while, 'She really does seem very nice—Miss Carter.' We had been walking on in silence.

But we had already, of course, discussed Miss Carter. Now Sylvia only added, 'Oh, we'll probably start to grate on one another in no time.'

'Well, that's just being defeatist,' I said.

'Now tell me something truly cheering: like, for instance, it's all just a snappy game of pretence and what fun it is to be a con-man. I think I'd feel much better for an inspirational word.'

Nevertheless she insisted—grumblingly—on obtaining a platform ticket; it seemed wholly masochistic.

I found a seat on the train and then remained in the compartment, standing at a window, with the ventilator open, because I thought that that would save the necessity of a kiss or an embrace—and a handshake seemed quite wrong. Even apart from that, divided as we were by glass, she somehow seemed more manageable. I said, 'Don't forget, Sylvia, that you're coming to stay with me this summer.' And the enthusiasm which I could hear in my own voice was not entirely, at that instant, sham.

'Bank Holiday,' she mumbled.

'Yes.'

Four months away. I almost said, 'Make it Whitsun if you like.' I kept remembering we had lived together—breakfast, supper, lunch—for nearly a quarter of my lifetime. A nicer person could not have said goodbye so easily.

'And you'd better let me know before then,' she said again, 'about something you want for the house.'

'Yes, I will.'

Perhaps one reason I was able to leave her so easily was that I felt I had salved my conscience. I had bought her a video recorder. I had given it to her just an hour or so earlier while the two removal men were still going in and out. I believed she was pleased; if pleasure was to be measured by the quality of gruffness, she was certainly pleased. Anyway, I thought, she'd never again be able to accuse me of meanness.

'Well . . . see you, then,' she said. The flag was about to be lowered. 'Don't forget to write or phone sometime if you feel like it.'

'The moment I'm connected I shall get in touch.'

She stood there awkwardly on the platform. I stood there awkwardly on the train. 'Christ almighty. Ten and a half years,' she said. 'I know,' I said. 'Isn't it incredible?' It seemed a terribly protracted moment, by far the worst of the whole morning, and I knew that I'd made a mistake: if I'd been on the platform I could so easily have thrown my arms about her—I found I'd even have been glad to—and so avoided these last desperately long seconds by making my way back to my seat. It would have been natural, spontaneous. As it was, we just stood there. Powerless. Separated by glass.

She didn't even cough. I realized a few minutes later, as I was taking my place in the restaurant car, that she hadn't once had a cigarette in her mouth since we'd left the flat. That had clearly been intended as a gesture.

But, contrarily, I felt annoyed rather than grateful. It seemed as if she hadn't quite played fair; both with that and with her final words to me—because afterwards she hadn't even said goodbye: just raised her arm, a little limply, as the train at last moved out.

'It must be nice,' she'd said, 'to have something to look forward to.'

I'd merely nodded vaguely.

'It must be nice,' she'd said, 'to have a home of your own.'

That was not the kind of trick that I admired.

12

I felt now that I had never had a real home.

The rented flat with my mother had certainly not been a home; it had been a prison. Or at least it had gradually turned into one, obscuring childhood memories of snugness and contentment and what had seemed unselfish love, just as my mother had gradually become a despot, obscuring behind scratchy veils the pretty, smiling face I had so much liked to look at, obscuring the fun and irresistible laughter when I was being tickled in my bed, or sliding down the back of the bath and causing floods upon the lino; and, anyway, whether prison or home, the only time I could remember even being consulted upon some question of its decoration my opinion had not been listened to, and after that I took no interest. Admittedly, when she had died and I was sharing another rented flat, this time with Sylvia, I had done my best—we both had—to make the place comfortable; but I had never particularly regarded it as expressing my own personality: Sylvia's had always seemed, up to that odd display of weeping and dependence, by far the stronger of the two.

Yet now it was different. My home-making instinct had

suddenly been roused. There was something so seductive about the atmosphere of that house in Bristol—the almost human voice which had bidden me welcome there—that it had caused a hitherto cautious person (for the most part) nearly to forget that such a quality as that existed. I not only rushed off to Olympia, for instance. I spent fascinated hours elsewhere, looking at kitchen units and bathroom fittings and track-lighting and window-boxes in one store following another. I was still a rather boring woman, perhaps, but my boringness—before I left London and there were still a few people to talk to—had at least taken off in an entirely new direction. As one slightly overbearing friend had put it when I went to say goodbye—well, really more a friend of Sylvia's than of mine—'Rachel, you used to be such a gentle, timid little thing. Repressed. One really wonders what's got into you.'

'Ah ha,' I said mysteriously. 'The influence of a house. Reaching out to me magnetically, the first time that I ever saw it.'

I laughed and opened my eyes wide and held my hands aloft with outstretched trembling fingers.

'Or even only heard of it.'

Even if I hadn't been on the point of leaving London I still feel I should probably have needed to make some new friends.

13

But first there were the more prosaic things: the damp, the rot, the applications to the council; the rewiring, the insulation, the central heating; the replumbing (the bathroom, on the second floor, hadn't been used for perhaps more than a decade); the new slates, the removal of the bunkers; strangely satisfying—the filling of the skip; et cetera, et cetera. It was like all those years of apprenticeship or deadly study that may finally lead to the work of art, to public recognition and the flowering of an assured, even a flamboyant, personality.

After that, the things that really showed, the fun things: the workmen with their long ladders, their trestles and their planks, their tins of paint, their buckets of paste; and the woman who was making the curtains; and the man who was re-covering the chairs; and the firm that was fitting out the kitchen, and the shop that was putting down the carpets. Every day had its excitements or preoccupations. 'All those years' reduced, basically, to just over eight weeks: one of the few advantages of the recession—the speed with which large jobs could now be undertaken, the promptitude to match impatience. For lovely though it was to have a whole new aspect, it was even lovelier when all its many details could be fitted into place together. One of the last things to be seen to was the giving of a final coat of paint to the front door. Its deep, gay yellow gloss, with the shining and winking new knocker and letter-box, was redolent of springtime and daffodils, and seemed to symbolize all the brightness and the freshness of my own new life, of my rejuvenated hopes and aspirations.

That yellow—it was a good choice, the *right* choice; though I had been a little worried about it.

'All things work together for good, to them that love God.' (I felt rather naughty: I set it to the tune of 'Pretty Baby'.)

And then, too, halfway through June, there was the young student who came to do the garden. He was very tanned and muscular and worked without his shirt, and though I watched him through an upstairs window I still found him almost unbearable to watch; and when I went out to speak to him, to settle some fresh point or to take him out some cooling drink, I was afraid of what my hands might do—that they might suddenly acquire an innocent and challenging life of their own; reach out to touch the moist dark-golden tendrils of his chest. Supposing that they did do that?—oh, what embarrassment! Whatever would one *say*? 'Oh dear, I am so sorry, I thought there was a fly.' It was like feeling a compulsion to punch a baby's stomach in the pram; or to use on someone standing next to you the carving knife you held. He was only twenty-two.

Despite such unsettling irrelevancies I felt so very blest to have him there: somebody straight and vigorous and clean, who might one day achieve eminence or fame and who would certainly, I thought, love widely and be widely loved, spinning a web of mutual enrichment from the threads of many disparate existences. An enchanting web—glistening and golden and sunsplashed—into which I too was now miraculously absorbed. He had created a garden—*my* garden—out of wasteland. The thread was indissoluble.

This was all extremely fanciful—I realized that. I have an extremely fanciful nature; but people had always said that I must hold it back. Did it now, however, with the carefree lifting of restraint, genuinely seem to burgeon into colour, as I half thought it did, vying apparently with the growing piece of land behind my house? Did it, I wonder?

Or is that just being too fanciful?

Begone, dull care. Begone, drab black and white.

Certainly the land burgeoned. The young man worked from a design of his own, so as to obtain, he said, the very best town garden; and I suggested variations. What I wanted, even in a place of only this size, was first and foremost my seclusion: my own kingdom, self-contained and free from life-destroying, frightening demands. Then I wanted an air of mystery—and romance: you shouldn't be able to see from one end to the other with a single look: there had to be arches and *trompe-l'oeil* and a path that enticed you with its possibilities. There had to be a fountain, because I loved water, and a bird-table, and some fruit trees, and an arbour with a small white bench. And along with all the greenery there also had to be flowers, cunningly variegated, so that there was something in bloom for as much of the year as possible, but never out of harmony. And, lastly, there had to be a certain hint of wilderness. In short—I wanted the perfect garden: in thirty by a hundred.

'I'm very much afraid, Roger, that it's a bit of a tall order.' Our plotting had almost a feeling of conspiracy about it: the two of us pitting our wits against nature, the elements, the world; for a fleeting period he belonged only to myself—this bronzed young hero from another sphere. I didn't want to learn of him anything terrestrial.

'But wouldn't you say that a tall order, Miss Waring, is just about the most interesting kind that there is?'

And of course it wasn't really so very different from his own blueprint, anyway. I had merely added some refinements.

'Do you believe, then, that you can . . . that you can really lick it?' There was pleasure even in a choice of word.

'I've always wanted to find something just like this—and then to start from scratch—just like this—and . . .'

I understood at once. 'Make it your own?' I said.

'Well, yes . . . in a manner of speaking.'

'The two of us are very similar, I think. We both want to leave the world a better place than when we found it.'

He nodded. 'We want it to be different for our having been here. I mean—positively and noticeably.'

The world of Rachel Waring was certainly quite different for his having been there: for the ten whole days that had been vouchsafed to me out of this glamorous life.

My garden, however, was not immediately the garden I had visualized. But it would grow—it would grow towards perfection; the potential was already there. And even in the meantime it was a worthy extension to the house itself which—if the garden was my kingdom—should logically have been my palace. But it was only a palace in the surely rather homely sense that the Sleeping Beauty's was: palaces in picture-books are usually more intimate and charming than in real life, more like quaint, turreted castles or châteaux. (Could you imagine thorns and trees and bramble and creeper growing up thick and protective around *Buckingham* Palace, for instance, impenetrable to all but the sleep-dispelling prince who'd bring to me the kiss of rebirth—and more importantly, of love?)

Yes, a worthy extension. It was quite a large house by modern standards but, despite this, palace, château or what, in whichever part of it I was I had never once felt troubled or on my own. It was strange. I felt as if I only had to call out—perhaps I'd be downstairs in the kitchen—and someone would hear me in the sitting-room on the top floor and send me back a friendly greeting. Elsewhere, of course, I had often felt troubled and very much alone.

It was a nice feeling to have about one's home.

14

And what had that vengeful fairy brought to my own christening? Ah. She dealt in negatives, and yet her gift was comprehensive: an inability to make the most out of my life. That was the curse of the spiteful fairy.

But *The Sleeping Beauty* had never been one of my favourite stories. I preferred *Cinderella*. And just before the War I'd seen *Snow White and the Seven Dwarfs*. I was most impressed by that; I told the little boy downstairs that someday *my* prince would come. I sang it all day long and at five years old I genuinely believed it. But Bobby was unkind. 'Mirror, mirror on the wall, who's the fairest one of all?' He laughed and pointed a grubby and derisive finger. 'Not you, Rachel Waring, not you! Besides, you haven't got a wicked stepmother,' he added a little more gently, as though this might really be a matter for condolence.

Some three years later—after my father had died, and all the tickling had stopped—Bobby's words came back to me. Snow White's father had been dead as well; at least, he hadn't been in evidence. And in the interim, I thought, I'd really grown much prettier. My grief had made me so. Therefore I began hopefully to chant, mainly at bedtime, the mirror incantation. Of course, this hadn't quite been Snow White's rôle, but in small things of that sort it surely didn't matter.

In some ways it was almost as well that the tickling had stopped. Handsome princes didn't usually come to maidens who were cosseted.

Not usually. But when I was much older I hesitantly went to a party at which—although I really remember it even better for another and not wholly unconnected reason—a group of us was choosing the person, living or dead, that we should most like to have been. 'Grace Kelly,' I answered shyly, when eventually it came to my turn.

I then had to say why.

'Well . . .' It seemed so very obvious. She came from a cultured, wealthy family. She was extremely lovely to look at. She'd had a huge success in Hollywood. And now she was about to marry a prince.

Champagne and Ruritania combined. Applause and celebration. A honeysuckle path, from cot to marriage bed.

'It just isn't fair,' I murmured, with a rueful smile.

They waited. One had no wish to sound self-pitying. What could I say that would acceptably explain?

'I'd really like to have been an actress, you see—play interesting rôles—belong to a nice company.' I was talking far too quickly and I knew I'd gone quite red.

'That's all,' I said, uncomfortably.

'Well, what's stopping you?' someone asked. 'You're only twenty-two—you've still got time, haven't you?' She gave a sidelong glance at those around us.

'But I haven't got connections.' I was aware they thought this very feeble.

'Connections? The ability's no problem?'

'I don't know.'

'We must find out,' they said. 'An audition.'

'What?'

'Recite something. "To be or not to be: that is the question . . ." '

'Don't be silly.' I was beginning, rather shrilly, to panic.

'A poem, then.'

'I couldn't.'

'Oh, don't be shy, Rachel. We think you're probably quite good.'

I could see that they weren't going to leave it alone. It was escalating unmercifully. I mumbled desperately for mercy.

'Silence, everybody. Rachel is going to say a poem.'

'No! No!'

I had a choice between rushing from the room, bursting into tears, or actually reciting something. Before the whole party should hear of it, I whispered, 'Just a few lines, then. Will that do?'

'Yes, yes,' they cried—greedy for at least an ounce of flesh if they couldn't get their full pound.

So I said my few lines. I said them, I thought, without enough expression or audibility, and definitely too fast. It was the first stanza of *The Lady of Shalott*; I had always felt very much drawn towards the lady embowered upon her silent isle.

But I had misjudged, apparently, my own performance.

'Oh, that was good. Wasn't that good, everybody?'

There was some vigorous clapping; they really did seem to have enjoyed it. 'You're poking fun at me,' I said. They swore that they were not.

'More! More!'

'You don't really want some more?'

'Yes, we do, Rachel. Please.'

'You're truly not just teasing?'

'Of course not.'

I knew that I could improve a good deal upon what I had just done.

Confidence came quickly; the more I recited, the better I grew.

> Or when the moon was overhead,
> Came two young lovers lately wed;
> 'I am half sick of shadows,' said
> The Lady of Shalott.

Unfortunately, however, my memory of the poem was far from perfect.

'Never mind. Just carry on. You're doing great.'

> Out flew the web and floated wide;
> The mirror crack'd from side to side;
> 'The curse is come upon me,' cried
> The Lady of Shalott.

Now I really was declaiming—and making good use of my hands as well. I had known that I had it in me to be an actress.

Yet the real test lay in the final stanza. I wanted if possible to bring the tears into their eyes. I ended on a quiet and very reverent note.

> But Lancelot mused a little space;
> He said, 'She has a lovely face;
> God in his mercy lend her grace,
> The Lady of Shalott.'

Even a school I had invariably found that a poignant finish. Now, again, my own gaze was so misted I couldn't fully tell how my audience was affected. But I certainly caught sight of the odd handkerchief; heard the odd blowing of nose.

And one triumph led to another—they just didn't want to let me go. Finally I sang to them. They were beside themselves with pleasure. At last I put my hands upon my chest; I went back a whole decade: to the one big popular success of my childhood.

> Although when shadows fall
> I think if only—
> Somebody splendid really needed me,
> Someone affectionate and dear . . .

It was sheer intoxication; a wonderful prelude to what was to happen later that same evening.

15

I went back to the chemist's. I wore my red dress, though this was now a little too warm for the time of year. And only the previous afternoon I'd had my hair done. It was a moment I'd

46

been continually aware of—and, squirrel-like, had been delaying.

Of course, as with nearly all such moments, there was the particle of grit in the shoe, so difficult to dislodge that one almost welcomed a particle in the eye as well: in this case the haunting knowledge of a poor night's sleep, coupled with the imagined unsightliness of make-up much too caringly applied.

I said, 'Good morning; how are you?'

'Very well, madam. How are you?'

At first it would have been almost a relief if the lumpish, shiny-nosed girl had been there instead; but as soon as we started talking I began to feel considerably more at home.

'I came in last March. You advised me that I ought to settle here. Well, I've taken your advice,' I told him—smilingly, to make sure he realized there was no reason to reproach himself.

'Oh, yes, of course, I remember.' It was rather clear he didn't.

I was wearing a light blue jumper with a darker blue skirt. My Boat Race outfit, as everybody called it! Oh, but of course I had my coat on, too. Camel-hair. And quite a pretty little hat—black, you know, and really rather smart.' I laughed.

He merely gave a gentle nod—boyish and abstracted—but it came as no surprise that he should be the strong and silent type. That was the kind of man which I had always found attractive, that and the witty debonaire sophisticate: beguiling, unattainable young gods—or devils!—whose rightful mates were only to be met with in the ranks of society's true princesses, relaxed participants in repartee, who could, reliably, match thrust with thrust.

And that, I knew, was never Rachel Waring.

I realized I would have to help him out.

'Of course, who am I to say my little hat was rather smart? A hostess doesn't praise her own cooking! Besides, smartness—like beauty—is just in the eye of the beholder, I imagine.' I did hope my laughter wasn't beginning to sound at all foolish.

47

He said: 'Well, well. So you've lately moved to Bristol? And do you like it here?'

A man came in behind me.

'Why don't you serve this gentleman first? I'm not in any hurry.'

The man bought a packet of man-sized tissues and some corn-plasters. I took note of everything. He was youngish and his jeans were nicely pressed but he was very down at heel: quite literally, I mean. That wouldn't have mattered so much. Yet didn't he *know*—he ought to have done—that when there was a shine on your shoes there was a melody in your heart?

Poor man. Perhaps if he bought polish he wouldn't need plasters. There was a connection. I pictured him out of work, keeping up a brave front (it was only in that one—admittedly important—detail that he'd failed), struggling in something rather like a garret to produce a masterpiece.

It was a lovely world. I executed a few unobtrusive dance-steps which hardly took me from the spot on which I stood. My own shoes were gleaming: high-heeled red sandals with lovely thin straps; almost dreamily delicate. This was just the second time I'd worn them.

I had very pretty feet.

It didn't matter that he hadn't recognized me. It was but the tiniest of disappointments.

A woman came in. That didn't matter either. She only wanted some Tampax.

Corn-plasters; sanitary towels. What a funny old world it was. I was so *glad* that I could see the humorous side of it.

'Yes, I like it here very much,' I said, as she put away her change—and before she should remember, dear gracious heaven, that she needed toilet rolls as well! 'I think Bristol must be one of the nicest towns on earth. Have *you* been here very long?'

'Oh—about thirty years,' he smiled. 'I came here when I married.'

There was a stillness: the sort of terrible stillness that may exist, I imagine, right in the eye of the storm. It was like being enclosed in a glass booth with an avalanche of melting snow cascading down the sides of it; or like being sealed in a crystal cylinder beneath the sea. Only a Houdini could discover a way out. With a start I found myself—no expert, sadly, in escape—staring through these transparent walls at a showcard on the shelf behind him. Things happened after a Badedas bath. You might be whisked away to Camelot, for instance, by a lovesick errant knight. It would be good to be that woman in the window.

She had to face no brutal truths.

No, not brutal perhaps. Unnecessary. Insensitive. It hadn't wholly eluded me, of course, he might be married.

But on the other hand . . .

'Ah, yes, I see. And is your wife still . . .?' I corrected myself; despite the numbing quality of such a shock, I hadn't yet lost any of my old cunning. 'Is your wife a native of Bristol?'

'Yes, she is,' he answered.

I bought the toothpaste I'd come in for. I decided that the Paracetamol would almost certainly be cheaper at Boots.

'Have you settled near here?' he asked.

'Buckland Street.' It was the first name that I thought of.

'Oh—just around the corner.' That, too, seemed an unnecessary scrap of information. I probably wouldn't come in here again. 'Then maybe we'll be seeing something of you. That's nice.'

It was almost what he'd said before. This time I wasn't fooled. They could make a dupe of you once per-haps—because, after all, you were only human. You didn't set out to be suspicious. But in their arrogance they supposed they could go on doing it—time after time after time.

At best he was clearly insincere; at worst . . .

I thanked him for my purchase with dignity and in a very natural manner, whose slighter degree of coolness such a person could hardly be expected to recognize. But that was good. I certainly didn't want him to have the satisfaction of thinking it to be important.

Outside, a few doors along, I passed the marriage bureau through which he'd probably met her. I had never under-stood how anybody, no matter how lonely, could be sufficiently lost to all sense of pride as to enter any place of that sort.

But I wreaked, I thought, a very subtle form of revenge. I went into another chemist's shop (it wasn't Boots) where the prices were most likely as inflated as his own—and possibly even more so—I rather hoped they were. And I not only bought the Paracetamol. 'Do you happen to stock Badedas?' I enquired, with a merry ripple of laughter. 'Because—if so—I'd like the very largest that you've got.'

16

Yet despite such inspired retaliation I knew that I needed to cheer myself up. I recognized the signs. I felt dangerously low—for the first time since coming to Bristol. Help. Quickly. I went to the library.

I almost immediately started to recover. The woman at the desk might have been no older than I was, but I thought that she definitely looked it. Someone could have told her, for instance, about touching up your hair or even about the invention of contact lenses. I wanted to say, 'You know, my dear—men seldom make passes at girls who wear glasses.'

I said, 'Men seldom make passes at girls who wear glasses.'

I tried to convey that it was a matter of absolutely no importance, yet that it was one which, even so, it might some day be as well to think about.

The very last thing one wanted to do was to wound anybody.

'Excuse me?'

And they only gave you any trouble for the first week. Contact lenses, that is.

I smiled winningly. 'Errol Flynn,' I said.

'Oh. Books on the cinema are over there.'

I saw that she hadn't got a wedding ring. I automatically liked her and despised her and felt sorry for her and was glad.

'Do you know, offhand, if you've anything here about Horatio Gavin?'

'Is that someone also connected with the cinema?'

'You're not serious?'

She led me across to the biography section. 'I'm sorry,' she said; 'what was that name again?'

It was all very well—she was certainly quite pleasant—but I began to feel resentful; both on his behalf and—more obscurely—on my own. The fact that I now owned the house where he'd once lived had clearly made me sensitive.

There was nothing on the shelves. 'I'll check the cards,' she said.

This was more successful. 'Ah, yes, there is something here. Oh? Was he a local man?'

I answered with relish and severity. 'He lived barely half a mile from this library. Why?'

'This book was published by a local press. I'll go and see if we've still got it.'

She returned three minutes later, empty-handed. And it didn't seem that they could get it in for me.

'Could you give me the name of the press, at any rate?'

'Yes, of course. But I'm afraid that it closed down, some years ago.'

'This is absurd,' I said. I felt prepared to make a scene. What had started out as almost an idle request had turned, within minutes, into a matter of some urgency.

'You could try the second-hand bookshops, I suppose.' But her tone lacked conviction.

'And I could advertise, too.' It had never in my life occurred to me to advertise for any book; the words just seemed to come to me. I felt a little smug.

'Yes, indeed.'

'I could even go to the council.' There seemed no end to my ingenuity. She nodded at me, a bit uncertainly, and I was going to enlighten her, but suddenly I didn't want to. It was nice to have one's little secrets; it gave one a feeling of superiority. This could be between Horatio and myself; just the two of us. I smiled. 'Well, thank you, anyway, for all your help. Goodbye.'

51

But on my way out I passed the shelves bearing the encyclopaedias. There was no mention of Horatio Gavin in *Britannica* but there were a few lines about him in *Chambers*. I felt a tremendous leap of the heart, like there might be on suddenly seeing a well-loved face in the crowd, when you hadn't thought there was much chance of it.

Gavin, Horatio (1764–1797), English social reformer associated with William Wilberforce in his campaign to eradicate slavery; died nine years too soon to see the longed-for abolition of the slave trade.

It was the shortest entry on the page—perhaps in the whole encyclopaedia—but what of that? I rushed back to the desk. 'Look,' I said. 'Look.' I pointed triumphantly.

I realized, a little too late, that there were two women who'd just arrived to have their novels stamped and that I had rather pushed in front of them. But that didn't seem important. Although the librarian read the entry more out of politeness than out of interest—although she merely said, 'Well, fancy! Yes. I'm glad that you found something after all'—although I was sure that the three women were talking about me as I returned the volume to its place—none of this seemed too important, either. I only felt that Horatio Gavin had been vindicated in some small way; and through my own efforts.

For the third time I approached the desk.

'Oh, by the way, I've found a tube of toothpaste here,' I said. 'I don't know if anyone will come to claim it.'

17

So he had been only thirty-three when he had died. I was mildly disappointed; not, I regret, for his sake, but simply because I'd been picturing someone a little older than myself.

Yet I adjusted quickly. In the library I had already felt protective. A good man; his name linked with William Wilberforce. I had known before, of course, that he was good—partly from the evidence of the plaque plus the few words of Mr Wymark, and partly from the very aura of the house (strangely, it had never once struck me that that aura could have come from any other occupant)—but the expression 'the good die young' now occurred to me with more immediacy, and more poignancy, than it had ever done before, even in connection with my own father.

I suddenly wished that I was younger. (Well, one wished that all the time, of course.) I had an acute feeling of loss: a momentarily nauseating realization that, no, there were very seldom any second chances. I had now missed out for ever.

'Just thirty-three,' I said. I spoke aloud. The nausea had briefly bent me double and brought a fine sweat to my forehead but now I continued, slowly, with the preparation of my lunch. 'What on earth could you have died of at the age of thirty-three?'

I paused again in the act of peeling my potato.

'Well, at that time I suppose you were one of the luckier ones—living even that long.'

And perhaps I was one of the luckier ones, too. A survivor. Unexpectedly strong.

After lunch I went around the second-hand bookshops. And I knew—I positively *knew*—just before I stepped into the third—that I was going to find it there; I was hardly dismayed at all when the owner shook his head. He was a little humpbacked man who invited me, indulgently, to browse. Yet I did so for barely a minute.

The man stared at the book a moment as though unable fully to believe this *was* what I'd been asking for. 'I thought I hadn't seen one of these for years,' he said. 'A little miracle.'

'It was right there in the centre; even the shelf was at eye-level.' I felt so pleased. 'It must have worked its way along, whenever you weren't looking.'

And I can't quite explain it, but I almost believed in what I was saying. Only when he answered, 'A little game of leap-frog, eh?' did it of course sound totally absurd.

But how my heart had leapt—and for the second time that day. Even despite my certainty.

There was no price inside the book. The man shrugged and said, 'Oh—20p.' I was immensely moved. He had seen that I had wanted it. He could have asked ten times that amount—even more—and I would willingly have paid it. People were sometimes . . . so very, very kind. I walked home in a glow, almost dancing, almost skipping, as much on account of people's kindness as because I had the book.

I didn't start reading straight away. I made myself a pot of Lapsang Souchong and carried it, as I did every afternoon (along with the extra cup and saucer and teaplate just in case of a visitor), upstairs to my sitting-room, which looked warmly inviting with its quantity of fresh flowers, bought twice weekly at the market, its many polished surfaces and softly filtered rosy light.

I set the tray on a small gateleg table with a red chenille cloth; stood at the window for a moment enjoying the view of my new garden—this was almost a ritual; glanced appraisingly in the antique mirror above the Adam fireplace (I had changed into a cooler dress before going out after lunch), poured my tea and carried it to my favourite arm-chair. I didn't want a biscuit. I sipped the tea appreciatively, then set it down on an occasional table beside the chair and—at last—picked up my purchase of that afternoon.

The book was less than eighty pages long; the print was large and spaciously set out. Even then the prose was precious and given to long paragraphs of philosophical comment that were absurd, irrelevant, self-congratulatory. I read the whole thing in a little less than an hour. But it was an hour in which I lived intensely.

There obviously wasn't a great deal known about Horatio Gavin. Where possible the author had consulted whatever records were extant, but a lot of the work was clearly supposition. One paragraph I liked in particular: 'He may have thought that fine spring morning as he cantered past the cathedral of all the faith and hope and backache that had gone into its creation, this immense project begun in one man's lifetime, perhaps not finished even in his grandson's—of all the myriad small miseries of daily life so erosively familiar to anyone in any age, like indigestion, constipation, piles or family tiffs; young Gavin may have thought of all these things as he rode by—yet on the other hand it seems unlikely that he did, since his mind must have been full of what he was going to say just then to Wilberforce.'

A book like that—even with nothing more to offer—must soon become a favourite on anybody's shelf.

But this one had a great deal more to offer; at least to someone like myself. It told the story, however fictional, of a lonely, brooding, idealistic young man, son of a merchant in Bath, who upon his father's death had moved with his mother to live near a similarly widowed aunt in Bristol. It told of his championship of the underprivileged, his entry into politics, his meeting with Wilberforce and of the instant rapport established between the two men. It told of his tender feeling for a Miss Anne Barnetby, and of the great blow when—on the eve of their betrothal—she eloped with some more worldly man: a shock from which (averred the Reverend Lionel Wallace) young Horatio had never quite recovered. When he died, as the consequence of a burst appendix (the author speculated), he had not found anyone to take her place.

'I say a burst appendix—another man might say a broken heart. I claim that other man, however, would be wrong. Hasn't the poor fellow yet discovered the balm of self-immersion in a noble cause?'

When I had finally closed the book I sat for a long time. I meditated, I conjectured. I wove a gaily-coloured tapestry. I began to picture myself as that woman he had so much loved—that sad, deluded woman who had thrown away the one thing of importance in her life, not realizing its worth. Yet if I really had been her how *different* it would all have been.

And then it suddenly occurred to me: supposing that he *had* found someone else? The departure of Anne Barnetby was factual; what came afterwards was mere surmise.

I'd once seen a play called *Berkeley Square*: about a man becoming his own ancestor of two hundred years before, and falling in love, timelessly, before returning to the present. Did I believe in reincarnation? I didn't know. But what a charming, what a fascinating thought. Supposing twentieth-century Rachel had been drawn towards this house, irresistibly, despite the choice of actual year being difficult to understand, because of what had once happened in it to her forebear: eighteenth-century Rachel . . . ?

I laughed—though not through sheer frivolity.

'No wonder, then, that from the first I've felt so very much at home!'

18

She was a gentle, thin-haired, deferential lady who offered me a jam tart with my cup of tea. On the telephone I had invited *her* to have tea with *me* but after a great deal of hesitation—and even some apparent reluctance that we should meet at all—she'd finally said that she preferred to stay at home. So I'd taken along a pound box of chocolates and half a dozen roses; and once I was actually there it was rather pathetic—the way that she kept on telling me how glad she was to have a visitor and thanking me for these small gifts and saying that really I oughtn't to have done it. She was very sweet, but I hoped that I should never become pathetic as I grew older.

'There was a picture,' I said, 'that Mr Wallace mentions several times: "The portrait that hangs above me as I write." Do you know what became of it, Miss Eversley?' I had hoped that I might see it as I walked into her small bed-sitting-room, but had known perfectly well that I shouldn't.

'Oh, yes—a great big gloomy painting,' she said.

I was surprised. 'But Mr Wallace said that he had a *nice* face, very handsome and with a lovely smile.' I remembered it precisely: 'A smile that somehow grew more pronounced, increasingly captivating, the better that you got to know the picture.'

She nodded, even before I'd finished speaking. 'Oh, I'm not saying anything against it really; I'm sure he did have a nice face, just like the Reverend Wallace said—but it was all so dark, so . . .'

'Sombre?'

'Yes, that's the word. It was so . . . sombre . . . that in certain lights you couldn't even see it was a face if you were standing in the wrong position. And the dust it used to gather . . . !' She raised her hands, and gave a little laugh. 'But in some ways I wish I was still dusting it right now. It wasn't such a bad life—not really.'

I had a vision, briefly, of the past she was remembering. To me it seemed a frightful life: the daily ministrations to some pedantic clergyman. Grey . . . all grey. Yet almost anything, perhaps, was better than old age. You might not even mind too much the thought of death—despite your doubts and your cold sweats at each new palpitation, pressure, pain about the heart: death itself could well be an adventure, or at least a rest. Old age, however . . . surely much greyer than most preceding greyness. Wrinkled fingers; dewlapped throat. No hope of change. How terrible no longer to have hope of change. No hope of finding love.

'More tea?' she asked. 'Another tart?'

'Not another thing. It was delicious.'

I wiped my mouth on my small handkerchief.

'Do you happen to know what became of it?' I repeated. 'The picture.'

'Well, you'd have to ask Mr Lipton, who came and cleared the house for me. I kept one or two little things, of course'— she gestured towards a chest of drawers, a wardrobe and her bed—'just enough to see to my needs here, but otherwise Mr Lipton bought it all; a very fair gentleman, I will say that.'

'Is he a local man?'

'Oh, yes. The Reverend Wallace said his shop was an Aladdin's Cave. He bought me this old tin-opener there, the best I've ever had.' And she rose with some difficulty, her cup of tea unfinished, expressly—as it turned out—to show me this very ordinary tin-opener. '10p,' she said. We both sat and admired it.

Then she told me how to get there. 'But if you'll forgive me asking something very personal . . .'

I told her the reason for my interest was that I lived in the house where Mr Gavin himself had lived; a fact which seemed to cause astonishment and pleasure. 'And I'd love to return your hospitality,' I said. 'I'm hoping that you'll very shortly come to visit me there.'

But she began to shake her head.

'I would arrange for a taxi, of course, to fetch you and to bring you back.'

'That's very kind,' she murmured. 'Perhaps . . . when the days draw out a little. When it gets a little warmer.' We were nearing the end of July.

'I see you have no television.'

'No. I never cared for it. Nor for the wireless, either.'

'I was just wondering, then, if you'd like to come and watch the Royal Wedding. In colour. Make a day of it.'

She was tempted; I could see that. 'I'll think about it,' she said.

'Shall I telephone next Tuesday?'

'We'll see. I don't know if I shall be able to come to the telephone next Tuesday.'

I was sure she said this only because she had no wish to commit herself. She meant—I may be doing some shopping; or—my room has to be cleaned; or—some shoes need to go to the repairers. But I suddenly wondered how it must feel not to be able to plan with any certainty from one week to another; how it must feel to know that every time you picked up a new novel you might never reach the end of it. I may already have had my last Christmas; or seen my last summer.

And thinking this, I experienced a great surging wave of gratitude: for having more life ahead of me. And I would make the most of it, I vowed. Of every minute! I was young! I had time! Today was the past that I would still be looking back to in a quarter of a century with nostalgia. I could have hugged her.

Apart from that I felt quite relieved that she would

probably not take me up on my offer. Myself, I didn't want to see the Royal Wedding. Not at all. It would have been a sacrifice; quite painful to have to sit through.

'Well, if not,' I suggested, 'perhaps I could sometimes come and see *you*? We could read the newspapers together . . . or simply sit and talk?'

'That would be very nice,' she smiled, with an expression, I thought, of genuine appreciation. 'I'll let you know when it's convenient.'

She held her finger to her lips.

'But sometimes they don't like it here if you get too many visitors. They're a bit funny that way. They get a little jealous—you know how it is—and say some very nasty things. One has to be rather careful.' She was still whispering.

'Who? The other residents?'

'And the wardens. But they're really very fair. On the whole. I will say that for them.'

She gave a smile and a shrug: in part an apology for being obliged to be so awkward.

Oh, dear.

Even though she was about to show me out I thought it best to change the subject. It was very frightening to see how people's own small worlds could contract into something so important that neither war nor flood nor famine, at least if sufficiently at a distance, could ever possibly intrude. And it was as sad as it was frightening, perhaps sadder, since—even then—their worlds were sterile, full of menace, petty regulations, disease-carrying insects; so immensely far-off from the Eden that you'd think they could have found. I said: 'But to return to what we were speaking of just now . . .'

For some reason she looked hopeful—as though I might supply the answer to a question which she hadn't dared or hadn't known how to ask.

'I'm also thinking of writing a book on Mr Gavin.'

'Oh.'

'Though I don't think it will be a biography, like the Reverend Mr Wallace's. No. It's going to be a novel. What do you say to that?' I had forgotten to keep my voice down.

'I was never a great reader.'

Oh, Miss Eversley. No novels; no television; the greyness of her life appalled me once again. The self-imposed greyness—even in a land of colour. No escape. No possibility of an escape.

Merely an inglorious retreat.

I laughed. 'All my life I've intended one day to write a novel.' I was so much wanting to infect her with just a little of my own new gaiety, my own new hope. 'And now, it seems, I've found my hero!'

She didn't laugh, but she certainly did smile. 'Thank you for coming. And thank you for all those lovely chocolates and flowers.'

'I know what I shall do!' I exclaimed. 'I shall go right out and buy you a large jigsaw!'

'A jigsaw?'

'Yes. They're such absorbing things. And you don't paint, do you? You don't work tapestry? Then you must have a jigsaw.'

'I wouldn't know what to do with it,' she said. She gave her head a puzzled shake.

'I shall buy you one with mountains and a lake, and a little village nestling on the slopes, and a castle and a church spire, and a café and a woman with a barrow selling flowers.'

She seemed a trifle overwhelmed by this.

'And an organ-grinder with a monkey! Why, Miss Eversley'—it suddenly struck home to me—'you haven't even got a record-player.'

'Oh, no, please,' she said. 'What should I want with an organ-grinder and a monkey?'

I was delighted with her sense of humour.

'Please not,' she said.

But when she actually opened the door she had her forefinger against her lips again, and then we only mimed the rest of our goodbyes.

19

I had hardly been home ten minutes and was just wondering whether to make myself a *proper* cup of tea when the doorbell rang and I had a visitor. (What an eventful day!—the employment exchange in the morning, followed by coffee and doughnut at The Good Hostess; Miss Eversley in the afternoon, my stroll back through the park, singing to myself,

> Ten cents a dance,
> That's what they pay me,
> Oh how they weigh me down.

—rather a melancholy song, surely, for someone who was feeling so happy and so very much alive; and now this—a visitor.) Or, rather, two visitors. Even three: a tall young man in a smart brown suit, his pretty wife—he had one arm around her shoulders—and, nestling at her breast, a sleeping few-months-old baby. They made a charming tableau, waiting on the pavement in the sunshine.

'Roger!' I exclaimed.

'Don't say that you recognize me, with my hair brushed!'

'What a lovely surprise.'

'May I introduce my wife, Miss Waring? This is Celia. And *this*—this normally rather noisy newcomer to the south-west—is Thomas.'

'How lovely. Oh, how lovely.' My vocabulary seemed limited. 'And I didn't even realize you were married. Do come in. I was just about to make some tea.'

'What terrific timing!' laughed the young man. 'I'm parched.' In a moment he was filling the hallway like a glowing Dane. 'But perhaps that wasn't very polite—I am sorry. Perhaps I should be saying I do hope we're not intruding but that we were just passing and—'

'We *were* just passing,' said his wife. 'Please, Miss Waring, pay no attention to my boisterous husband.'

'I assure you that I won't,' I said. 'Is he always like this?'

'Yes!'

'How unbearable! But at least get him to wear off some of his energy by holding Thomas for you. I'm afraid my sitting-room is two flights up.'

He said, obediently taking his sleeping son, 'But tell her, Miss Waring, I don't need to be all stiff and formal with *you*—tell her that we're old buddies.'

'We're old buddies, Mrs Allsop.'

'Celia,' he said.

But she was too busy looking all about her, it seemed, even to have heard. 'Oh, this is charming, Miss Waring. It's so delightful. Have you done it all yourself?'

They were my first real visitors, to my first real home. I felt very proud, but tried my hardest not to show it.

'Well, at least I've had it all done myself.'

'And in the ability to delegate,' said Roger, 'lies the hall-mark of true genius.'

She exclaimed over nearly everything she saw; so did her husband. It was the most intoxicating stuff. And I too exclaimed: over their handsome, adorable baby. We all appeared very pleased with one another. I went away and made the tea. The baby had awoken on its journey up the stairs and, in my absence, she fed it. She changed its nappy in the bathroom. She seemed so capable and organized. While we drank our tea and they ate little cakes that I had dashed out to the teashop for, Thomas cooed and gurgled peace-fully—this noisy little newcomer to the south-west—and clutched his father's finger. (How I wished that Sylvia could have seen us.) 'Oh, you are such a *strong* little boy, aren't you?' said his mother. 'Such a powerful little grip already.' I visualized those tight little golden curls under the crisp beige shirt where his head was resting, and, feeling myself begin to flush, looked away abruptly.

'Do you realize that we haven't told Miss Waring yet the reason for our visit?'

'My goodness,' I said, 'did there need to be a reason?'

'Well, *now* I realize not,' he answered. He grinned apologetically. 'But anyway I was boasting to Celia about that garden which we'd created—'

'Which you created.'

'No,' he said firmly, 'which we created. Very much a team effort: you the brain, me the brawn. And I suddenly thought—I'd like to see that garden again; and I'd like Celia to see it, to appreciate my cleverness.'

I laughed, delightedly. 'Our cleverness.'

'Yes. Cross my heart.'

'So, young man? You're only here to see the garden?' I felt the most outrageous flirt, but the flirtation came quite naturally, even here right under his young wife's eyes—of course, it certainly wouldn't have, without her there. 'You didn't want to see *me*.'

He bowed his head.

'I'd forgotten how nice you were,' he told me, in one of those crushing moments when you are wholly taken aback by plain sincerity and you don't know what to say.

'Of course you may come and see the garden,' was all I did say.

We sat out there for some time, close together on the white bench, Roger in the middle, and I was most terribly aware of the contact of our thighs.

'I remember you're a student,' I said, my voice sounding unnatural in my own ears, 'but for the life of me I can't remember what you're studying.'

'Law,' he answered.

Had I ever asked him? I said how interesting.

He nodded. 'But another three years to go. That's the hard part. I just can't wait to get started.'

'Yes, it must be hard.' I leaned forward slightly, looked across him to his wife. 'How ever do you manage?'

She replied, easily, 'Oh, we do manage. Somehow. Roger, of course, works at the landscape gardeners during the spring and summer vac.'

I smiled, not quite so easily. 'What it is to be young.' I hadn't realized that I was going to say it aloud.

63

'Well, we've got our health,' she said. 'And we've got Thomas. And we've got each other. Money isn't that important.'

Yes. And during the night money wouldn't seem important at all.

I wondered if he wore pyjamas.

And I wondered how often . . . and how it . . . Sitting there in the balmy evening air I felt momentarily sick again with deprivation and with jealousy and the bitterly recurring knowledge that I would never ever know—never now—I would die without knowing—that experience which . . . was meant to be . . . above all others . . . Oh God, I thought. Oh God, oh God, oh God. For a second I was afraid that I'd said all that aloud as well.

But the desperation of the moment passed. We talked some more about the garden. Celia said, 'I really think it's lovely. But—this may sound blasphemous within my husband's hearing—it's the house I truly go for. It's one of the most delightful houses that I've ever seen. And not only that; it's got such a marvellous atmosphere.'

'Ah. You noticed that?'

'Well, who could fail to?'

She had gone a long way towards making more bearable that moment of bleak desolation. I liked her. I liked her despite that gleam of loving pride whenever she looked in her husband's direction.

'Then you must come and visit me here often.'

'We should love to,' she said. 'And you must come and visit us.' She added impulsively: 'What about lunch next Sunday?'

'Darling, didn't your parents say that they might be coming over on Sunday, with Simon?'

'Oh, damn—'

We left it, for the time being, in abeyance. I was really just as glad, although extremely touched to have received any invitation, especially one of so much warmth and spontaneity. But I felt there was no hurry. I would perhaps enjoy the mulling over of it even as much as the occasion itself, when it arrived.

She made a face. 'My parents want us to have young Thomas christened.' He was making happy little noises and sucking his thumb and drumming his heels and looking contentedly all round him, on a plaid rug which I'd brought out and laid for him upon the turf his father had put down. (How I had liked the way his lean back rippled when he was lowering the turf into position.) 'We ourselves can't see the urgency. But I suppose'—she laughed—'anything for the sake of a quiet life . . .'

'I've never seen a more angelic baby,' I smiled.

'Would you like to hold him?'

20

I passed a largely sleepless night, for various reasons. In the first place I had fevered, wakeful dreams of having—perhaps—God willing—almost acquired a new family. Roger and Celia Allsop wanted three more children; which was a lovely—comforting—horribly disturbing notion. Being an only child myself, I too would have wanted a large family, if things had only been a little different. By the time I was seventy, I calculated, those four children would be either in their twenties or approaching them; by the time I was eighty they would probably have children of their own. What would they call me? Aunty? Aunty Rachel. I'd be such a sweet old lady. They'd come to me with all their troubles (in my mind the generations grew a bit confused): things they couldn't speak about at home. Aunty Rachel was such a *sport*. You could always rely on *her*. Her house was such a hive of activity as well—an ever-open door—people coming and going at all times—and so much *fun*. Not only that. She was always so very generous, too. (Though where the money for that was going to come from, I couldn't for the moment think.) Dear old soul. Nobody quite like her.

My hectic imagination pictured birthday parties—mainly, but not exclusively, for the children—Christmases: merry, traditional Christmases such as I had never known; ever since I could remember, it had been just my mother and me, or Sylvia and me. I saw myself doing a little song and dance, the centre of a loud admiring group,

> Sometimes I think I've found my hero,
> But it's a queer romance;
> Come on, big boy—ten cents a dance,

my pretty twinkling feet still as pretty and twinkling as ever, my ankles just as slim, my footwear just as elegant. 'Oh, I would never let any man drink champagne out of *my* slipper, no matter how he begged! Only think, my dears, of how it would squelch afterwards!' I would turn into such a character.

And there'd be weddings, too. By then I wouldn't mind the thought of weddings. I'd be able to flirt with all the handsome young men—and even older ones—and they would flirt with me—and there'd be nothing but sheer enjoyment in it.

At some time after four o'clock I fell into a different dream, and in this dream Roger was walking up the stairs towards me, naked. He was dark and didn't look at all like Roger but I knew that it was he. I was waiting for him at the top of the staircase, in a long white garden-party dress, and I was aware without any feeling of surprise that I had changed as well: I was younger, I was very beautiful. But the stairs seemed to go on for ever; there must have been a hundred flights. And at the top they were spiralled, worn steps between chilly stone walls, as though I lived in a high tower. And I became afraid that he would take so long to reach me that all my loveliness would fade even as I waited. I would not merely grow old, but ancient. Haggard . . . The lovely dream became a nightmare, directed by Hitchcock but without his penchant for the conventional happy end.

When I awoke I felt drained, unhappy. I remembered for some reason how it had felt, early that same evening, to hold Thomas in the garden.

66

I remembered how it had felt, less than a year before, when my monthly periods had stopped coming.

Unused. Wasted.

I remembered that I had cried, on and off, all through one wintry Sunday afternoon, when the realization had (quite belatedly) hit me.

But—as if all that wasn't enough—there was another theme which ran through my restlessness, concurrent with the first: the book that I was going to write: the idea of gradually getting to know another life, a decent and attractive life, of working my way in, *feeling*, with a wonderful and enriching instinct for the creation of links. I visualized myself—here, too—as being on the verge of a new relationship, undoubtedly the most important of my life, on one level, as perhaps the other could turn out to be on quite a different one. Indeed the two themes almost merged. It struck me at some point that the naked man on the stairs might not have been Roger, after all. It might have been Horatio Gavin. I was in that midworld between wakefulness and sleep where such a notion didn't really seem too wildly fanciful, or even particularly far-fetched.

The face of the man, strangely, had become a blur. My own face remained clearly in my mind. It was the face of Scarlett O'Hara.

Of Vivien Leigh.

And when I finally awoke in the morning—because, there, there was something concrete to keep it in my mind—it was the image of myself at the top of the stairs that I remembered best. Vivien Leigh in a low-cut white crinoline, with frills at the shoulders and a sash at the waist. Kittenish but strong.

21

Although I felt refreshed, rejuvenated and thoroughly happy
once more, I was also mildly annoyed that it was half past
nine and that I had overslept by two hours.

But, even so, I didn't hurry. Things had to be done nicely;
especially nicely from now on. My breakfast table, with its
single rose; my lightly boiled egg, my thin crisp toast, my
little jug of real coffee. The housework, my warm scented
bath, the careful brushing of my hair; the application of my
creams and make-up. Yet none of it was wasted time—far
from it. Even while I dusted I looked about me for things that
he might recognize, for segments of a shared experience.
There was the moulding on the ceiling; this he would have
known, might have sat and gazed at, as I, almost two
hundred years later, gazed at it, traced its convolutions with
attentive eyes. The moulding—the very shape of the room—
the mantelpiece; yes, that too was original. Also, the fireplace. Right here he might have stood—surely did stand—
arms resting on the mantel as mine now were, one polished
boot upon the andiron, his eyes staring dreamily into the fire.
He had been twenty-one when first he came to this house
with his mother: I saw the back of his bent head, with its
thick, healthily gleaming hair, the broad shoulders and the
narrow waist, the long sturdy legs, the shining leather boots.
I imagined, underneath the fitted coat, the play of muscle
down that lean back.

Or in 1785 would the fashion still have been for wigs—and
shoes? I wasn't sure.

Yet details such as that were superficial and could easily be
checked.

And as I ate my egg, I knew the chances were that he must
have—hundreds of times—eaten a boiled egg. His bread

would have been coarser, his coffee from perhaps a different bean, but the taste of a softly boiled egg (mine was free-range, very fresh) must have been identically the same then as it was now.

So, with almost everything I did, I was preparing myself to see things, feel things—taste, smell, touch and hear them—as nearly as possible in the way that he himself would have done. It didn't seem too hard . . .

It was nearly twelve when I went out. I had a short list of boring things I had to get, but I went first to a stationer's. I looked at the ledgers, the account books, the minute books— how beautifully bound and tooled they were. None of the plain exercise books (no, that seemed totally the wrong word—*exercise*) quite came up to the same standard, but there was one, the most expensive, that had a rather lovely feel when I took it in my hands. But was it thick enough? And weren't the lines a shade too closely ruled? I replaced it on the shelf, with some reluctance. It had to be just right.

I went to Smiths. Again I hesitated. I made something of a tour of the city. I ate a ham salad with a glass of orange juice and a piece of French bread in the restaurant of a department store, and I reviewed the possibilities. In the end I went back to my starting place and bought the volume I had liked at first.

With that decision taken (no, with the book actually bought) I felt a great deal better, and as though I had made the best choice.

It was a less agonizing matter—slightly—buying the right pen. I had thought about a dip pen, being the closest thing to a quill, but memories of how the nibs had so often scratched small lumps out of the paper at school, and left unsightly blobs, directed me towards the ballpoints. I already had one, of course; but for this enterprise I wanted a new one, and a better one.

I bought a notebook for my handbag, and a giant pad of rough paper.

I went into the library again; took out a book on Bath and one on Bristol, another on eighteenth-century social history and a fourth on costume. I was glad the spinster with the glasses wasn't there.

I returned home feeling well satisfied with my purchases and borrowings. A light rain was falling. It was un-important. The gardens would be freshened, and perhaps there'd be a rainbow. On my way, I popped into the grocer's, bought quickly and extravagantly, without my normal comparison of quantities and prices, and didn't even stop to count my change. When the man at the bacon counter said, 'Not quite so good today—eh, madam?', I replied, 'Oh, I don't know. Where you see clouds upon the hills, you soon will see crowds of daffodils,' and even though we were nearer August than April, I thought it seemed a jaunty, wise and almost witty thing to say, and indicative too of the springtime which had come into my own life, just a little late, and was still on its way. And the man said, 'You're right, madam. I only wish that more folks were a bit like you,' and I felt like a combination of Wordsworth, Al Jolson and Walter Huston, only luckier than all three of them, and then I remembered that Huston was connected with 'September Song', not 'April Showers', but that too fitted in quite nicely with my frame of mind and I found myself singing it on the rest of my way home, not loudly, but obviously loud enough to make one or two people glance at me in amused surprise. Well, let them.

> And these few vintage years I'll share with you.
> These vintage years
> I'll share
> With you.

I also took good care, of course, only to set my feet well within the boundaries of each paving stone and not to mess up any of the joins. 'Bears,' I exclaimed a couple of times—crafty, jolly and almost impossible to hoodwink (I believe that on the second occasion somebody actually heard me! But what did I care if they did?)—'Bears, just look how I'm walking in all of the squares!'

Yet I quite forgot—rather foolishly—to keep a watch out for the rainbow.

I liked pavements. In London I had often imagined each flagstone to be hidden beneath the work of a prolific cockney artist, so that the whole pavement stretched off into the distance like a gaudy patchwork quilt made for some giant's bed. And I had thought that, Mary Poppins-like, I might some day walk right through one of those paving stones into a crudely chalked land of happiness and sunshine, where the colours would grow softer with every step you took. It was just a pretence, of course—though since coming to Bristol it was one that I hadn't at all indulged in. Perhaps—since I seemed to have outgrown it—I was now no longer a child but was indeed turning into a young lady!

You had to laugh.

I was still singing, in fact, as I dusted the table—for the second time that day—by the window in the sitting-room where I would sit and write my novel. I took the book out of its paper bag and laid it ceremoniously upon the polished surface. (Perhaps I ought to put the red chenille cloth there?—no, the colours would clash.) I corrected its angle slightly; put the new ballpoint pen beside it. I brought over an Anglepoise—fortunately there was a socket—and my big Longman's dictionary. Also the rough pad and the four books from the library. The Reverend Lionel Wallace's *Life*. Lastly I fetched the tiny vase which I normally kept for my breakfast table and my supper tray and placed it carefully on a doily—I would put a new rose in it in the morning; perhaps a yellow one. 'There!' I said, as I stood back and surveyed the whole arrangement with some satisfaction. 'All for you!' I glanced humorously towards the fireplace and then back towards the garden. 'I trust it meets with your approval.'

I felt I ought to drop a little curtsy, but didn't do so. Really, that would be *too* absurd.

Yet then I laughed. Where was the harm in a little absurdity? One didn't want to be solemn. Serious—but not solemn. I had the feeling that Mr Gavin, like Mr Darcy, might very possibly err, just a degree, to the too serious side; a little playfulness might be the perfect complement, the very thing he needed to lighten his personality the merest fraction.

I dropped a rather graceful curtsy.

Irreverent but full of fun.

It was four o'clock. I had my cup of tea and petit beurre. I moved my armchair just a short way over, a foot or so nearer to the fireplace. They said that it was better for the carpet, to shift your furniture occasionally.

22

No television that night. No novel. No newspaper. I had begun on my research.

I slept extremely soundly; got up a little earlier than my normal time. Broke with tradition and went out to the market *before* breakfast, to get myself some flowers, especially my yellow rose. It was a lovely morning once again.

I had intended to be seated at my 'desk' by ten o'clock. And indeed I was. As a preliminary to starting work I dropped the mantelpiece a curtsy—it was to become a feature of each day's commencement, a reminder of the need for levity. But on this first morning, though easily seated by ten, I was up again and going for my gloves and scarf by twenty past.

This wasn't a bad omen. Nor was it in any way an admission of defeat—although admittedly I hadn't yet thought of quite the right opening. But I had suddenly decided that for entirely optimum working conditions I needed, if possible, just one more thing. In fact it was a signal of victory rather than of defeat.

I could have gone to Mr Lipton's shop on the previous day—*should* have gone—but I'd felt nervous. Now I saw that timidity should play no part at all in any area of this undertaking. If Mr Lipton didn't still have that portrait, tucked away in some dark corner and just waiting for me there, as the Reverend Lionel Wallace's book had been waiting for me a few days earlier; and if he couldn't remember to whom it had been sold or help in any way to put me in touch with it

. . . then just too bad, at least I could still advertise; and if my advertisements brought no greater success, then again too bad, at least I still had the Adam fireplace and my intuitive vision of a friendly, dark-haired young man standing, with his back towards the room, gazing reflectively into the flames. I had seen him there again this morning, just as vividly as yesterday. I even had the distinct sensation (uncanny but in no way frightening) that one day he might actually turn round.

I found the shop without difficulty; Miss Eversley's directions had been entirely lucid. I saw the portrait in the window.

I laughed, out loud. I laughed right there, standing on the pavement: a spontaneous burst of laughter that was partly the effect of my ecstatic recognition of *him*, and partly an aid to his more sober recognition of *me*: an easy, quite informal greeting, in mature contrast to that clash of cymbals and full celestial chorus which, as a girl, I had often daydreamed would announce to the startled, awe-struck world, as well as to our own two selves, the eternal importance of that first meeting of eyes across the crowded—suddenly stilled— room or shop or station concourse.

And that wasn't all. For partly, too, my laughter was a message to the passers-by that even when you momentarily lost your faith you were reprimanded in the most loving, gentle, *generous* way.

I had thought, without too much conviction, that the picture might be waiting for me *in some dark corner*, just as the book had been. But how could I have forgotten already?—the book had been waiting for me within easy reach of my hand, at the very centre of the shelf. And I had said to myself doubtfully, 'Eighteen months since the house was cleared?' but the bookseller had said, 'I'd have thought I hadn't seen one of those in *years*,' and I still hadn't understood. Dear Lord. I was tempted not merely to laugh out loud on the pavement, amongst those absorbed and frowning shoppers, but even to go down on my knees on the pavement, inadequately to express my thanks and to appeal for forgiveness.

73

And he was exactly as I had expected—except perhaps for the wig: a handsome clean-shaven face that bore a wistful, sympathetic smile (the smile already captivating but one I could quite well believe would grow yet more so); a proud, determined chin; broad shoulders and the look of height. The picture must have been painted, I thought, when its subject was in his middle twenties.

And it was, too, just as Miss Eversley had said, superficially a sombre picture; and yet that made it all the more exciting when those vital grey-green eyes looked right out at you, fixingly, whichever way you moved—or, at any rate, whichever way *I* moved—as though, almost as though, now that the pair of us had finally come together, he had no intention whatsoever of allowing me to get away from him. Not ever.

I rushed into the shop. There was a man with a large, gingery, drooping moustache who wore a brown overall.

'That picture in the window,' I gasped—yes, as if I had run there every inch of the way and on nothing less than a matter of life and death. 'How much is it?'

(Irrelevant question.)

His eyes screwed up in a kind and lively smile that seemed at variance with the tired moustache. 'You mean my old friend, the unknown gentleman?'

That, afterwards, would make me smile. *Unknown? His* friend? 'Yes, yes,' I said.

'Eight pounds to you, madam.'

'Oh—thank you!' I said.

I paid by cheque—not because I hadn't got the cash on me, and not that I could ever forget, in any case, the date of such a purchase, but because I wanted to have it written there upon the counterfoil, a monument in black and white, 'Today I met Horatio—in the flesh!'

Today I met my destiny.

While I made out the cheque, Mr Lipton took the portrait from the window.

'Well, I can see that he's going to a good home.'

'Are you a psychic, Mr Lipton?'

'What, madam?'

'Yes, today's the day he's coming home.' But I didn't want to explain too much. 'You're quite right.'

'All the same—we're going to miss you, my old chap.'

I was torn between slightly resenting this easy familiarity (but, after all, eighteen months did confer on you, I supposed, a position of some privilege) and feeling amused and rather proud that such a display of friendliness could only have been evoked by a natural propensity, on the part of its recipient, to inspire friendship.

Again, the sheet of brown paper—which wasn't even new—and the length of thin white string that had just been lying there untidily, a remnant, amongst a scattered mass of bills, seemed out of tune with the momentousness of the occasion.

'No, no,' I cried. 'Don't shut him in. You just don't know how bad it feels.'

'Madam?'

'To be cut off. In semi-darkness. To have to fight for life.' I laughed—I don't know why—it wasn't funny. I shuddered. 'Imagine being buried alive!'

'No, thank you, madam.'

'I saw a film once. A woman was entombed. She did finally manage to break out, but—'

'I'd say, then, that she was definitely one of the lucky ones.' His tone sounded a bit abrupt, but then he gave his crinkled, kindly smile. 'You're really quite sure, are you, madam, that you wish to take it with you? We could deliver, if you wanted, by twelve o'clock tomorrow.'

It! As though I could bear to be separated from him now for twenty-four minutes, let alone twenty-four hours!

'But perhaps I'd better let you order me a taxi.'

A quarter of an hour later I was standing in my own sitting-room. I should obviously have to find another place for the Pissarro, that had lived above the mantelpiece. Although I had wondered very briefly about positioning Horatio (did that sound, perhaps, a little *too* informal?) in a spot where I should see him last thing at night and as soon as I awoke each morning, I knew instinctively that there could really be no question about his rightful place. And, yes, indeed. The very moment he was hung there, he truly did seem to have come home.

Besides, I couldn't help thinking that the bedroom, though nice in many ways, somehow wouldn't have been *quite* the thing.

Not really.

That morning, by second post, I received a polite but rather chilly letter from the bank. I was overdrawn by £15— could I please make good this deficiency as soon as possible? This came as a complete surprise and just two or three days earlier, although I had a few shares left to sell, would have been a very nasty shock indeed and might well have made me quite depressed. (Yet I had not, even once, felt lastingly depressed in this kind house.) Today, however, my reaction to the news was more surprising than the news itself. I felt that it simply couldn't have mattered less. I felt gay about it. Defiant. I was ready to take on the world—and that included bank managers. I knew that that handsome, strong-faced, utterly *trustworthy* man who had had his thoughtful, smiling gaze turned full upon me as I read the letter was—without question—going to look after me from now on.

'Oh, thank you for coming home. Thank you for waiting for me.'

I laughed. My delight was effervescent and irrepressible. I lifted my feet off the ground and hugged my knees. My eyes never left his face.

'But how does it *feel*,' I asked, 'to return home after nearly two centuries?'

(Yet why was I automatically assuming that it was as long as that?)

'You *have* been here before.' I meant the picture, just as much as I meant the person. I clicked my shoes together, in continued glee. 'And in my heart—earlier—I was criticizing poor Mr Lipton. But how do you even start to make a homecoming after two hundred years seem properly momentous? Someone should have fired a cannon; I haven't even cracked a bottle of champagne. But I *shall* go out and buy

76

one, shortly—a fig for Mr Butcher! Thank you for coming home,' I repeated. 'Thank you for waiting for me. It is so *good* to have a man about the house!'

23

He was born after a difficult pregnancy and a long and painful labour to a woman who was then approaching forty—nearly an old woman, for those times—but who, despite twenty years or more of fearing that she would never conceive, had still been so *determined* that she was going to have a baby. (When I thought of that determination I became quite weak with gratitude at the reminder that Horatio's life had depended on such a network of fine threads—though I had never felt that way about my own; and I almost loved her, loved her as myself, while I wrote about her suffering.) After the child's delivery the midwife went down on her knees, thanking her Maker—and his—over and over again, with hot tears coursing down her face, good honest woman that she was. Horatio's father, elderly and sensitive, was also much affected. '"My dear, we almost lost you. Mr Trelawney says . . . that this young fellow here . . . our very last attempt . . ."

' "Mr Gavin," his wife answered, "the good Lord has harkened to our prayer; and what a miracle He has vouch-safed us! So great a blessing as this would make me appear greedy indeed, were I even to *think* about desiring such another."

'And she smiled up at him with so much simple goodness on her adored and loving, courageous, lovely features, that he quickly had to turn away, for fear of causing her soft heart a moment's consternation . . .'

By five o'clock that afternoon—even though I had not properly started until two—I had covered fourteen sides of my rough pad! And by nine o'clock, when I had copied them up neatly—with not one single crossing out!—over six sides of my finely bound exercise book. (But oh, how I had hesitated before inscribing my first fateful word upon that awesome snowbound land, a land which as the springtime thaw advanced might burgeon into richness. A timeless enchantment, for both the writer and the reader. Indeed, as a reader, I never embarked on any serious novel without still hoping, half hoping, to find between its covers the solution to all of life's important mysteries and ills: a story somehow so self-contained and comprehensive and engrossing that it would render the reading of all others totally superfluous. My first word—apart from 'Chapter One'; as yet I had no title— was 'On'.) When I at last laid down my pen, I made a playful feint of collapsing; and how my hand and fingers really did ache! But I felt marvellously elated by the act of creation; I hesitate to say 're-creation', since it was, of course, a novel, although 're-creation' is what I knew it really was. The *details* might be wrong—for the Reverend Mr Wallace had in truth mentioned nothing of Horatio's birth, other than the fact that he *had* indeed been born, nor had he given me, for example, the ages of Horatio's parents—but the spirit was entirely right. And even the details . . . well, I had from the first moment the strongest feeling that I was being guided; led on and inspired in the same way (I am aware that this may sound presumptuous—but why, when you truly think about it?) that the Gospel writers must have been led on and inspired; my brain, my hand, my pen the media through which some higher agency was aiming to communicate. Oh, yes—I can promise you. It really was a great and glorious feeling.

I hadn't stopped for supper—and even my afternoon cup of tea had been just *that*, a cup of tea, poured in the kitchen and carried up with two biscuits on the *saucer*! I laughed at this and said that art on all future occasions must not be allowed to interfere with civilization; but that, for this first afternoon only, I had a special dispensation. And I knew *just* what the Reverend Mr Wallace meant: Horatio's smile really did seem to grow a little wider, in appreciation of this gentle joke.

At first I intended to eat out; I rather fancied something light and delicate at a good restaurant. Indeed, I had already put on my coat and was standing before the mirror in the hall adjusting my—rakish, rather saucy—hat, when the idea came to me: if there *were* going to be any celebrations, how unfair to think of holding them away from home. Unfair, and thoughtless. I took my things off quietly, as if by doing it stealthily enough (idiot that I was!) I might avoid having my intentions guessed, and I went to look in the refrigerator. There was a little cold chicken, some ham, I could open my one tin of asparagus, there was even a bottle of white wine on the top shelf of my store cupboard. And this time—making up for my relapse—I did it all very properly indeed, even to the second wineglass (which I hoped was a nice, forgiveness-seeking gesture) and the clean damask napkin folded into a sort of tricorn. Even the yoghurt looked rather pretty, poured into a sillabub glass with a stem and sprinkled with cinnamon, and of course I had the freshly polished silver that my mother had inherited from *her* mother. I had already applied fresh make-up but I tidied my hair again, now that I'd removed my hat, and as I walked upstairs and into the sitting-room, bearing the tray carefully before me, I felt in the proper festive mood, happy, expectant, even perhaps a little nervous, just as if this were a proper party. And from now on, I thought, any true celebration would always be held at home. It was almost a promise to him.

24

I hadn't been to church in years—perhaps in the whole course of my life I had only gone a dozen times—and certainly the last two or three occasions had not been for purposes of saying thank you. What prompted me on this particular Sunday I didn't know. One could just as easily say thank you elsewhere.

Besides, I felt embarrassed as I entered. Where to sit? There were already lots of people and I felt their eyes were all immediately upon me. Who is she? A resident? Someone on holiday?

Yes, yes, I wanted to say; the answer to each alternative is yes. Life should be a holiday.

I chose a place quite near the front. This was a mistake. I couldn't see most of the congregation without turning round.

On the other hand, perhaps it wasn't such a mistake. I was wearing a very dashing sky-blue skirt and jacket. White blouse and scarf. I had taken a full two hours to get myself ready.

I followed through the thought about a holiday. If you had enjoyed a holiday you didn't mind the fact of going home. It was only if you felt you hadn't made the most of it that you saw its end approach with anguish. This time a week ago, you said . . . This time ten days ago . . . It could all have been so happy if I'd only tried; if I'd only made light of all the silly irritations.

I should come to church more often, I reflected. I had merely been here a few minutes and already I was having worthy and profound ideas.

Yes, life was *just* like a holiday. Imagine coming to the end of it and thinking, Oh if only I had realized; if only I had been determined to be cheerful, to capitalize, to beat the odds.

How different it could all have been!

Just imagine the sheer *awfulness* of it: of only finding out the truth (or what you thought to be the truth) when it was far too late.

Well, I, thank you, was having a lovely holiday . . . now. Yes, enjoying myself immensely—progressively discovering more and more about how to get the utmost out of each new day. *I* had not left it too late, mercifully. I was busy creating my past.

Should I go up into the pulpit? It was very close; I could do it oh-so-easily. And wouldn't people get a surprise! I should love to see their faces.

'Ladies and gentlemen. What is a storm in the bathwater?'
(Pause for dramatic effect.) 'I'll tell you what it is. It's a
shipwreck; it's a desert island. It's a fortnight in a sarong.
Now . . . whom would you want to spend that with?
Another question you must ask yourselves is this. When
finally your Book of Life is closed—will it be a success story?
For that's what everybody wants—isn't it? A success story.
And every day's a page. Go home and splash your bathwater.'

How that would have shaken them up!

But unfortunately the service started while I was still
thinking about it. A lady started playing the organ.

It was a long time since I'd heard an organ. Yet why should
it take me back to the Odeon in Leicester Square? A trailer—
just a trailer: 'I wonder who's kissing her now; I wonder
who's showing her how . . .'

At the time I had never appreciated that old Wurlitzer. I
think I'd even been a little bored by it.

What sacrilege!

'The Lord be with you.'

'And also with you.'

Good gracious, we *had* started. Where was I?

The minister was young and not bad looking, in a beefy
sort of way. That no doubt added a little pep to the service—
no wonder there were so many women present. I might even
come again myself, next Sunday. He had nicely shaped
hands—well-manicured—and their backs were dark with
hair. His wrists as well. He probably had a thickly hairy
chest.

'Almighty God, to whom all hearts are open, all desires
known, and from whom no secrets are hid . . .'

I did my best to concentrate.

As a matter of fact it wasn't Almighty God whom I ever
worried about: his knowing what went on inside my
mind—or even inside my bathroom. It was my father, mother,
Aunt Alicia, Bridget, et cetera. (Sweet Bridget—
whose nephews had once wanted to marry me.) Would
they all have his understanding? I'd have felt shy in front of
Aunt Alicia; but not at all in front of God. Wasn't that absurd? I shook my head and laughed at the absurdity of it.

The minister glanced in my direction.

Oh, dear. I should have to apologize to him afterwards.

We had a hymn.

> Dear Lord and Father of mankind,
> Forgive our foolish ways . . .

That was nice. And at least I knew that my singing voice was undeniably an asset.

'I'm so sorry that I laughed. It wasn't disrespectful. I was simply having fun.'

'Miss Waring, that's exactly the kind of sound I want to hear inside this church. It was like a breath of—well, between you, me and the gatepost, Miss Waring, I must confess we don't normally get enough of it. The congregation at St. Michael's—perhaps I shouldn't say this, in view of their kind hearts and good intentions—has always been, well, quite frankly, a little *stodgy* up till now. And I do hope that we're going to be seeing a great deal more of you. I heard your singing, by the way. May I ask—do you sing professionally?' He added as a postscript: 'And may I say, too, how lovely I think the colour of your suit?'

He was a most pleasant young man. During the reading of the Gospel I asked him a few questions. He was delighted by my quick intelligence—by my refusal merely to accept. I told him something of what Mrs Pimm had said: about the man who had thrown himself from a skyscraper and landed on a passer-by. 'Vicar, do *you* believe in second chances? You see, I keep getting this picture of the flat man being given *his* second chance. Don't laugh. It's like the resurrection of a Silly Symphony. He goes loping off down the street, a cardboard cut-out of a paving slab, grinning rather foolishly.'

He did laugh.

'I say it again, Miss Waring. A positive breath of spring.'

'Now, Vicar. You just keep your mind on business. You haven't heard my question yet.' I rapped his knuckles with my fan. 'Supposing that he *didn't* get that second chance? Would you say, then, that he was simply in the wrong place at the wrong time—or would you actually believe that it could have been the right place, at the right time?'

82

I smiled.

'I also want to ask about King David—and Bathsheba.'

'My goodness! I can see you're going to be a full-time occupation! But listen, Rachel; standing here over coffee isn't really the moment for deep metaphysical discussion. You know the vicarage? Well, I'm afraid it's mostly a shambles, because my housekeeper, dear old soul though she is, isn't quite the world's most dedicated cleaner—nor cook; but if you can find it in your heart to overlook such shortcomings as these . . .'

It was all just agreeable nonsense, of course. I hadn't brought my fan.

He was now mounting to the pulpit. I prepared myself, quietly and without fuss, to listen to his sermon. First I smoothed my skirt out under me and crossed my legs—there was so little room—arranged my hem below the knee. Then I smiled, with shared expectancy, at those about me. (They didn't seem too friendly.) Lastly I cleared my throat and looked all eager and attentive. I even bent forward slightly, so that he should see how I intended not to miss a single word. Vicars, after all, were only human; they, too, grew happier with encouragement. 'It's just like talking to your flowers,' I whispered to the woman next to me. In my own case, however—how should she know?—it was a great deal more than that.

'We clergymen are always a little behind the times!' he began, quite mystifyingly. (There was a small but appreciative ripple of amusement. I myself laughed, I think, more loudly than anyone.) 'If you will forgive me, I should like to quote to you from an Epistle we had much earlier in the year.' *Forgive* him? For something so immeasurably considerate? He knew, of course, that this was my first time there and that I hadn't had the opportunity of listening to it on the earlier occasion. 'Beautiful words can sometimes become so familiar that we almost stop listening to what they mean.'

That was very true. I nodded my approval. I felt inclined to call, 'Hear, hear!'

'"Though I have all faith,' he said, 'so that I could remove mountains . . . and though I bestow all my goods to feed the poor . . . and have not charity . . .'"

There was a long and telling pause. He appeared to be looking straight at myself.

'"It profiteth me nothing,"' he said.

He spoke the words deliberately and clearly and with force. I could see his knuckles white upon the rail, those very knuckles that, just a minute or so before, I had wanted playfully to tap.

'It—profiteth—me—nothing!'

For the sake of appearances he swivelled his head slowly, from right to left, but I knew full well that my own eye was the only one he was genuinely intent upon catching.

'In other words,' he said, 'without love I would still be worth nothing at all.'

I could hardly believe it. He went on to talk about the hunger strikers in the Maze—did I actually even know the precise number that had died so far? How persistently had I prayed for any one of them? How many policemen and rioters had been injured at Toxteth? What was the name of that six-year-old child wedged down a well in total blackness for three days back in June? When was the last time I had passed a mental hospital or a shelter for alcoholics, or indeed even an ordinary hospital, and thought at all deeply about any of the unknown people inside it? What did I know about the oldest victim—or the youngest—who had been killed in trying to get across the Berlin Wall?

From there—somehow—he went on to talk about how I might so easily just be whistling in the dark, how I needed to take a long hard look again at my priorities, how he felt about *Clash of the Titans* or *Excalibur* or Shirley Temple for all I know—I really wasn't listening. He stood there looking so pious and dynamic, with his hairy hands and his hairy chest and his hitherto honeyed tongue, and of all the messages of comfort that he could have chosen as a happy and a loving welcome he had deliberately gone and picked a text like that, and at only a moment's notice! How cruel; how unspeakably cruel! To have made me think that he was genuinely glad to have me here: a leavening and stimulating influence, a charming touch of spring: and then to have shown only too plainly . . . What was it—jealousy? Was no one but himself permitted to invigorate? Well, he could keep his invigoration. He could keep both his hairy hands *and* his hairy chest; *I* didn't want any part of either of them.

'"And now abideth faith, hope, charity, these three; but the greatest of these is charity."'

'Some hope!' I said—I thought, quite wittily—staring around me in defiance.

He ended—as though he had just thrown it in for good measure—'"For now we see through a glass, darkly."'

There was a pause. I picked up my handbag and gloves and almost walked out, right there and then, before he had even turned round and begun to leave the pulpit. *That* would have caused a stir. Yet just in time I stopped myself. People must *not* be allowed to see the extent to which they had hurt me.

But, during the next hymn, I didn't sing.

Oh, yes, I moved my lips all right; it was just that I let no sound emerge from them. I could see him looking at me in pretended consternation, and how I rejoiced.

'Oh, have you strained that lovely voice of yours, Miss Waring?'

'I think I should make it absolutely clear to you, Mr Morley, that I am no longer fooled by that rather smarmy way of yours. Please go and practise it, therefore, upon somebody else.'

When the collection plate came round I did not put in the pound notes I had planned. I almost put in nothing. But then—far more subtle than that—I saw I had some silver in my purse; and I put in precisely 35p. I thought that he would realize the significance.

I began to feel a little better. By the time everybody suddenly and inexplicably started shaking hands with one another (they were obviously a friendlier bunch than I'd supposed) I had sufficiently recovered—by dint of ignoring, blocking out, trying to think only of pleasant things—to be fully able to participate. Indeed, I did so readily and with aplomb, considering that I was somewhat taken aback: 'How do you do? Don't you find it rather cold in here?' What a lovely way of making contact; now *this* really was welcoming.

'Hello, do you come here every week? My name, by the way, is Waring.' Unfortunately—how very British—people didn't seem too overwhelmingly responsive: hands, yes, smiles too, but nothing that went any deeper. Never mind. I found it by far the nicest part of the service—well, that and singing the first hymn. I had been feeling happy then.

Afterwards, the vicar placed himself outside the door; but that was one hand I certainly had no wish to shake. 'No, thank you,' I said—though quite politely. (I totally ignored his Good morning, I believe you're new here.) He looked really at a loss: piety, dynamism, invigoration—all. 'Er . . . there's coffee in the church hall, if you'd like some.' Because he so clearly didn't expect me to accept, I nodded graciously and answered, 'Thank you, yes, I'd like a cup. But please don't worry. I think I can take care of myself.'

Perhaps he wasn't *quite* so bad as I had drawn him. I had always been taught the overriding importance of good manners: I felt I ought to make amends to some extent: I went back, while he was still, I noticed, gazing after me, and said, 'Incidentally, I forgot to thank you for the wafer and the wine. You may be surprised to hear that I believe in the idea of transformation; at least, I think I do. Not, of course, that I'm a Roman Catholic.'

'Er . . . no,' he said.

I made a little joke. After all—I wasn't likely to forget our first ten minutes of comradeship; not quickly at all events. 'And I don't suppose you are, either?'

'Er . . . no.' He had no sense of humour; and, in reality, not much conversation.

I went in to have my coffee.

The hall was fairly crowded. I joined a little queue at a small counter. There was an older woman just in front of me; she was looking in her purse for change. 'How much is the coffee?' I asked. I hadn't realized that they would want me to pay.

She smiled at me in a very friendly manner. 'Five pence,' she said. 'I hope that you enjoyed the service. Oh, excuse me a moment: I see that little monkey of mine is making a pest of herself again.'

86

But her three- or four-year-old came across obediently enough, as soon as she was called.

'Well, I can't say that I thought very much of the sermon.'

'No,' she agreed, 'I didn't either. I'm afraid you hit an unfortunate week as far as the sermon was concerned.'

Which amply confirmed for me, of course, what I already knew.

She laughed. 'I quite expected it to be about the Wedding. But not a single mention of it from start to finish.'

'Oh, well . . .' I murmured. One could learn to be philosophical about these things. There was some good to be said of everyone.

We got our coffees; her daughter had a squash. We stood together a short way from the counter, suddenly not appearing to have very much to say to one another.

'Let's hope the weather's nice and sunny for next Wednesday.'

I smiled, and nodded.

'I do think Lady Di looks such a charming girl.'

'Do you?' I said.

From her expression I might have announced that I'd just left a bomb in the vestry. 'Well—don't you?'

'Oh, I daresay she's pleasant enough.' I laughed. 'But you must admit she's very ordinary. Very ordinary indeed.'

I sipped my cup of coffee. It was particularly revolting.

'Oh, well, yes, perhaps. In a way. I suppose she is. But that's what makes it all rather nice, isn't it? I mean—he's marrying the girl next door!'

'Precisely,' I said. 'That's just my point.'

At least I had the satisfaction of seeing her, too, look a bit perplexed for the moment. But then it was suddenly as though she'd discovered a trump in her hand which she'd almost forgotten that she'd got. 'She certainly appears to be a very popular choice,' she remarked.

'Yes, you're right. But I just can't help it if I am out of step. I really don't see what all the fuss is about.' It was a relief to be able to say it, to a perfect stranger whom one would probably never meet again.

'Well . . .' She smiled, a little vaguely. She seemed to be

87

looking around for someone else to join our group. 'At least much better than some foreigner,' she suggested—with a brightness that sounded oddly forced.

'I'm not so sure.' She had obviously not followed my argument. 'An Englishwoman—well, it could have been you, or me, or anyone. Just picture it,' I laughed, to add a little levity, a little reassurance, because for some reason she was looking slightly flustered. 'Coming out of St. Paul's. Riding through the City in an open carriage. Thousands lining the route, cheering themselves hoarse, waving flags, holding their children up to get a look at you. Loving you like the Queen herself. But *why*? Where is the fairness of it? Why *her*, and not you?'

'I am a *degree* older than she is.' The woman laughed; I had cheered her up again. Once more, it was a victory for politeness.

'But you do see what I mean, don't you? She doesn't even dress well.' I shrugged: my good-humoured bewilderment at the folly, the sheer excess, of it all. 'And Dr Runcie has asked for the prayers of the entire nation to be offered during the ceremony. Why? Haven't they already got enough, without our all being expected to pray for them as well? But of course'—I smiled—'to them that hath shall be given.' It was the old, old story.

I never got an answer. Before she could give one her little girl had made an abrupt turn and jerked her mother's elbow. The woman's cup of coffee was knocked out of her saucer— and threw most of its contents down my skirt. I shrieked.

The next few minutes were chaotic: someone with a tea-cloth doused in cold water, half a dozen more offering remedies and opinions, anecdotes and concern; the scolding of the child; the cleaning of the floor.

The little girl cried—the mother had been sharp with her, and she no doubt felt baffled, frightened and defenceless. The woman herself was close to tears. The two of them each received as much consolation as I did. More.

It was the first time I had worn it. It was ruined.

'Are you all right?' somebody asked me. 'I'm sure the stains will all come out.'

88

'Yes, thank you,' I replied. 'I'm perfectly all right.' I added, with a wryness they would not appreciate: 'I've had my little bit of fuss.'

I noticed that the vicar was carefully keeping his distance. How very typical, I thought. In times of joy, some people had the Archbishop of Canterbury; in times of stress, others didn't even get the vicar of St. Michael's.

The *victim* didn't cry until she got outside the church and began walking home with the damp cloth cold and heavy and unyielding against her legs. She didn't cry, indeed, until she'd walked at least a hundred yards.

The *other* victim, perhaps one ought to say.

The sky had a large dark cloud in it, with spiky runs towards my knees.

But, when I got home, I knew at once the cloud would soon disperse. I was so glad to get back to Horatio. The more I saw of other men—most other men—the more grateful I was for what I had. I had been very blest. How could I have forgotten?

25

The best thing about the Royal Wedding day—apart from my work on the book—was undoubtedly *The Sound of Music*. For the first time I was struck by the line '. . . like a lark who is learning to pray.' Somehow, I thought, it seemed quite applicable to myself. A little message, almost. A nod of encouragement on the way. It was an oddly appealing idea.

Afterwards, on ITV, there was another film. It was very feeble. I didn't watch it all. The only thing I approved of was its title. *The Lady Craves Romance*.

Poor Miss Eversley, though. I felt a little shifty. I hadn't phoned her; I hadn't bought her a jigsaw. Of course, it seemed she hadn't wanted either of these things. So perhaps that was all right—I had been totally sincere in both those offers. But, whatever happened, I must never become a person who didn't keep her word. Larks who were learning to pray must always be straightforward—free of cant. Someone to rely upon.

And I should never be short of inspiration. I had the perfect example in front of me. Above the fireplace. And sometimes, even . . . when I was being particularly blest, particularly receptive . . . *at* the fireplace, too.

Dear Lord. If *I* couldn't finally win through, there-fore—given circumstances like these—well, who on earth could? I sometimes felt that I'd been singled out for glory.

More often than not, however, I felt I simply didn't stand a chance; though—now—it didn't seriously depress me. Strange!

I was a sister to the Wandering Jew; a well-loved face aboard the *Flying Dutchman*.

A charmed life that carried a curse—or a cursed life that carried a charm?

In short, I knew neither what sort of person I really was, nor how well I fitted in; nor if there was any hope for me in the place where I was bound.

26

All through the following weeks he *grew*, though not quite with that wonderful fluidity which had attended his birth; and at the same time, obviously, the novel grew as well.

It was clearly going to be a long one; before I was done, I should need to buy perhaps another *two* of those impressive thick volumes. But that didn't dismay me—quite the reverse. I was so far from being in a hurry to finish it, indeed, that I would have to ration myself to only three hours' writing per day. Even now, with that finish maybe still *years* in the future, I didn't know what I would do when eventually it came. My life, I thought, would once again be empty; although I did realize with a part of my brain that it could never now be that. Emptiness came only with achievement forgotten; with thinking that one was alone and quite uncared for—that one's passing from the world would go unheeded. I need surely never have any fear of that.

And I didn't crave critical or popular acclaim; or not particularly. If it arrived, of course, that would be pleasant—and not simply on my own account, either, indeed far from it—but we were not impatient for it. Even unpublished, the three wine-red volumes would still look very good, immensely distinguished, in their place of honour, between book-ends, on the mantelshelf. And in any case the journey was what counted. Always. I could know for sure that, while it lasted, my life was his life. His life was mine.

So when he went swimming naked in the creek, with other boys his own age, I was there with them as well, enjoying it all as much as they. And when he scrapped, his hurts were my hurts, his victories *my* victories. My tears fell like his when he saw beggars dying in the streets, or heard about the injustice of the lawcourts, or the misery inflicted by the press-gangs. My entreaties were added to his when he pleaded with his father for money, with his mother for articles of clothing, with Nancy for food, to pass on to the homeless, the crippled, the drunk, the desperate. I got a headache to match his own when he worried over his Latin verbs or his algebraic formulas, or when the sad wife-ridden Mr Tole got one of his periodic bouts of choler and none of his pupils could do anything right. But my joy was surely as great as his, too, when he first heard Mr Handel's music and his heart leapt in exultation; the experience in itself surely just as revelatory. For I, on my own, had never much enjoyed 'good' music. This was now incomprehensible. I wondered at my blindness—or, more properly, of course, my deafness (this was one of our silly little jokes; we were gathering quite a store of them)—and more especially, far more guiltily, at my great selfishness. It should have *occurred* to me, right from the start, to play the music of Handel and Mozart and Gluck and Haydn (these last two names didn't come to me immediately, any more than those of earlier composers, like Purcell, Byrd, Scarlatti). Even stating it at its lowest, it would have seemed a sensible thing to do, when one thought about creating the right atmosphere. (Unnecessary, unnecessary.) While from every other viewpoint . . .

For the first time in my life I felt ashamed to own no classical music whatsoever. I couldn't afford to *buy* all the records I now wanted, for although I was not a bit worried by the low state of my finances I was at least being sensible, but very fortunately the main public library included an excellent record section. No sooner *had* it occurred to me, so belatedly, than I rushed round, breathless, without even any scarf or gloves, and brought away as many records as I was allowed. (They almost made me go home for my stylus; I said a little prayer; they waived the rule, for this occasion.) And from then on the eighteenth-century house was filled with eighteenth-century music. Or earlier.

But not exclusively.

'I am getting more and more to appreciate *your* music,' I would say, 'and I realize that a great deal of my own time's is rubbish, but, all the same, it won't do you any harm, you know, to get a little better acquainted with at least some of it . . .'

And playfully hectoring him in this fashion (oh, how I nagged the poor fellow!—'I feel sure that Mr Tole would sympathize with you!'—but he was always extremely good about it) I would put on Jack Buchanan or 'Gypsy' or, just for old times' sake (a tribute, I had thought sentimentally, when I had bought it, both to an over-painted maiden aunt and to an undervalued time of childhood), a selection from *Bitter Sweet*.

> I believe . . .
> The more you love a man,
> The more you give your trust,
> The more you're bound to lose . . .

Or even (but not from *Bitter Sweet*):

I really must go . . .
But, baby, it's cold outside . . .

And I never once saw him wince—although I half expected
it. I was pleased. Education was a two-way process. We had
so many things to give each other.

And occasionally I would dance a little too—usually to the
strains of some rather dreamy waltz. (I could never have done
that if I'd kept even half of Aunt Alicia's furniture.) And I
would hold my hands out, as if I were being moved slowly
around the floor in the arms of some invisible partner, sometimes imagining that I actually felt the pressure of his left
hand upon my right, actually felt the pressure of his arm
half-circling my waist. And on each occasion I was held more
closely.

There were even times when I wasn't so sure that it was all
merely in the imagination.

27

The Allsops came back —though not, I must confess, nearly
as soon as I'd expected. Not that that mattered; I'd had so
many other things to occupy my mind; and the thought that
they might have temporarily forgotten me had caused me
little heartache. Yet when I saw them standing on my doorstep again I felt so pleased.

'What can you think of us?' asked Celia. 'Saying you must
come round to us in a few days—and then not getting in
touch with you for nearly three weeks.'

For nearly five weeks.

'What nonsense!' I exclaimed. 'You're young. You've got
your own lives to lead. I don't expect—'

'Oh, it isn't that,' said Roger. 'But we've all been down
with summer colds and there seems to have been just one

thing after another—what with all my studies, and that wretched job of mine . . .'

He looked even more golden and more Viking-like than ever.

'Well, I'm sure that you know how it is,' he ended, with a grimace of utterly irresistible charm.

'Oh, I do, I do. Really, you don't have to explain a thing.'

'Just so long as you don't think that we're insincere,' added Celia. 'We really couldn't bear that—could we, darling?'

She looked at him devotedly—that same old smile of doting admiration—but I didn't find it quite so disturbing any longer, and, realizing this, I felt even happier. There was just no reason any more to be envious of anyone.

'No, I would plunge a dagger in my heart,' he confided, 'rather than think that you thought that.'

'Oh, a little drastic—surely?'

'In fact, madam, it's all your fault,' he declared cheerfully, the penitent stepping with ease into the shoes of the accuser. 'If, like sensible people, you only had a phone—'

'Oh, that's unfair,' I broke in, gaily. 'The Post Office keeps promising that they're going to connect me. I want to be connected. Should I go down on my knees and pray to be connected?'

For an instant he himself went down upon one knee, his hands imploringly upraised, like Jolson about to give us 'Mammy'. 'Connect me with the human race! Oh, please connect me with the human race! Somebody—somewhere—must want to hear from me!'

'Yes. Sylvia,' I smiled. But my heart sank. She would be here with me on Friday.

'That would be charming,' he said, as he got up, 'but I'm afraid that it mightn't accomplish very much. Unless, of course, you went right to the fountainhead—no intermediaries—addressed your prayer to Buzby. But failing that it would be quicker to become a doctor. Or even—if you must, I suppose—a clergyman.'

'Don't listen to him, Miss Waring. Darling, I think you might be being offensive.'

'Oh, not at all.' I denied it with a laugh. 'Just absurd. And anyway . . .' I was about to point out that although I might not have a telephone as yet I certainly did have a letter-box; but I just stopped myself in time. *I* didn't want to make anything of their not having been in touch. It was they who were making so much of it. 'And anyway—enough of all this nonsense. Let's talk about important things. How's my little Thomas? May I hold him again, Celia? And then I'll just pop down and put the kettle on.'

'Your little Thomas,' said Roger, 'is just about as good and sweet and angelic as . . . well, I don't know . . . as his father is.'

'No longer, then, the noisiest little thing in the whole of the south-west?'

'He never really was.'

'He's certainly getting a lot heavier.'

'Oh, he's going to be so big and strong and bonny. Aren't you, Tom? Just like your old dad. Disgustingly healthy. Never a day's illness from one year to the next.' He laughed and poked his son merrily in the tummy. 'Do you mind if I take my jacket off, Miss Waring? It's rather warm, isn't it?'

'Oh, *please* . . .'

I added—perhaps a little outrageously: 'After all, I have seen you in the past, not only without a jacket but even without a shirt!'

He grinned. 'Well, I'd forgotten you'd had that treat.'

I said: 'I hope you don't put on a suit and tie especially to come and see me?'

He seemed about to deny it but then he spread his hands. 'I think one should always pay one's friends the compliment of trying to look one's best if one knows one may be going inside their houses.'

I inclined my head, graciously. 'And I feel honoured by that compliment, I really do; but I'm surprised—surprised *and* delighted—to find that someone of your generation should think like that. Yet, all the same, Roger, the next time that you come . . .'

'No,' said Celia, 'the next time, *you* are definitely coming to us.'

'Besides,' enquired Roger, 'why do you say someone of *my*

95

generation? That makes it sound . . . I don't know . . . as though we came from different planets, as though you were Methuselah. I honestly don't see it that way. Nor does Celia—do you, lovie?'

'Not at all.'

'That's very sweet of you both. But . . .' But what? 'How long *is* a generation, anyway, come to that?'

'Oh . . .' He shrugged. 'Isn't it something in the region of twenty-five years?'

'Well, in that case we don't even belong to different generations. Nothing like.'

'Who said we did?'

'But the fact remains that I call you Roger. And Celia. You call me Miss Waring.'

'What was that, Rachel?' He bent towards me, frowningly. We all laughed.

'I didn't even realize that you knew my first name.'

'Ah. I bet there are other things you never realized about us.'

'I'm sure there are.'

He shook his head. 'No, that's utterly the wrong cue. You're meant to say, "Like what?"'

'Oh, your daddy!' I said to the baby in my arms, giving him a merry shake, which made him laugh. 'Oh, your funny old daddy!' But of course I did what he wanted.

'Like, for instance, the fact that we'd very much like you—if you would—we'd really be so very happy—if . . . No, *you* tell her, Celia.'

'No, *you*, darling.'

'Well, if you'd be that pickle's godmother . . .'

28

Here it was then: the true start of that other road, which would soon unwind across the poppy-filled landscape like yellow thread, a road running companionably beside a river bank. When (at long last) I went to put the kettle on, I half danced my way downstairs—in the hall holding Roger's jacket out in front of me, a sort of scarecrow partner from the Land of Oz, en route for a coat-hanger and a coat-peg. Celia called down after me: 'May I come and give you a hand?' 'No, you stay there with Tom,' I answered—it would have spoilt it all.

I hung up—I smoothed out—his coat. I filled the kettle.

'Dancing in the dark,
With a new love;
I'm dancing in the dark,
Here with you, love . . .'

'Caught you!' said Roger. 'Caught you red-footed! And what a pretty voice you've got.'

'Oh, you villain.'

'I wish you wouldn't stop.'

'Well, you don't really expect me to carry on before an audience, do you?'

'I'll tell you one thing. You're certainly not Methuselah.'

'Twenty-three,' I said. 'Next birthday.'

'Really? As much as that? You surprise me.'

'Sycophant.'

He laughed. 'Now tell me what I can do.'

It was fun. He got out the milk jug and the sugar bowl and the teaspoons—though I could have done it all far more quickly myself—and he shook some more sugar lumps out of the packet, and he filled the jug and sliced a lemon; then he went off across the road—'But I insist, Roger, that you take this.' 'And I insist, Rachel, that I do nothing of the sort'—to buy some cakes. While he was gone I went to see if he'd taken his jacket, and, finding that he hadn't, I slipped two pounds into the breast pocket. My life seemed incredibly full; my heart felt as though it would quite burst from happiness. I buried my nose for a moment in his jacket.

Upstairs they spoke about arrangements for the christening, and some of the people who were likely to be there. 'It will all be very *dull*, Rachel, but afterwards you and we and a few of our more special friends will have a bit of a knees-up to atone.' I could hardly be insensible of the magnitude of the compliment. My hand shook slightly as I poured the tea.

'Are you expecting someone else, Miss Waring?'

'Rachel,' corrected Roger.

'Because you may think Thomas *very* advanced, but he doesn't yet handle a cup and saucer with total confidence.'

I stared at the fourth teacup. 'Oh, that's your husband's fault. He was so busy playing the fool down there that he got me quite mixed up.'

'No; I noticed that it happened last time, too.'

Then, frightened perhaps that I shouldn't like to admit to absentmindedness, she quickly put another question—it must have been the first thing that came into her mind.

'Perhaps I shouldn't ask—I'm always far too curious—but . . . who is Sylvia?'

Roger laughed. '"What is she, that all our swains commend her?"' His laugh had relieved any slight suggestion of awkwardness.

I looked at him questioningly. 'Shakespeare?'

He nodded. '"Holy, fair, and wise is she."'

For a moment I held my head a little to one side. 'Wholly fair?' I said. 'Hmm . . .'

'"Is she kind as she is fair? For beauty lives with kindness."'

'No—don't,' I begged. I was beginning to giggle. 'You'll make it so that I can never look her in the eye again.'

He giggled with me. They both did. 'Who *is* Sylvia?'

'Sylvia was my flatmate in London. She isn't *quite* as you

describe her; at least I don't think that she is . . .'

'But, Rachel. You can't quarrel with Shakespeare.'

'I beg his pardon.'

(How he seemed to have the gift of drawing from me repartee.)

'It appears, then, there are just two possibilities. Either when in London you saw only through a glass, darkly'—I hoped that I didn't start—'because to be frank in my book there's nothing surer, whatever people may say, than that familiarity *does* breed contempt; or else—'

'Yes? Or else?' I think it must have seemed, almost, that I was interrupting.

'Or else he just got the names mixed up. He was describing the wrong flatmate.'

Well, if I coloured now, it was certainly not from any too painful association.

'All these compliments!' I managed to get out, eventually. 'I'm really not quite used to them. But, "Thank you, sir," she said.' (I would have dropped a curtsy.) 'Which play does it come from?'

'I think—*The Two Gentlemen of Verona*. It's not a speech, by the way; it's a song.'

I nodded. Just so long as I knew where to look for it, afterwards.

Mirror, mirror on the wall, who's the fairest one of all? Not you, Rachel Waring!

> *The other day upon the stair*
> *I met a man who wasn't there;*
> *He wasn't there again today;*
> *I do wish that you'd go away!*

He.

No. You, *Bobby.*

'You'll have to learn to sing it,' he said.

Celia may have thought that her husband was getting a little too carried away (if so she was probably right) because she now changed the subject, rather abruptly. 'These are such pretty cups,' she said. 'I meant to mention it the last time that we came.'

'I believe you did.'

'Did I? It must get boring. Everything here is just so pretty. So . . .'

'Attractive,' said Roger. '"Pretty" is such a milk-and-water word.'

'I was going to say "perfect". You must excuse us, Rachel.' This time she got it right. 'It must be very bad form to enthuse all the while; at the very least, a bit lacking in sophistication. But the real problem is—I seem to have fallen in love a little with your house.'

'Well, you *know* you don't have to apologize for that,' I smiled. 'Who wants sophistication?'

'That picture's new, isn't it?' said Roger.

I nodded. I didn't trust myself to speak.

'We've been admiring it.'

For several seconds the three of us gazed at it in silence.

'One of these days I'll tell you all about him,' I said.

'Ah. Is there a story, then?'

'There certainly is. But not for now. I'm only going to say—at this moment—that if it wasn't for him I myself shouldn't be here.'

'You must be joking!'

'I can assure you that I'm not.'

Then how they tried to draw it out of me! But I wouldn't let myself be coaxed—not this time—not even a little way; I was determined not to compromise. It was far better, I often thought (despite my natural inclinations), *not* to give everything away too quickly.

29

Poor Sylvia. When I'd left London, August had still seemed a long way off, and I'd hoped that after several months of our being apart it would probably be very pleasant to have her spend three days with me and let me show her Bristol. For, after all, to begin with, we had got on rather well. But when her letter arrived at the start of August I had thought: three days without writing, three days without privacy, three days of weighty talk and cigarette smoke and ceaseless coughing; how can I bear it? Three days of profanity and sensible down-to-earth attitudes . . . tainting everything. And I had wondered if I could perhaps make some excuse to save myself from such a purgatory, the thought of which grew daily more oppressive. *Any* excuse—it wouldn't much have mattered if she'd seen right through it. But as soon as I'd reflected I had felt ashamed. *He* wouldn't have made one. And did a mere three days really represent such a terrible sacrifice?

'I will be good,' I said. 'I will learn. Please don't despair of me. I must have my little grumble.'

No, I mustn't.

'I shall be gay and full of laughter, then, no matter what. No one will ever know. Except you.'

Yes. Poor Sylvia. After all that foolish trepidation of mine, when she finally arrived, late-ish on the Friday evening, it *was* very pleasant. I felt quite remorseful—and exceedingly relieved. She obviously liked the house, even if her praise was never totally unqualified and usually had to be fished for a little; she was funny about her new flatmate (though not too maliciously so—and in any case when was I ever likely to meet Miss Carter again?); and with all she said about the intrigues in her office and about some of her adventures on the underground and buses, I kept thinking how very blest I was to be out of it all, how very blest I should still have been even if the blessing had been a purely negative one.

But she—evidently—didn't see it in quite that light.

'Christ. What do you do with yourself down here all day?' I hadn't yet told her about the book. (I'd decided, since her arrival, that in fact I might.) 'Apart from listening to the bloody *Archers*?' she added.

I laughed. 'I haven't been listening to *The Archers* for some time.'

'Streuth.'

'It's just astonishing how the time goes. Well, first there's the house itself, of course . . .'

'Don't tell me you've become a woman for going out and *joining* things. I'd never believe it. Do you mind if I smoke?' she said.

At least she asked these days—even if, from her actions, she assumed automatically the answer would be yes. Some day she might become a positively reformed character.

I passed her an ashtray. We had brought our coffee cups upstairs and I had drawn the curtains and put a divertimento on the record player, quite softly and unobtrusively—which was perhaps, as Roger had remarked at our last meeting, not really the way to play classical music.

'Nice,' she said, letting out a long sigh of contentment and, miraculously, not coughing. 'Though I didn't know you went in for any of this highbrow stuff.' I only smiled, non-committally. 'You'd better eat some of these things,' she added; 'in any case don't leave them too near me. Obviously *you* still don't have to worry about your bloody weight. It's damned unfair.'

Besides the box of liqueur chocolates, she had brought with her a frozen chicken and two bottles of wine. When I'd remonstrated over this she'd said, 'At least *I*'ve still got a job. Such as it is.'

Yet she hadn't brought me any housewarming gift—unless these things could be counted as one. Of course, I hadn't let her know of anything I wanted; but then, she hadn't reminded me. It wasn't that I was mercenary: an inexpensive present would have been most welcome, if I could only have believed it had been chosen with some care; and she *had* spoken about getting me something. So it was rather a shame: despite my unexpected pleasure at seeing her again, I still had to keep trying very hard not to remember what that video recorder had cost me—especially since it was money I could well have done with at the moment.

Well . . . never mind.

Now she quickly grabbed one of the chocolates before they left her side too finally, and repeated her earlier question.

'But what on earth do you find to do?'

'Oh . . . this and that. I've made some friends, you know.'

'Oh, yes?' She bit into her chocolate and then tilted her head back to drain the half she was still holding.

I smiled. 'There's a very nice chemist.'

She made several appreciative sucking noises and then unscrewed the little label which she'd cast into the ashtray. 'I can thoroughly recommend the Benedictine,' she said, and picked up her cigarette again. 'Not *tradesmen*, my dear?'

'He says I've changed his life.'

'*Does* he indeed? Good for him. Good for both of you.'

'And then there's a deceased clergyman's wife. Widow. I had tea with her the other day. That was very nice.'

'Did you read *The Lady*?'

In the early days I had often found Sylvia's sense of humour one of the most attractive things about her. Then, notwithstanding its coarseness, it had seemed the cause, or effect, of an enviable ability to laugh at life—rather than simply at people.

'Also a rather *physical* vicar who complimented me upon my singing and my intelligence, and all but suggested that I drop in to cook a meal for him.'

'He did what?'

'A sort of candlelit tête-à-tête. Of course, I very firmly sat on that idea.'

'Well, more fool you. And, anyway, what do you mean by *physical*?'

'You know perfectly well what I mean, Sylvia.' I reproved her with a laugh.

But I had saved, of course, one of the best things till the last.

'And then there's a charming young couple, Roger and Celia, who—would you believe it?—have asked me to be the godmother to their firstborn: young Tommy—he's adorable. The christening is to be next week. A very crowded, rather plush affair, so I believe.'

I could see that, this time, Sylvia was really impressed, despite her every effort to conceal it. I immediately went on to tell her what Roger had said about the probable dullness of this great occasion and his suggested remedy. 'I swear they think I'm quite as young as they are!'

Sylvia said: 'I can see why they're so charming!'

She glanced about her and I got up and fetched her another ashtray. She accepted it with a rueful grin. 'I haven't *quite* managed to fill this one yet.'

'Anyway,' I said, as I sat down again, 'you're as young as you feel.'

'Obviously.'

'It's my new motto.' I laughed.

> Stay young and beautiful,
> It's your duty to be beautiful . . .

It was strange—we kept on talking but even when the Mozart had come to an end, that perky little tune was still irresistibly in my head, making it impossible for me not to tap my foot. I hadn't thought of it in a long time. Now, however, I was sure that I'd remember it. It would be rather nice to have a theme tune. Like Aunt Alicia had had *her* theme tune.

And it was perfectly true, of course: I'd always been happier when I had a motto.

Even now that I felt so assured of happiness, a motto could only be a choice and desirable extra ingredient.

> Don't forget to do your stuff
> With some powder and a powder puff;
> Stay young and beautiful
> If you want to be loved . . .

'I know what you've got on *your* mind,' said Sylvia. 'You and your corny old tunes.'

I smiled, affectionately. 'I remember how you used to call me the Croaker.'

'Well, one of your most infuriating characteristics was that habit you had of humming under your breath—totally out of tune and on a monotone. How it could drive me crazy.'

I didn't understand.

'Why did you do it? That's what I'd like to know. Did it seem to you beautiful?'

'What do you mean?' She was smiling, too—well, if not affectionately, I should at least have said amiably. You had to get to know Sylvia.

104

'All those dreary tunes. Why were you always singing—still are, of course, for anything I know about it?'

I stared at her.

'Surely it's the right thing to do, isn't it,' I answered coldly, after a pause, 'to try and face life with a song?'

'Oh, Christ. Pollyanna!' She coughed, then shrugged—and even laughed. She had always been amazingly impervious to changes in the temperature.

'Anyway, why on earth do you say under my breath and out of tune? I should think I could sometimes be heard all through the house; and . . .'

But I suddenly caught his eye—or, rather, he suddenly caught mine. I looked down at my hands; I looked up again. I made an effort.

'And?'

'And . . . I'm sure you *don't* know what was on my mind.'

'You're forgetting, my girl, that I lived with you for close on eleven years—for my sins.'

'All right, then?'

Clearly, she couldn't have expected such persistence. But Sylvia-like she was determined to make good her boast—or at least to go down fighting. The first was an almost impossible assignment; one admired her spirit—even while one was mystified by her choice.

> 'Fairy tales can come trew-ew-ew,
> It can happen to yew-ew-ew,
> If you're young at heart . . .

Well, I'm not bloody Frank Sinatra. I only wish I was.' She gave a caustic laugh. 'Not that he should go around getting too big-headed about that.'

Poor Sylvia. Suddenly I did understand. I didn't know who had first called it the green-eyed monster—but they were surely right. Sylvia's eyes were flecked with green.

'Yes, you're perfectly correct,' I said. 'You're really very clever.' I had stopped my toe-tapping. (Of course, long since.) I remembered when I'd seen that film.

She let out an incredulous guffaw—triumph taking over from astonishment. I wanted to change the subject. I said:

'Did you know that Howard Hughes once sat on the lavatory for seventy-two hours? Adventurer, playboy, film maker. And unbelievably handsome, as well. But later . . . Three days, three nights, of battling with his constipation. Imagine. Could you really call *that* a success story, I wonder?'

Sylvia looked at me most oddly. Well, she had certainly stopped crowing and I had certainly managed to change the topic.

'I must remember that as a gambit,' she observed, 'when I'm next asked out and can't quite think what to say. I've always been so shy with strangers.'

But *she*, I knew, wasn't, in fact, whatever she might say, asked out very often.

'I didn't know you even used words like that,' she said. 'Lavatory. Constipation. I didn't realize you were aware that they existed.'

I smiled, but said nothing: a woman of mystery.

Indeed it sometimes seemed to me that I did have a gross streak which perhaps I ought to keep my eye upon. I sincerely hoped, anyway, that on this occasion I had not caused any offence.

Sylvia, I thought, would have been delighted, rather than offended.

I was right. 'I can remember,' she said, 'when *I* sat on the lavatory for forty minutes. One gets all sweaty with frustration.'

'Oh, *Sylvia*!' I exclaimed. 'No—don't! Please.' Automatically, my eyes had travelled upwards.

'Well, you were the one to bring it up, my dear.' She smiled, a little grimly. 'Association of ideas, perhaps? Come on—you'd better tell me all about your romantic chemist. I realize you've been dying to. How old is he, for a start?'

I struggled not to take umbrage.

'Oh . . . I don't know. Early thirties?'

'My God, you *are* cradle-snatching.' She was very jealous. 'Does he sell love potions on prescription? If he does, I think I'd better have one.'

'No, he . . . he helps the poor.'

'That sounds a barrel of fun.'

106

I realized, of course, that she was scoffing, but I didn't mind—or not sufficiently to stop me. It was so lovely to be able to talk about him. I now wondered why—woman of mystery or not—I hadn't in fact done so last Tuesday, with Roger and Celia.

'You see, he's got this idea that because he was born with—well, comparatively—a silver spoon in his mouth he must always do what he can to help those . . . less fortunate than he is. I think he sees it as his duty. Do you remember, by any chance, *Magnificent Obsession*?'

She nodded—with a queer little twist to her lips. 'Both versions,' she answered. 'Do you want to say he's more Robert Taylor or more Rock Hudson?'

'Oh, neither. He's himself. Just as good looking as either of them, of course, but . . . he's got such lovely eyes; they seem to suggest that there's *nothing* he can't understand, nor forgive. Above all, he's a very sympathetic listener. I talk to him by the hour. And, as a matter of fact, if you'd really like to know what he looks like . . .'

'Yes, I would. Obviously I must meet this paragon.'

'Oh, you can't.' Foolishly it hadn't occurred to me that she might want to meet him. 'I mean, he's gone away for the weekend. Gone home, to Bath.'

'Hope you offered to scrub his back for him?'

'What?'

'In the bath?'

'Oh, I see.' I laughed, but very dutifully. 'No—Bath, home. You'll see him another time, maybe.'

'Home—to his family? To his wife and children?'

'No, of course not. Home is where your parents are. It's the place where you were born.' I added irrelevantly: 'His father's dead.'

'I don't believe a word of it,' laughed Sylvia, but in my relief at having escaped, quite easily, what could have been an awkward situation, I overlooked her somewhat gruff unkindness. 'Oh, his father may be dead,' she conceded.

I didn't deign to make an answer.

'And you're one of the poor, I suppose, that he's been trying to help?'

'Don't be stupid.'

She suddenly had a prolonged paroxysm of coughing—her first really bad one of the evening. It was useless to ask her if she *never* meant to give up smoking.

When she had finished she happened to be looking, watery-eyed and still slightly wheezy, above the fireplace. 'What a bloody awful picture,' she suddenly remarked. 'I feel the two of you are sitting there in judgement. And I honestly don't know when I last saw anything so gloomy. I meant to comment earlier.'

It was the final disintegration of our friendship; on my side, anyway. And there were still a whole three days to run—or nearly so. It was going to be even *worse* than I had imagined. 'Oh, help me!' I said silently; suddenly quite desperate. '*You* will probably forgive her. But I don't believe that *I* ever shall.'

30

There were things, that night, which I remembered.

(There were things, most nights, which I remembered.)

I remembered, for instance, lying awake on light summer evenings with the sound of music floating in through my open window from the pub across the road—a narrow sidestreet called, ironically enough, since in those days it was still very much a slum, Paradise Street. Often I didn't merely lie awake, either; I'd get out of bed and kneel beside the window, my knees, only cotton-protected, on the hard lino, my elbows—or sometimes my arms and cheek—upon the cool sill. The music was so jolly: even when it was something sad, like 'There was I, waiting at the church . . .' everybody standing around the piano (although I couldn't actually see in) and joining in with such gusto—how much I wished I could have been amongst them. Sadly, by the time that I could have had my wish, the singsong round the pub piano seemed to have gone out of fashion—though I don't suppose, anyway, that I'd ever have been brave enough to venture in. Never mind: at least I'd profited upon those bygone summer evenings—indeed, upon the winter ones as well, for many a time, once my mother had departed, had I raised high the window, then huddled up inside my bedclothes, like in a small snug leakproof boat upon a stormy sea, and heard the words more clearly. There had been a warmth about those hazy lights in winter, the imagined cosy conviviality around a log fire, especially towards Christmas-time, that I wouldn't willingly have done without, even for the softer summer air. And I had learned songs—so many songs—which, whenever heard in later life, would instantly bring back such potent memories of childhood resilience and expectancy and illusion and innocence—of so unbounded a potential for happiness, indeed—that one could almost believe, in fact very often did, that one had actually been happy, with an unclouded type of happiness that one was ever trying, afterwards, to recapture, no matter from what base of contentment; oh, my, how distance lends enchantment . . .

I remembered my bedroom.

It was a small, cream-coloured rectangle, almost box-like, with a boarded-up fireplace and cheap furniture. But it had my window at one end and it had my pictures, more than a dozen of them (the wall alongside my bed was very nearly covered), for when I didn't simply cut them out of magazines and have them framed—very cheaply, in Paradise Street, he was only quite a young man but he was always so extremely kind and gentle, and with a rabbit hutch in his back yard—I saved up my meagre rations of pocket money and bought them for 1/6d. or even half a crown, mainly at junk shops but sometimes at the nearby Woolworth's in Oxford Street. I nearly always spent my pocket money that way, except when I had to buy my mother a birthday or a Christmas present (when my father was alive I got extras for things like that) and except when I once bought a large secondhand book about films or when I used to get, again from Woolworth's, cigarette cards of the stars or a pin-up in a photo frame; and except when, occasionally, I had to pay for my own cinema . . .

(He was knocked down and killed, that gentle young man with the club foot, just before I was fourteen; I never knew what happened to the rabbit. I was too shy to find out. And *I* couldn't have kept it, anyway.)

I remembered how I would sometimes sit before my mirror (or, rather, lift it down from my chest of drawers and sit with it upon the bed) and wish that I was beautiful; but how, for long periods, too, I would try to avoid mirrors totally, like Queen Elizabeth, and live in a blemish-free land of hopeful possibility.

I remembered how, when I was older, I used sometimes to dream about Gary Cooper or Gregory Peck or, mostly, a fair-haired athletic young B-picture player whose name these days I just can't bring to mind. But in the only film of his I saw he spent most of the time in a swimsuit or shorts, perhaps because he had such well-shaped, muscular legs. When he came to see me in my daydreams he was usually wearing shorts as well. Sometimes, he wasn't . . .

But, chiefly, I remembered something else. What I remembered longest, that night, was the party. That party, and its aftermath . . .

31

His very first words to me.

'Hello—I'm Tony Simpson. I just wanted to say . . . I think you did that *Lady of Shalott* thing awfully well.'

'Oh—did you like it?'

'I thought it was excellent. You know, you've almost sort of made history at this party.'

He seemed a bit hesitant, though—almost shy—which is perhaps the reason that I very quickly felt at ease with him; but which later I did think a little strange when I learned that he was training to be a representative. But he was very young, only nineteen, which could well explain his occasional nervous glances behind him, almost as though I were the first girl he had ever paid a serious compliment to and he was needing to cut the apron string that tied him to his friends. I liked that. He was perhaps a little too thin for my total satisfaction and his nose, as well, was perhaps a trifle beaky, but otherwise he wasn't bad looking; he had nice hair and quite a sensitive expression. And he was no mean hand with the compliments. He followed up those first ones almost immediately by saying, 'As a matter of fact you ought to be an actress.'

'That's what I want to be.' The flush of success was still upon me. For the moment such an ambition seemed nearly a possibility.

'Not just because you recited that thing so well'—he appeared to be growing more confident as he spoke—'but because you also remind me a bit of Vivien Leigh.'

'Really? Do you mean that? But Vivien Leigh is *beautiful*.'

'She's my favourite film star,' he said. 'I've seen *Gone with the Wind* four times.'

'I've seen it twice.'

'I'd go and see it again tomorrow if it were on.'

'So would I.'

There was a pause. I was suddenly terrified that he might simply nod and move away.

'Do I *really* look like her?'

'Hasn't anyone else ever told you?'

'No.'

'Well, I think so, anyway.'

Pause.

'What did you mean, when you said I'd sort of made history at this party?'

'Oh, nothing much.' Again that nervous glance across his shoulder, that search for reassurance from a phalanx of his friends—he didn't even know that he was doing it. 'There's a sort of catch-phrase going around,' he said, uneasily. 'I bet you must have heard it?'

'Catch-phrase?'

'Yes; I don't know why.'

'What?'

He hesitated. '"The curse is come upon me."'

'". . . cried the Lady of Shalott."'

'Yes.'

'Oh, that's nice.'

He seemed heartened. 'It's like a sort of password: it gains you entry into any group.'

It was fast becoming the loveliest evening of my life—in every way. I even liked his beaky nose. But it was to grow still nicer—who said that selfish prayers were never answered?

(It wasn't, of course, a wholly selfish prayer.)

'Would it be all right,' he said, 'if I took you home after the party? I have a car.' He suddenly sounded so decisive.

A little later I did hear someone use that catch-phrase; Tony was perfectly right. It was a man, though—which did in truth make it sound a little absurd, and no doubt accounted for the screams of laughter, both masculine and feminine, that greeted it: 'The curse is come upon her!' he said. But he was certainly admitted entry to the group, most cordially, and I was delighted to think that it was *I* who was responsible for all that hilarity and good feeling. Well, I and Tennyson together. We made a fine team. Tennyson and I, with Tony Simpson in support, cheering us on so loyally.

In the car he said, 'And perhaps it *is* on somewhere!' No more defiant or panicky or jubilant glances across his shoulder, because, of course, none of his friends was in the car with us, and now, as well, with perhaps no little assistance from myself, the umbilical cord had been very cleanly cut, it seemed.

'*Gone with the Wind?*'

We were marvellously attuned.

'Yes.'

'Perhaps it is.'

But I wasn't taking any chances.

'As a matter of fact there's another film I'd very much like to see, called *Young at Heart*. It's supposed to be very good and it's on at the Astoria in Charing Cross Road.'

'*Is* it?'

'Last week it was at the Tivoli in the Strand.' I felt this somehow rather clinched the matter.

'You know, I'd really like to see that, too.' Oh, God *was* in his heaven. All *was* right with the world. The following morning my mother said:

'It must have been a fine party—in spite of all that fuss you made beforehand. Aren't you grateful to me, I said you had to go?' She sounded very jaundiced.

'It *was* a fine party. Why?'

'You've got a sparkle. It makes you almost pretty.'

What praise!

'Who is he?'

'A man called Tony Simpson. He's going to take me to the pictures.'

'Why—does he think that you've got money?'

'No, of course he doesn't.'

'Well, just don't let him make a fool of you, that's all.' She poured me out a cup of tea and pushed across the toast rack. 'Though he'd be something of a fool himself, I suppose, even to want to.'

'Why?'

'Oh, for heaven's sake, don't pick me up on every word I say.'

Young at Heart would have been a special film under nearly any circumstances. It was charming, funny, tender, sad: about an ordinary middle-class American family (no 'characters' or eccentrics) to which anyone in her right mind would have given almost anything to belong. Doris Day was one of the three daughters, Ethel Barrymore the amused, no-nonsense, understanding aunt, Gig Young the good-natured irresistible newcomer the whole family quickly fell in love with. Added to all of this, there were some very good songs.

It was so enjoyable, indeed, we saw it again the following night! My mother was *astonished*! And even when, a whole week after that, we went out together for the third time, she was still quite clearly at a loss to understand it. (And didn't I relish, didn't I revel in, didn't I wallow in, her amazement!) Each time it was wonderful, despite that tiny bit of disappointment I always felt when first I saw him—which just ten minutes later, anyway, was all forgotten; but the third time was the best of all, even though the film was much less entertaining and even though, at the very end of our evening . . . Well, anyway. In the cinema we held hands; for a lot of the time; and even when we didn't, our arms were very close together on the armrest—it was early summer and we both had on short sleeves. Afterwards he kissed me, in the car. It was heaven. We had a coffee and a Danish pastry in an espresso bar and we talked, oh how we talked, of all *sorts* of things, I can't remember what, but everything we talked about we agreed upon, and we found that we had so many unexpected things in common, and though he never actually mentioned children when we spoke about what we most wanted out of life, or even marriage, and though I couldn't yet quite be sure he loved me, and though I kept on telling myself, so unavailingly, that it *might* be a mistake to wear my heart upon my sleeve—still, I thought, still, it really did seem as if he must be growing in affection, in esteem; indeed I was certain of it—we had to be turned out of the café when they wanted to close; it was just like one of those romantic comedies where the members of the orchestra are beginning to yawn more and more because the starry young lovers don't even realize that they're the last couple on the floor, the last couple in the restaurant . . .

They stroll away with a giggle and a wave; maybe a fur stole trailing . . .

And when he reached my home, instead of stopping the car in Marylebone High Street, as he had done each time before, in front of our rather drab main door (our flat was on the third floor, over MacFisheries), he turned into Paradise Street and drove down to the end of it, where there was a public recreation garden—in which I often used to read—with ancient, nameless gravestones, the statue of a little boy, an unused bandstand and some playground swings. He pulled up before the locked gate. It was after midnight and the streets were quite deserted.

'I really ought to be getting home,' I said—but without too much conviction. 'My mother doesn't turn her light off till I do.'

'Oh, just another ten minutes,' he suggested. 'Please. Another ten minutes won't make a lot of difference.'

He was (just like Gig Young; well, no, perhaps not *quite* like Gig Young) completely irresistible.

'We could get into the back,' he said, 'if you liked. It would be more comfortable.' His voice held that very same uneasiness—yet now combined with a dryness, a brusqueness, almost—that had drawn me to him at the first. Poor Tony. It sounded so very far from casual.

> 'Ten minutes more,
> Give me ten minutes more,
> Only ten minutes more,
> In your arms . . .'

I said—or rather sang. 'Tessie O'Shea,' I added brightly. He wouldn't see that I was nervous.

'Yes.'

We cuddled on the back seat. His hands were everywhere. For the first few minutes I was more than just nervous—I was even scared—and could only sit there, rather stiffly and passively. But, even simultaneously, I was thrilled—if that were possible. I thought, 'Rachel Waring, this is you—the first time—a complete woman—a real live man with you, doing all this. Enjoy it.' And gradually I did relax; most of my apprehension left me and my whole body began to tingle with anticipation. By the time his lips were upon one of my breasts, glinting white above my pushed-down brassière, I felt quite weak with longing. I heard myself moan and was so happy—such a reflex must absolutely mean this was the proper thing—and I began to writhe (well, as far as I was able, the car not being a very large one) and my hands began to fumble with his clothing, moved caressingly beneath his shirt—what did it matter if his chest was thin and flat and smooth?—along his trousered thighs—even as his own hands fumbled their way under my skirt, kneaded a little, suddenly pulled at, almost tore, the garment which I wore beneath it. Oh, God—it was such bliss. A man's hand, warm, hard, questing, unpredictable, where a man's hand had never been before. We didn't talk; we only moaned—yes, actually the two of us; who wanted talk? But when I realized that one of his hands was just then trying to get his trouser buttons unfastened I did just say, 'Oh, do you think we ought?—have you any—?' or perhaps I only thought it, because I can remember thinking, too, that a new life resulting out of this would be the most glorious thing I could imagine—I didn't want to be conventional—and a baby, anyway, must surely mean that he would marry me. I waited—there was a brief hiatus, a giddy moment of suspension—feeling more positively alive than I had ever felt before, alive with sheer expectancy and love and a sense of culmination. It occurred to me suddenly, with both my hands upon his chest, that I couldn't picture, wouldn't want, a chest more beautiful.

There was, unexpectedly, an exclamation. A second afterwards I was aware of something rather warm, felt its warmth even through nylon—a fluid, which spurted along one of my thighs, slipped down the inside, copiously, some just above the stocking top, dripping and growing cool between suspenders. 'Oh, *God!*' he said. 'Rachel, I'm *sorry!* I *am* sorry! Oh, *God!*'

It did take me a moment to adjust, but the first thing that I recognized—perhaps even before the fact of my own disappointment—was *his* misery. 'It doesn't matter,' I cried, 'it doesn't matter; darling, it doesn't *matter*.' And I soothed his damp brow, tried to ease away its creases (that I could sense rather than see), ran my hands around his ears, stroked the back of his head and neck, endeavoured to comfort him in every way that I could think of. 'Oh, darling, it doesn't matter. And I enjoyed myself, I really did. Was it . . . was it . . . quite good . . . for you as well?' I think he gave a sob.

'It was a farce,' he said.

'Oh, no, don't call it that. It was a wonderful experience.'

'I couldn't even get it into you,' he remarked; I was surprised at so much bitterness. 'Here—here's my handkerchief. You'd better clean yourself up and then I'll get you home.'

I took the handkerchief; it was larger than my own. 'I'm sorry for the mess,' he said. His voice was rather toneless. He started readjusting his own clothes.

'But you mustn't be sorry. Not for anything. I truly don't mind the mess.'

I added after a moment—it didn't strike me as being crude:

'In fact I really enjoyed the feel of it. Shooting out like that. All devil-may-care and . . . and imperious. You know, in some ways it's quite a compliment: that he was so excited; just couldn't wait . . .'

I tried to make an even better joke of it. 'All nicely chambré-ed, too. The perfect temperature.'

I even capped my own pleasantry—I so much wished to see him smile.

'The perfect womb temperature!' I felt inspired.

'It didn't get there,' he said.

He got into the driver's seat while I was tidying up and just sat there a short time, till I was ready and had begun with some silly, gay remark to open the door. 'No, you may as well stay where you are.' It took him less than a minute to drive the length of Paradise Street—even allowing for turning the car round.

'I'll wash this out,' I said, 'and let you have it back the next time that I see you.'

He shook his head. 'It isn't worth it. I'll throw it away.'

'But it's a *lovely* handkerchief. I wouldn't let you.'

I got out of the car. He crossed the pavement with me, stood outside my door.

'Rachel.'

'Yes, darling?'

He faltered. 'If you should ever meet any of the others . . . and they should *say* anything . . . you wouldn't let on that it was such a farce . . . would you?'

'Of *course* not, Tony. Of course not. Besides—why should—why ever—such an occasion . . .?'

But I wasn't hurt that he had asked me. I had read about

the tremendous vulnerability of male vanity in matters such as these, and he was very obviously upset and not himself.

No, I wasn't hurt. What, afterwards, had the power to sadden me far more (a little absurdly?—no, not at all absurdly) was the fact that I had once been so very close to a man—almost as close as any person *could* be to one— almost at the very root of him—and I had never even . . .

I couldn't believe that it was possible.

So close and yet I had never even touched it. Never placed my hand around it.

Yet that wasn't the thing that really hurt. What made me cry with vexation more than once—actually sob into my pillow with the crippling awareness of opportunity wasted— was . . . no, not the fact of never having had it drive powerfully up and down inside me, close packed, oh-so-tightly a part of me . . . no . . .

I cried for something simpler than that.

I cried, because I had never even seen it.

32

I felt that, almost from beginning to end, the Bank Holiday represented a pure travesty of hospitality. For the first time in that house I seemed to have lost nearly all my inner peace.

To make matters worse it rained, on and off, all through the holiday, and Sylvia—never at the best of times an outdoor person—didn't seem at all disposed to come out and explore. She sat around and read the newspapers and looked at television and did the crosswords and the air appeared to get thicker and bluer by the hour. I opened as many windows as I could but along with the rain there had sprung up a driving wind, and I seemed to be faced with the alternatives of either getting everything drenched or having all my cushions and furnishings forever redolent of stale tobacco. But, in reality, there was no alternative. Sylvia enjoyed a fug.

'Is it *always* like this in Bristol?' she asked, with quiet satisfaction.

'No—quite the reverse. We've had a lovely summer.'

She laughed, derisively. 'Strange—when the rest of the country seems to have had the coldest, wettest one on record.'

Also, she liked to belch; she was an inveterate loud belcher. '"Whoever you are, wherever you be, always let your wind go free,"' she had formerly been prone to quote at me. '"For not doing so was the death of me."' She claimed it was a factual epitaph. 'I still don't see why you have to be *quite* so flagrantly earthy and natural about it,' I used to complain, in some way or another, whenever I felt driven to it—and once, wittily, 'But *your* letting it go free will probably be the death of *me*.' And this weekend, it appeared, she was extra intent upon remaining alive. Or had I just forgotten? In any case, during the whole of those three days, at least until the Monday evening, I don't believe that I even once raised my voice in song.

Fortunately the television set was on the ground floor, in what I called my breakfast room, so for a great deal of the time I was able to get her downstairs. ('*Some* of us still have to make do with black and white,' she announced, with the same somewhat gloomy satisfaction. 'But of course *I*'m not one of the gainfully unemployed!' Well, really! I thought, remembering the video.) Yet though the radio was there as well, and I kept on returning the crumpled newspapers, folded as best I could, to the table where we ate our meals, and left one bar of the electric fire on all the time, she *would* keep drifting up the stairs again, as though even she, despite her blindness and bad manners, was somehow drawn uncomprehendingly to be often in his presence.

Indeed, as I saw that she appeared to be quite fascinated by the picture—because she couldn't ever leave the room, if I was there, without at least some casually disparaging remark—I did, a little, begin to soften towards her again. After all, who had hated Christ more thoroughly than Saul of

Tarsus? And I began to think that even for slovenly Sylvia there might come her slightly soiled Damascus. Despite my carefully suppressed sensations of resentment, and unwillingness (now) to share, I began to be intrigued to see if it might possibly come about by Monday evening—that opening of the sky and great blinding flash of revelation. 'You could do it,' I thought. 'I know that you could do it if you wanted.'

Not that it seemed very likely. After breakfast on Sunday, looking for some distraction on the radio, I happened to catch a few moments of the morning service. 'Tom Lehrer once said that modern maths was so simple that only a child could understand it,' was the preacher's first comment that we heard. 'Well, it's precisely the same thing, you know, with prayer—and with trust. They're so simple that only a child can understand them! And that's exactly why Jesus said we must all become like little—'

'You can't really want to listen to all this muck,' said Sylvia. She reached across and turned it off.

'I thought that it might entertain you.'

'I don't *need* entertaining. You're my best friend. You shouldn't have to work at entertaining your best friends, you know.'

Then, inexplicably, she flipped it on again. They were now singing a hymn.

> 'Christian, seek not yet repose,'
> Hear thy guardian angel say;
> Thou art in the midst of foes;
> Watch and pray.
>
> Principalities and powers,
> Mustering their unseen array,
> Wait for thy unguarded hours:
> Watch and pray.

'Oh, no, you really *can't* want this,' she cried again. 'I shan't allow it. It may be all right for infants and loonies, but as *we* don't happen to be either—at least not yet . . .' she said. She switched it off; and this time very finally.

'No, I'm not honestly so sure if you *could* do it,' I thought, with quite commendable humour.

But I continued to seem cheerful, as I'd promised him that I would try to do.

I even relented so far in my attitude towards her as to suggest, on the Sunday afternoon, that she might like to come and help me window-shop for Tom's christening present.

But I was quite relieved when she declined.

'You go if you want to. You can leave me here.'

'No. I'll have plenty of time during the week.'

Though it would have given me an hour or two of rather glorious respite, I was reluctant somehow to leave her in the house alone.

I don't quite know what I imagined. Certainly she wouldn't have done anything, I felt convinced, to harm my picture.

Perhaps I thought that she might have snooped and come upon my precious stiff-covered volume, where I had carefully hidden it away. That would have seemed like grubby fingers in a drawer of underwear, after a case of break-in and entry.

(There had been many instances of this recently; the police had issued repeated warnings to householders in the area. It was one of my greatest worries; but not, of course, for the sake of my underwear. Fire worried me for the same reason. So did ants. I kept fearing that ants might eat my manuscript; or some other hoard of tiny nameless insects, less visible, that feasted on paper like woodworm on wood. Each night I blew between the pages and inspected carefully for the onset of attack. But none of my precautions could ever totally allay anxiety.)

Besides, through jealousy and malice, she might decide to change things—and suppose that she contrived it so skilfully as to utterly defy detection? What then?

So we stayed indoors and somehow managed to pass the time. ('My God, you're a compulsive polisher! You were never that at home!') We talked—desultorily; I would almost have welcomed some of those earnest topics which—in anticipation—I'd decried: apartheid in South Africa, our responsibility towards the animals, our ceaseless consumption of junk foods. (Yet she had bought for me a battery chicken and a box of chocolates.) Even on the Saturday evening, when there was little to watch on TV and when we opened one of the bottles of wine, 'in an attempt,' she said, 'to cock a snook at the President of the Lord's Day Observance Society and shock him with a touch of hopeful bacchanalia' (for the first second or so it simply didn't occur to me whom she was referring to), even then, our conversational flights remained obstinately earthbound. There was only one exchange in any way worth recounting—and that, certainly, not for the sake of its intellectual content. It came a minute or two before she decided, anyhow, that she'd do better to go and watch the cricket downstairs.

'I've been thinking recently,' I said, 'that I might start to wear a brighter shade of nail polish.' I held out my fingers as I spoke, and regarded them meditatively.

'Yes,' she said; 'I saw mention of it in the paper.'

'In London I always wore colourless, of course; since coming here I've been wearing pink. Now I'm wondering about something deeper—scarlet, do you think? My toenails, too. Or does it all sound—still—a bit too jazzy and modern?'

'My dear Rachel,' she answered. 'Bristol may be a bit of a backwater, but I can assure you—'

Suddenly she broke off.

'No, I don't care if it *does* sound too jazzy and modern.'

'You know—something's been bothering me; I've only just now realized what it is. At times it doesn't even sound as if you're actually talking to *me*.'

'What on earth do you mean?'

There was a pause. She shrugged. And then she gave her rather brusque laughter.

'Search me. I said it on the impulse. Perhaps I'm just going slowly round the bloody bend.'

She heaved herself, rather wearily, to her feet.

'Or perhaps it's that romantic chemist,' she added, inconsequentially.

Late on the Monday afternoon I was clearing away the tea things while she was just packing her suitcase, as I supposed. But suddenly I heard her heavy tread on the stairs and she came into the kitchen with a really magnificent cut glass bowl dangling from one hand.

'Ah ha! I bet you thought that I'd forgotten.'

'What?'

'Housewarming present!'

'Oh, Sylvia!' I quickly wiped my hands on my apron and took it from her, reverently. 'But it's *exquisite*! It must have cost you a fortune! Oh, really, you shouldn't have.'

'Not quite the £39,000 one that Charles got from the Reagans.'

'But not far from it!' I laid it down with great care, put my hands upon her shoulders and kissed her fondly on the cheek. 'I shall treasure it for ever.'

'I hope you don't mind,' she said, after a moment, as I turned away to examine it again. 'I used the box for something else, and I really couldn't be bothered to wrap it.'

'You could never have done it justice.'

'Of course, it had my nightie and things round it in the case. A new kind of presentation pack . . .' We laughed together, companionably, as in the old days. Then she said: 'But I bet you were telling yourself that I'd forgotten.'

'No, really. I hadn't given it a thought.'

Yet suddenly I smiled, and nodded once or twice.

'Yes, I did believe that you'd forgotten. You see—I'm aiming towards truth!'

'Oh, Christ!' she said—not because I had been honest, but because I had told her that I wanted to be so.

'Is that so terrible?'

'Yes.'

'Why?'

'It's infantile,' she said, 'and nauseating and bloody dangerous.'

I was not sure whether she was making a joke or not, but sadly, by the time we set out for the station only ten or fifteen minutes later, I was having consciously to hold on to my feelings of recently awakened affection—my belief that, after all, there just might be something there between us to resuscitate. Then—still more unfortunately—as I locked the front door, she appeared to notice the plaque for the first time. 'Philanthropist!' she said. 'Politician! Haven't we got enough of those already, without our having to commemorate them? Do-gooders, it seems to me, have always been something that we could get along better without.' She shifted her suitcase to the other hand.

In view of what we had spoken about on Friday, it was perhaps a little tactless, to say the least.

No, I thought, as far as the outward signs went she had certainly not been vouchsafed a vision. And on the whole—I do have to admit it—I was glad. It would have been a confirmation of his power, yes definitely—but what need had I of that, anyway?—yet, too, it might have subtly spoiled something if Sylvia had been permitted even the briefest glimpse of it. I was almost pleased that her last words to him had been: 'Goodbye, Sourpuss. I can't exactly say I've grown accustomed to your face.'

In effect they were also her last words to me—even without that business on the doorstep.

Had she acknowledged him at all it might have been different (though I didn't *want* a fellowship) but as it was I felt little compunction about saying to myself as the train drew out, 'Well, maybe that's the last I'll ever see of you, best friend.' The decision was not untainted by the shadow of regret, of course—particularly in view of that magnificent present.

I walked back—still through a light drizzle, though the evening was calm and mild and it seemed the sun might soon be breaking through—feeling carefree and refreshed and as if, although the remains of a particularly dreaded and mostly awful party still had to be cleared up at home, this was certainly a small price to pay for the restoration of our peace and privacy—which, from now on, blessedly free from all trespassers, we should possibly value even more than we had ever done so in the past.

33

When he was twelve Horatio got lost—not in the Temple
—but in the Assembly Rooms in Bath, as the result of a dare,
and caused *his* parents, too, a vast amount of worry. But that
was nothing, of course, to the worry he occasioned them a
few months later, when he nearly died. He contracted a chill
one day when swimming with his friends and, like young
boys will, neglected it; pneumonia resulted. But, this time, I
identified with the mother. The fact that every churchyard in
the country was filled with the graves of babies and children
—sometimes one after another out of the same family—did
nothing to accustom you to the idea of loss; or, rather, resign
you to it. I imagined how it must feel to watch the relentless
decline of the child that had been denied you for years and
years but who when he finally came was everything you could
have ever hoped he'd be—healthy, good-hearted, intelligent
and caring. I, of course, had never had a child myself, but
now how my stomach felt a steady ache of fear and wild,
rebellious grief—one wouldn't let it happen, one *wouldn't*, it
couldn't, not to him. Was there no God? Of course there
was a God. Didn't He *know* what type of human being
Horatio was, couldn't He *see* his value for the future? Wasn't
He aware how greatly he was loved, and how great was his
own capacity for loving? Had He only given, and after such
travail, so soon to take away? She wasn't Sarah. She couldn't
bear so to be tested, she couldn't stand up under it. Oh, yes,
if she had been *Sarah* then perhaps she could have, but if she
was to be Eliza Munday or Anne Armstrong or Eleanor
Jenks, each of whom had stood at more than one pathetic
graveside in the last few years—well, *then* she couldn't bear
it. (And *they* had all had other children left at home and were
still capable of having more.) And she had always been led to

believe that God was good, all-powerful. Oh, she didn't question it—she *couldn't* question it (for that way only despair and surrender and madness lay)—but where, then, was His mercy?

You see, although I had no child, I *knew* what it was like. It would be like someone taking from me my book, my object, my power to start again; my portrait, my hope, my belief in the purpose of humanity, the purpose of life itself.

And I was more than simply mother: it was as if she saw, Jane Gavin, that not only would she lose her son, but husband also. Jeremiah Gavin was now almost an old man, far from being robust; the son's death would surely be the husband's too.

But God *was* merciful. And although with one part of my mind I had known all along, of course, what would be the outcome, the enormity of her relief, of her thankfulness, the blessed sense of *calm* after the tempest of such wild emotion, was nevertheless nearly as much the reaction of Rachel Waring as it was of Jane Gavin—the woman who had stood to lose real flesh and blood, and bone and heart and smile and soul and muscle. The two of us had known something of the same desperation; the two of us now felt the same glorious return to life.

For I had not enjoyed the days it took to write that section of the book. Perhaps it had come too much on top of Sylvia's visit; and perhaps the strain of *that* had pulled me down more than I had realized.

I don't know.

But I just couldn't forget, somehow, the fate of poor Alfredo. Alfredo Rampi. (You see, Reverend Mr Morley, I *was* concerned; you had no right to tell me otherwise. I had gone out to the library just the following day and asked for their back numbers and read up all about it. I had read up as fully as I could about the Maze prisoners, too, and about Toxteth; I had borrowed a book upon the Berlin Wall; and I had actually taken the bus and stood outside St. Lawrence's and *prayed*—only briefly ducking behind a tree when I saw Mrs Pimm come out of the entrance. So that really did prove it, didn't it?—I was *not* just whistling in the dark; and I was not, repeat *not*, uncaring!)

And I couldn't quite get it out of my mind all the while I wrote about Horatio. I heard him sobbing in terror down there in the darkness, that little six-year-old, crying out and whimpering for help, wedged fast but not so fast apparently that he couldn't slip some more, trapped there during three unimaginably slow and dreadful days of hell . . . until he died. And I kept reliving that moment when a volunteer cave explorer, slim himself like a child, who had forced his body head first down the narrow well, had managed to drop a handcuff round one of Alfredo's wrists, a handcuff with a rope attached. It must have seemed such a breath-taking, God-praising moment, when success had been virtually assured and the prayers of thousands almost answered . . . Ask, and it shall be given you; seek, and ye shall find.

Yet not always, perhaps, in the manner you'd expect from a merciful, all-powerful God: small though the handcuff was, the child's hand had been still smaller. All that earnest supplication, all that straining effort, all that anguished clinging on in horror but in hope—vain. And while we struggled for Horatio's life I tried very hard not to listen to the prayers of Alfredo's parents; and not to be dismayed, either, by the violent attack of nervous indigestion from which I had now been suffering for well over two days.

34

The day of the christening came. It wasn't to be held until the afternoon but even in the morning I did no writing. I spent a long time soaking in the bath, then giving myself a beauty treatment. After all I was going to be meeting many of Roger's and Celia's family and friends; I had to look my very best.

I'd considered buying a new outfit for the occasion; had

even gone back to my special shop. But they had nothing there that really took my fancy: except the sweetest, loveliest wedding dress you ever saw—oh, it was adorable!—with hundreds of tiny roses embroidered all over it; but *that*, perhaps, would not have been entirely suitable. The assistant who'd been there the first time (it had been another who had served me with the sky-blue jacket and skirt) must have seen me gazing at it, and fingering it too—lovingly, a little awestruck. She crossed and stood beside me, companionably.

'Yes, isn't it quite gorgeous?' she said. 'It seems to have that effect on nearly all of us.' I don't believe she recognized me.

'What effect?'

'Total absorption. It's a real heirloom, that: the sort of thing one would hope to hand down to granddaughters, great-granddaughters . . . it rather makes you want to weep, doesn't it?'

I smiled, politely.

'But you know one of its really most delightful features? It's so simple that without the train your daughter could almost wear it as an evening dress. The effect would be so charming. It would make every other woman look quite dowdy.'

We continued to stand there admiringly. It occurred to me that for some reason I didn't like her so much as I had in March.

'So you see it wouldn't even need to be put into mothballs after the wedding. It could still have a long and very exciting life ahead of it!'

'Yes. I . . .' She couldn't see my hands, of course, hidden as they were by gloves. I was gratified—but not at all surprised that I looked married.

'And the really incredible thing, madam, considering all these advantages, is how very reasonably priced it is.'

'How much . . .?'

'Less than £200.'

'Really?'

'Yes.' It was a penny less than £200. She nodded,

beatifically. 'May one enquire, madam, when it is that your daughter's . . . ?'

'Oh, the date's not settled yet.'

'You'll have to bring her in,' she said. 'But I would certainly advise against leaving it too late.'

'Yes. Thank you.' I bid her farewell with—apparently— great sincerity. But I laughed very quietly as I walked from the shop. I considered that I had most decidedly outwitted her—that over-keen, rapacious saleslady. I felt mischievous, clever, triumphant, sad; though the dominant emotion, I suppose, was really the last. I felt like a mildly melancholic Mrs Machiavelli, already growing ashamed of her own duplicity.

But I liked the alliteration. I chanted those four words as I walked along the street, wondering how rapidly I could say them without stumbling. As I did so, I unthinkingly passed the chemist's shop—so unthinkingly that I almost didn't notice.

'Badedas!' I said.

Like a very naughty child I had a strong impulse to open the door, just put my head through the doorway, cry 'Badedas!' very significantly, so that the meaning of it couldn't help but pour all over them, whoever might be there—then simply disappear. It would be, oh, so glorious.

At first I resisted it; but this, of course, was purely upbringing. What was naughty, what was harmful? In fact, quite the reverse was true. For let them only pause sufficiently to ponder the full implication of what they heard . . . I almost had a duty.

I did it. There were four customers in the shop—and him, thank heaven, not the girl. But I thought that I should have done it immediately: before I'd deliberated, before I'd conceived it as my duty. I now felt slightly nervous.

'Badedas!' I shouted—as succinctly as I could. But although there was a fairly satisfactory, instant silence, and all heads jerked in my direction, I knew that I hadn't managed to inject the word with all the rich weight it should really have carried. It ought to have been heavy with the distillation of experience, the kindness of constructive criticism. I simply don't believe it was.

A young man and his girlfriend were standing nearest to the door—they'd been looking at something on a shelf. The young man was the first of all of them to speak.

'And bananas to you, too!' he said, cheerfully.

His girlfriend giggled. (A pert little blonde, she reminded me of Una at the office.) I withdrew—having first, with slightly feigned high spirits, quickly blown my friend a kiss or two, on the assumption that if he'd been labelled romantic it couldn't, in all fairness, have been totally for nothing.

I had to admit that it was not one of my most brilliant, unqualified, spectacular successes.

The young man must have thought I had a cold.

Well, never mind.

Back to the dress.

I couldn't really have afforded a new dress, anyway. (I wasn't thinking of the bridal gown!) I had spent far more money than I should, already: on Tommy's christening present. I had bought him a silver napkin ring and a lovely little eggcup—to which I would add one of my own silver eggspoons and an inscribed copy of *Pride and Prejudice*. (While in the jeweller's—such an odd week this was for me, what would be the third thing?—I saw a wedding ring, so much prettier and more delicate than those you normally see; my heart quite ached to hold it, let alone possess it! I joked to the jeweller, 'That third thing will probably—now—be an *engagement* ring!' He was by no means a beauty but he was such a pleasant little man, immediately and unquestionably very much upon my own wavelength. 'Yes,' he answered, clearly totally in agreement. 'Would you like to see our selection of engagement rings in that case?' 'Oh, yes—what fun—why not?')

But that wasn't even all. Young Thomas would get scant pleasure for the time being out of a napkin ring and an eggcup—even *though* they were doing a rush job to engrave them for me, ungrateful little monkey!—and if he couldn't yet handle a teacup and saucer with insouciance and mastery it might still be a year or two, as well, before he could fully appreciate Jane Austen. I realized that. So I got him, too, a large and wickedly expensive cuddly: rather appropriately, a cheeky-faced monkey, in a checked and natty waistcoat! I was sure that he would get costly presents from his grand-mothers and aunts and other godparents, et cetera; but his *godmother* certainly didn't intend to be outdone, either now or later. Maurice the Monkey had more sheer character—and impudence—a far greater potential for growing into a lasting favourite, a reverently-handled, much-loved member of the family—than any mere, ordinary, *teddy bear.*

I shouldn't even mind too much, come to that, if *my* monkey called *his* monkey Rachel! Even the waistcoat didn't have to make him masculine—not these days. 'If he really is dead set upon it—the insolent young pup!' as I later laughingly told Roger.

(I think, in the end, they called the creature Michael. It wasn't of such good quality as I'd been led to believe when I had bought it.)

But—anyway—I decided that I'd wear my green. That was very soft and smart and people had told me in the past it was becoming; although in London, actually, I wasn't always sure that it had suited me so very well and Sylvia had pronounced it a mistake. Now when I first tried it on I saw it in a wholly different light—one that had almost the freshness of revelation about it. Some premonition must have made me keep it; for either I had changed or the dress had changed or perhaps we both had—if the picture of Dorian Gray could do it in an attic the dress of Rachel Waring could do it in a wardrobe. (Joke, of course: the portrait of Dorian Gray was inherently evil, whilst both my wardrobe and my world were thrown wide open to the begged-for influence of good.)

Before my bath, I coloured my hair. I took a risk, I suppose, switching from Brasilia to Naples for an important occasion like this without a trial; but I'd suddenly felt like a change (it wasn't a very large one) and what better time for that than immediately prior to a big event? (At least if the risk turned out to be justified!—and this one did.) Normally, of course, I wouldn't colour my hair *and* bath all in the same morning, but there are few things so pleasant as breaking with custom—even in absurdly minor ways. It gives one the sensation of making progress and defying dullness in some way. Predictability—not age—is the enemy of youth; predictability, and the death of hope; an end to looking.

It was a happy morning, full of pleasant anticipation; and this, despite the fact that I made what would at one time have been a most mortifying discovery; and one which—even as it was—needed the summoning up of all my resources to deal with adequately.

No, not merely adequately; rather well.

On the back of my left leg, just above the knee, I had several tiny swellings; and further down, now that I looked more carefully—and these were visible on both my legs—little lines of blue.

Varicose veins.

My father, apparently, had suffered from them, young as he was; and he had inherited them, in turn, from his father. Ever since my mother had first mentioned this (needlessly and unkindly, even maliciously, it had seemed to me) it had been one of my greatest fears.

And now that fear had been realized.

But I was sensible about it. I admired the fortitude with which I coped. The philosophy. I admired and was surprised by it. I was becoming quite a girl.

'You're becoming quite a girl, Rachel!'

It was a pity that there was only myself to say it.

I shook my head a little sadly—*humorous* in even such a situation. 'No, it's no good, I just can't see *you* using slang; or hear you, more to the point.'

And I laughed, brightly.

In any case, I thought, there was no real reason, was there, why they should get worse? Hadn't I even heard somewhere that vitamin E—regular doses of it—could often clear them up? And anyway there were ways of disguising these things. Leg make-up. A slightly thicker denier; not *thick*, for heaven's sake; just a degree less fine. Besides. My skirt lengths would never be *above* my knee; and I had never much cared for swimming.

'Oh, I don't know. They must have used a certain amount of slang in your time. Our time? And, of course, you *have* been listening to Bing Crosby!'

This was ridiculous; I wasn't even in the sitting-room.

Yet what better approach was there, anyway, than via the ridiculous? The whole of life was ridiculous. Varicose veins were, most certainly, ridiculous.

And to illustrate this I did a little Charleston, right there and then, in my petticoat.

> We dream about,
> We scheme about,
> We have been known to scream about,
> That certain thing
> Called the boyfriend,
> Vo-di-o-do!

Oh, what a hoot it all was!

'Yes, you *could* say that you felt proud of me.'

I listened a moment, and then I dropped him a curtsy.

'Thank you, kind sir.'

I didn't need to be in the sitting-room.

'"Life without him is quite impossible—quite devoid of all charms . . ."'

Oh, how you could ride anything, when you were gay: not just the *big* challenges but the petty, unworthy, often sordid things as well—like, in this case, wanting his approbation but not wanting him actually to know the cause of my deserving it. I sometimes felt quite repelled by certain of my blemishes.

Though veins, of course, had nothing to do with age. I knew of someone who'd had an operation at only seventeen. Seventeen! Why, it could happen to a child.

I must admit it, though: my body had always been something of a problem to me. But that's what came of having looks; they left you with expectations, even with responsibilities, and naturally with fears. (Is it better to have never had, one wonders, than to have had, come to depend upon— and lost?) For it actually appeared to me on occasion that *body* was more important than *personality*; and that having a nice shape automatically equalled being found desirable; and I worked very hard to keep my nice shape. I was terrified my dainty breasts would one day start to sag.

I reached for the nail polish. '*Red-Letter Day*—for that extra glow of excitement, that extra bit of colour in your life.' And I certainly had that. I somehow had no doubt he would approve.

(I looked up sharply—thought for a moment I caught a glimpse of him within my mirror—and, as befitted the apparent zaniness of the occasion, wagged my finger at him playfully. '*Not* in the bedroom!')

And then it crossed my mind: And yet, why not?

This, after all, *was* the latter half of the twentieth century.

When my fingers were dry I started on my toes. (Was that the wrong way round? Never mind. I was such a beginner. In all things. I would learn.)

Oh, pretty feet, I thought. Pretty feet. I sounded like a parrot.

(Did varicose veins ever move down to your feet? Oh, no. No. No. No.)

> Stay young and beautiful;
> It's your duty to be beautiful.
> Stay young and beautiful . . .
> If you want to be loved!

Young . . . and beautiful . . . and with a Marcelle wave in your hair. (No, on this occasion, I thought, I might just do without that—forgive me.) Well, how do I look? I pirouetted. Do I pass muster? Do I look almost as if I could possibly be . . . one day . . . (not everybody has to think me so) . . . well, just perhaps . . . 'When you go dancing, you look so entrancing, they call you the belle of the ball . . .' Do I?

Thank you, Roger and Celia, thank you both so much, for inviting me to Tommy's christening. For inviting me to be godmother. For inviting me to be belle of the ball. I gratefully accept your invitation.

Well, as my mother had always told me, 'Laugh and the world laughs with you.' *Look for the silver lining, whenever clouds appear in the blue.*

But *she*, unfortunately, had never seemed to profit from her own good advice.

Remember
Somewhere
The sun is shining
And so the right thing
To do
Is make it
Shine for you.

Oh, yes. Dear Lord. Always.

35

After the church service we all went back to Celia's
parents' house. I had a place of honour, indeed, in
Colonel Tiverton's own car. 'Wasn't he such a good
baby?' Mrs Tiverton kept asking me. (She posed almost
this exact question at least five times—it was as though
she couldn't think of much else of any relevance to say to
me. She seemed a bit *perplexed*.) 'And that lovely way he
gurgled at the font.'

There was one slightly embarrassing moment, when I
was standing near her at the house and someone said, 'You
must be feeling very proud!'

Well, *I* was holding the baby when he said it. It
seemed only natural that his words were meant for me.

'Oh, I *am*!' I answered—with a lot more conviction,
actually, than Mrs Tiverton herself, who was a half-
second behind me and must have worked off some of her
enthusiasm by then in telling me what a *good* baby he
had been and what a lovely gurgler at the font.

We all laughed, but I did feel a little silly. (And Mrs
Tiverton didn't look enormously amused.) The only way
I could fully recover my composure, indeed, was by
thinking in what a lively fashion I'd be able to retell the

incident at home, along with a few witty character sketches and an account of what we'd eaten.

Celia's family *was* a bit stodgy; it seems ungrateful to admit it. And even Roger's wasn't a great deal better; how did someone so very much alive—and wicked—and amusing—spring out of such a thoroughly conventional background? Was he outrageous only to shock: to shock his and Celia's relations, I mean: retired military, stiff Civil Service, even a rather stuffy younger generation? (It appeared almost as if they were mounting a demonstration of block solidarity—to keep outsiders out, initiated babies in.) Roger shone golden through the midst of them; the vitality of his colouring alone seemed nearly an affront.

Perhaps, I thought, it was a take-over bid from outer space; and he and I would be the world's saviours.

But then, of course, there were his friends, his and Celia's—I mustn't lump *them* in with the rest—although, surprisingly, they weren't so easy to distinguish from the general crowd as I'd at first assumed they might be.

'Friend or foe?' I asked a tall and rather handsome young man—whom I considered to be one of the more likely contenders. 'In place of a Masonic handshake,' I laughingly explained.

'Excuse me?'

'I mean, friend or . . .?'—'family?' I almost said. Luckily, at the eleventh hour, I remembered my diplomacy. 'Well, if this is an invasion of the body-snatchers,' I put it, brightly, 'are you one of the bodies, or one of the snatchers?' I laid my hand upon his sleeve; at parties—well, at parties especially—it was one's duty to be as entertaining as possible. 'Of course, it does occur to me that I'll have to examine your answer very carefully. For would a snatcher admit to being a snatcher? Wouldn't he, rather, try to palm himself off as a body?'

'Er—I'm sorry—I don't quite . . .'

I nodded. 'It *is* rather a conundrum,' I laughed. 'Oh, what am I to do? And who will save me?'

'. . . understand,' he said.

I took my hand off his sleeve. Despite his quite attractive face, I had obviously made a mistake. 'Oh, it really doesn't matter. Please don't worry. Allow me to recommend these delightful little vol-au-vents. Extremely tasty.'

He wandered off, with a vague smile and a slight shake of his head (perhaps he didn't care for savouries), and I was glad that at least I hadn't put my foot in it. A moment later I was casting round for a further possible ally.

But before I could greet one, I myself was greeted.

'Good afternoon, Miss Waring. This is an unexpected pleasure.'

'Why, it's . . . Mr Wymark!' I was so pleased I could immediately recall his name.

'I had no idea you were related to the Allsops.'

'Oh, I'm not. No, not at all. I'm just a . . . well, a friend of Roger's and Celia's.' I tried to make my voice sound casual.

'Ah . . . I see.' He nodded smilingly and, to my relief, it was in vain that I looked for any slight sign of surprise.

'And Thomas's godmother, of course'. He must have missed the service, it occurred to me. 'Well, actually, I don't know if that does make me a relation of a sort. Are you a . . . a member of the family?'

'No, no,' he said.

'No—and I can't *really* claim relationship, either.'

'Then you and I, Miss Waring, will always know from now on how it truly feels to belong to a minority group. Won't we?'

We laughed. I felt we shouldn't have done, but we laughed—with gathering momentum. I hadn't suspected such a side to him when first we'd met.

'Mr Wymark,' I said, 'I think that you're being naughty.'

(Ah, this was so much more like it.)

'Not at all,' he answered, 'but *friends*, in this situation, are a little like those orphans bragging to their school-mates: "They had to have you. But they really *wanted* us."'

I had heard that joke before, yet it seemed to make no difference. It must have been the champagne. 'Oh, dear. Please don't. You're going to make my mascara run, most dreadfully.'

'It looks perfectly in place at the moment,' he reassured me. 'In fact, may I take the liberty of saying, Miss Waring . . .?'

'Rachel.'

'. . . that you look extremely nice? The best-dressed woman here.'

Again I tried to hide my pleasure. I felt that his compliment was extravagant—but not, perhaps, so entirely wide of the mark. And it was, certainly, a very pretty shade of green.

Gold and green. Green and gold. I wondered if I, too, really did stand out; was fit to take my place beside him.

Damp golden curls around the nipples.

What was sure was that if they could only read my mind they'd all—undoubtedly—find me every bit as shocking. I thought I had at least a fair portion of his vitality. Did I, too, shine with . . . expectation? A refusal to look dulled, muted, accepting—as if it were all already over for me?

I very much hoped so.

Rachel, you—are—quite—a—girl!

'Well, thank you, Mr Wymark. Thank 'ee kindly, sir.' I gave him a rather modified version of my curtsy.

He accepted the tribute with a slight, gracious inclination of the head. (Yes, he was certainly well qualified to be a member of the company: the fun-group, the life-enhancers, the anti-stodge.) 'Well, among friends, you know, if you're Rachel I'm Mark.'

'Mark Wymark! Oh, I don't believe it! From now on I shan't believe a single word you say!'

'But I'm afraid it's true. A nasty little joke on the part of my parents. Or perhaps they—just—never noticed!'

My mascara was in grave jeopardy again.

'I'll tell you something else they say about friends, of course,' he remembered, after a minute. 'They're God's way of recompensing you.' He paused. 'For families.'

I said, 'I wish I'd known you were like this the day that I first came up to Bristol. We'd have had a so much jollier time.'

'I wish I'd known that *you* were like this, too.'

'You wouldn't come for coffee.'

'It will, from this day forward, be one of my major regrets.'

He was a clown. He had a charming personality. He hadn't the looks of either Roger or of Horatio . . . but he was certainly a clown.

'Did you know that Petula Clark got a fifteen-minute ovation last month for *The Sound of Music*?' I asked.

'Really? I shouldn't have thought that she could spare the time. After all, she's *already* a bit long in the tooth for such a part—isn't she?'

He was a gem.

'I say, you must let us in on all this merriment. We've been dying to know what's going on.' Family.

'Oh,' I said gaily, 'just a series of silly little jokes. Little things please little minds. You must know what I mean.'

'Such fun!'

'Godmother's Follies!' I explained.

Obviously the eyes of the whole room had been upon us.

'*Not* Grandmother's Footsteps,' I hurriedly pointed out, with merry anxiety—having suddenly realized that I could possibly have said the wrong thing and if so wanting only to expunge the memory of it and set the record straight as quickly as I could. 'Not the tiniest connection, of course!'

Mark Wymark had been taken over. I caught his eye again a little later, when he raised his hand in salutation from a group across the room, just as Mrs Tiverton, a conscientious hostess, was purposefully approaching me once more, and I'm afraid I got the giggles.

It was no reflection on my godson.

But . . . 'Mark Wymark?' I thought, shortly afterwards. Could he really be having me on? It was rather strange I hadn't noticed earlier. Yet perhaps, it came to me, he didn't sign his Christian name in full; only the initial. I was satisfied by that.

36

And then something rather awful happened. It had all been so nice. And Roger and Celia so charming, so very pleased to have me there. Yet—suddenly—it just . . . sort of fizzled out. Up in the air one minute; nose in the ground another. Roger came over to me and put his arm around my shoulders (I felt electricity zoom through me) and said, 'Well, Rachel, it's been great!' Then, with appealing timidity, as if almost seeking reassurance: 'It has been, hasn't it?'

'No other word for it,' I answered happily.

'Thanks for making it so swell.'

All these Americanisms.

'Swell?'

'Yes—swell.'

I joyously concurred.

'Celia and I are awfully grateful. And so's young Thomas, of course.'

'And so he should be. I shall expect nothing but gratitude for the next half century.'

'Fine. A deal. Look—what I wanted to say—is it all right if my father-in-law sees you home? Celia would quite like to get back to the flat as soon as possible—after all this excitement, you know—and have young master in his jimjams and ready for his bed.'

'Yes, of *course* that's all right. It's very kind of Colonel Tiverton.'

'Good. Well, then . . .'

I expected him to say they'd pick me up a little later; or

else give me directions on how to get there. I waited to be told of the arrangements.

Instead he bent forward and kissed me on the cheek. (There wasn't quite the same high voltage.) Celia, who had come up just then with Tommy in her arms, also kissed my cheek. She held up my godchild, warmly squirming and reluctant, to administer something of the same treatment. But that was all. It was over. No mention of a knees-up.

And I had no right to complain, of course—none whatsoever; after all, I'd thoroughly enjoyed the whole afternoon; but *that* was the part which I had most been looking forward to, even so.

'See you,' he'd said.

'We'll be in touch quite soon,' Celia had added.

No chance even to give the little invitation that I myself had been planning. In the car with Colonel Tiverton I felt a trifle flat.

But I'd seen Roger again just before we left. He had waved to me, with a broad grin and a bit of jolly clowning and not the faintest idea in the world that anything could be wrong.

Well, I thought, as we drove away, a poor memory in one's friends was definitely an inconvenience—but not something one could fairly blame them for with any real conviction, let alone bitterness. And they certainly *had* provided me with a lovely afternoon, and an opportunity to shine.

'Young Thomas is a grand old chap,' said Colonel Tiverton. 'Wouldn't you agree?'

37

And, after all, it was good to be home.

It really was. I wasn't just saying that.

I flopped down in my usual armchair. I kicked off both my shoes, to display my newly painted nails—hardly visible within the reinforced tip, of course. I wriggled all my toes.

'Yes. Be it ever so humble . . .' I said.

I frowned—though not with impatience, obviously; merely with surprise.

'Oh, surely you know it? "Be it ever so humble, there's no place like home . . ."' And then I realized my mistake. 'Oh, what a fool I am. Is it only a nineteenth-century song?—I was thinking it was older. Sometimes, you know, I think I can distinctly remember my father singing it to me; I'm sure it's not just something I was told.'

I smiled, nostalgically. I felt utterly relaxed.

Indeed, the sense of anti-climax after the party, succeeded now by this feeling of tranquility at home, had made me rather drowsy. I yawned, my hand across my mouth. 'Oh, do excuse me.' I smiled again, and began to sing.

> 'Flow gently, sweet Afton, among thy green braes,
> Flow gently, I'll sing thee a song in thy praise.
> My Mary's asleep by the murmuring stream,
> Flow gently, sweet Afton, disturb not her dream.

Isn't it strange—I'd have said I didn't know a single word of that, apart from its title?'

My Mary's asleep by the murmuring stream . . .

Didn't that sound just so tender and protective and considerate and trustworthy?

'You can't really trust many people, can you? Not deep down. Not in small things. I suppose we're all really thinking more of ourselves than of anybody else.'

I yawned again. I laughed.

'Your Rachel's nearly half asleep, as well. "O, my love is like a red red rose, that's newly sprung in June . . ."'

'Of course, when people are married and they have each other, it may be rather different. I mean, a *good* marriage. Presumably they do really care—and very much—about what happens to their wife, or to their husband. The death of one of them could almost be the death of both. They lie at night locked in each other's arms, entangled in each other's legs, heartbeat close to heartbeat, and they tell each other how they care. Passionately. And sometimes—frequently—it must be true. How lovely to be loved.'

I looked up at him, wistfully. I remembered Roger's tiny but amazing revelation of his need for reassurance. I seemed to get a nod.

'And, also, parents care for their children—don't they? I mean again, *good* ones, a mother like yours, for instance. Mother love . . . One almost automatically thinks of the tigress, leaping like a roused fury to the defence of her young, the very instant one of them's in trouble.

'Oh, the understood vulnerability of a child . . . The understood vulnerability of a loved one . . .

'I was in love once. Yes. He told me I reminded him of Vivien Leigh; and he was very much in love with me . . . Oh, Vivien Leigh, of course, was an actress; an extremely pretty one. Next time I go to the library, perhaps, I can find a book that has a photograph. She . . .'

At breakfast, surprisingly, my mother wasn't cross that I had been so late the night before; and—again, contrary to expectation—she hardly questioned me at all on what we'd done. Instead, she informed me that my grand-father was ill (she'd had a call while I'd been out) and that we were therefore travelling down to Winchester by the midday train.

'But I can't.' I was aghast. 'I take my examinations in another month.'

'You can study there just as well as here,' my mother said. 'We shan't be away for much more than a week, I daresay, and you can write a note of explanation to the Principal.'

'But can't I stay here, Mother? Wouldn't it be easier? Besides—who's going to water the plants?'

He had said he'd telephone that night, long-distance.

'Mrs Fowler will water the plants. And if I really thought, Rachel, that either they or even your examination results meant more to you than your own grandfather, who is very clearly dying . . .'

And he himself wasn't even on the telephone at home; and if he had been, it would not have done me much good: he was at present on his way to Edinburgh, and even his firm wouldn't be able to tell me in which little guest-house he'd be staying there. I just couldn't reach him.

'It isn't that,' I said; 'but I'm expecting this very important phone call, you see . . .'

'From Mr Heart-Throb?' Her tone was unexpectedly sympathetic. I felt a moment's hope.

I nodded.

'Look, darling, so much the better. It's *fatal* always to be at the other end of the line just waiting for them—take it from somebody who knows. If you seriously want to hook him you've got to give him a few anxious moments. Play a little hard to get. That's the thing which really brings them running.'

It was funny that she should have said that. I hadn't at all discussed with her my feelings on the matter; I'd hardly once mentioned his name in her presence. (To anyone else who would listen, or even on my own, I must have spoken it, on average, twenty times an hour.) And an enforced absence was certainly the only thing

144

which would give me strength to keep him guessing.

It would only be a week.

And I could write to him.

'Of *course* you could write to him, after a day or two.'

But Grandfather seemed no worse than usual. He'd been bedridden now for several years and he'd always been complaining and hypochondriacal; even Mother had said so. I almost suspected, indeed, that it was a ploy on the part of the woman who looked after him—just to get herself some help in the house. When I said as much to my mother, however, she only answered tiredly, 'Look, write your letter to the boyfriend—more importantly, write one to Mrs Greenwood—and I'll go out and post them both as soon as you've done so. I could certainly do with the fresh air.'

The week turned into a fortnight. When I hadn't heard from him after ten days—ten days of hope and disappointment and living on my nerves that had put *me* into my bed as well as Grandfather—she suggested that I write again. She was really rather sweet. 'After all, it's just possible it could have gone astray. Letters do, you know. Suggest that he should come and see you here. Let him know that you've been ill.'

In the end we stayed in Winchester for nearly three months. I didn't even take my exams; typing and shorthand and business management seemed completely unimportant to me now (in fact they always had)—both to me and, less foreseeably, to my mother. Grandfather recovered; or at any rate appeared to. 'Dying?' said the doctor when I met him one day in the town. 'That old fox? No, he could last a good ten years yet.' 'That isn't what he said three months ago,' Miss Wilkinson later protested, vehemently. 'Oh, dear me, no. No, not at all.' It was a strange look I intercepted, between my mother and herself.

And I seemed to recover, too—after a fashion. But I had certainly lost that 'sparkle'.

I met Tony just once more—within a week of our return to London. By then he was unofficially engaged:

to the schoolfriend at whose party I'd first met him.

Letters? No. He had received no letters. He had tried to get hold of me each evening for a week, he *said*; had finally been told by a plant-watering neighbour that we'd gone away for the remainder of the summer— though she didn't know exactly where; and had decided that I clearly wasn't interested—was probably having far too good a time elsewhere.

It didn't matter now, of course, but the only other person to whom I'd written from Winchester was that same schoolfriend. I knew that *her* letter hadn't gone astray, because in fact I had received an answering short scribble, addressed to the flat for some reason but sent on—with all our other mail—by Mrs Fowler.

Many girls, of course, would have got themselves a job, left home and had a life of their own. There wasn't a week that passed, throughout those early years, when I didn't consider it. But what could I do? I was un-qualified, had no experience, no inclination to return to college. As a shop assistant I *might* have earned £6 or £7 a week—hardly enough, without other resources, to set oneself up independently. Besides, I *wasn't* inde-pendent: timid, without much character or know-how, and always a little frightened. Frightened of the unknown. The unknown could be lurking anywhere— anywhere outside our main front door. (But it was Sylvia, later, who helped me to push back the barriers of it and to clear myself a very elementary pathway through —a path that was extremely narrow at first yet would gradually, painfully, grow wider, until at last, with the news of the coming of the handsome prince, who would finally demolish the thicket, I found I had no further need of her and could now step out in total confidence upon the yellow brick. Yes, it was Sylvia and the letter that I found. Sylvia and that letter and a sudden resurgence of the will to survive; faint, stumbling, but ultimately strong.)

I believed at that time that I might always be

frightened. And of course, basically, I suppose one nearly always is—no matter what. There are degrees of trepidation.

Therefore we had a rather joyless and destructive relationship, my mother and I, of hopeless inter-dependence. God knows why she needed me: she was perfectly capable *then* of sweeping her own floors, making her own bed, doing her own shopping, her own washing, her own cooking. (And I'm not suggesting that it all devolved on me; we used to share it, more or less.) Perhaps she had some prescience of the incapacity to come—she had never been robust, and how my father would have pampered her—or perhaps it was simply a question of *anyone's* company being preferable to none. (We often went to the cinema together—occasionally to the theatre; it wasn't, I suppose, all gloom. We made conversation to one another.) But more dominant, even, than her need for a companion or a nurse or a servant—so I believe now—was quite possibly her need for power. She had to control someone.

And I, for all my many envying looks towards the outside, my reading of advertisements, my reading of romance, my secret play-acting ('I'll tell you what I want. Magic! Yes, yes, magic! I try to give that to people. I misrepresent things to them. I don't tell the truth. I tell what *ought* to be truth. And if that is sinful, then let me be damned for it!')—I needed, I suppose, someone in control of me.

It was a bleak kind of life, then, we led throughout all of my best years: a perpetual petty seeking for retaliation, on both sides.

But in the end it was I who had the higher score. The verdict was a simple one of Misadventure.

Lucretia was the daughter of Lucretia.

Amongst her effects, much later, I discovered the second letter. I don't know why she'd kept them.

I don't know why she'd kept them separately.

It didn't move me nearly as much as the first. *That*, after the sleeping sickness of fifteen years, had been like a second prick of the spindle, even sharper, entering more deeply, the rusted blood of one and a half decades bringing with it, fleetingly, both stimulation and madness.

My Dear,

Did you believe that I'd deserted you? I hope you didn't ring and ring and ring and stay awake all night. Or, rather, perhaps I hope you did, a little! *I*'ve hardly slept a wink—for worrying about you and thinking of all the uncertainty you might be going through. 'You walked into my lonely world; what peace of mind your smile unfurled!'—recognize it? The rest of it is just as true: 'My love is ever you, my love, now and for ever you, my love . . .'

Talking of love, don't laugh but I'm so very glad I've got your handkerchief. I keep it under my pillow at night, and bury my face in it a dozen times a day, thinking exuberantly that *your* nose has been exactly where *mine* is—well, I don't know too much about the law of chance, but I imagine it must have been at some time, don't you?—I sort of work my way around it. Also, of course, this precious handkerchief absorbed your love, the other night ('absorbed', perhaps, is not entirely the right word—poetic licence!), and I really felt quite loath to wash it!

I keep remembering the way that your hands just went *wandering* all over me—so possessive, so proprietorial; upstairs, downstairs, in My Lady's . . . whoops! I can't wait until I feel those naughty scampering fingertips again! Or perhaps I shouldn't say that—am I being too forward? But we don't want to have any secrets from each other, do we, ever? Except for little white lies, we want—always—to be spendidly free of hypocrisy; at least that will be our aim. And as an earnest of good faith . . . it doesn't worry you, does it, that you're a *little* younger than I am?—a mere year, maybe two. (That little joystick of yours certainly didn't seem too awfully worried by it!) And, anyway, just through knowing you, I shall now most probably grow younger day by day; you'll have to watch out—they'll say, 'Who was that *child* I saw you with last night?'! I'm so happy, by the way, that *that* was the first film we happened to see together—aren't you? I'm sure it must have been meant. Thank heavens that it wasn't *Gone with the Wind*!!

This is, of course, the first love letter that I have ever written. Imagine that! I am enjoying it so. (It almost makes our separation worth it! *Almost*, I say . . .) But now, I suppose, I'd better get down to boring *facts* for the moment, and tell you why I couldn't be at home when you telephoned—has it been a little naughty of me, to have kept you in suspense all this while? My most heartfelt apologies! And how I wish my grandfather were only on the phone . . .

I couldn't bear to read it all; there were more than twenty sides. Here and there some of the words were slightly smudged—my biro must have been getting to its end. A comma had smeared across three lines; one full stop looked like the hangman's noose. I imagine I just hadn't cared—in the way that you stop worrying about how you look when you are feeling exhilarated.

I told Horatio all of it; *all* of it; though in a funny way I had the feeling he already knew.

And understood.

We finished with some more songs; after I had cut myself a sandwich.

> Gin a body meet a body
> Coming through the rye;
> Gin a body kiss a body,
> Need a body cry? . . .

I smiled. I said, 'I read the book of that. I liked it; but I couldn't see—*quite*—what all the fuss was about. Not like when I first set eyes on James Dean. Now that was an entirely different matter. And it wasn't until about five years after his death, as well, would you believe it?' . . . At first I could have bitten my stupid tongue off. And then I thought: But why? Just be natural. People were not so very easily hurt, unless you set out deliberately to hurt them.

I felt like singing him a song of my own choice after that.

> After the ball is over,
> After the break of day . . .

Nothing strident or bouncy or out of keeping with our mood; even something a little melancholy: a lament for lost innocence and artlessness and for the fragile gossamer little hopes that everybody takes with him throughout the early part of his life.

> Many the lie that was spoken,
> If you could count them all;
> Many the heart that lies broken . . .
> After the ball.

A lament, yes—a wistful seeking to return and put it all right and not have to come away again, because you had the key.

And as I sang I danced—to a slow and sadly thoughtful, dreamily haunting refrain. I was very aware while I did so of the presence of Aunt Alicia—and Bridget—and Miss Havisham—and Sylvia, poor disappointed ladies all, who for one reason or another had each, metaphorically speaking, been left there waiting at the church, waiting at the church. I could have cried for them; my heart was overflowing. Because there, I knew only too well, there but for the wondrous grace of God . . .

> Oh, the days of the Kerry dancing;
> Oh, the call of the piper's tune . . .

It was a gentle, pleasant, homespun evening; comforting, companionable, snug.

Better far than any knees-up.

38

That night I dreamt that I killed Celia. Like a similar dream I'd once had, it should have been a nightmare, but instead was something I didn't want to wake from. I stood with her on the suspension bridge and pointed to the beautiful reflection of a star upon the water. As Celia leaned over . . .

I watched her plummet, and waited till she'd gone down for the final time (un—deux—*trois*! I counted rather prettily); then I straightened my shoulders, briskly brought my hands together as if—no, not to clap—simply to brush away her dust and screams; pulled the collar of my ermine cape more snugly round my neck, then walked back to the carriage, in which Tommy sat waiting patiently to take me to the palace. He said not a word but he gave me a nod, and a reassuring smile (I knew it wasn't wind), and then he drove me hell-for-leather through the moonlit night, until at length there I was, running up the marble steps to the ballroom, my lovely slippers twinkling like glass upon my flying feet, underneath the raised silk skirt. The dancing floor was open to the sky, although many chandeliers hung blazing in the void, and there were columns, presumably intended to support a roof. It was deserted—save for the orchestra. Almost immediately, however, a solitary resplendent figure emerged from the outer darkness of—perhaps—a terrace and came towards me with his arms outstretched. As I ran towards him the cape slipped off my shoulders, and he gathered me into his embrace and kissed my waiting lips, tenderly yet passionately and long. Then we swayed together, almost as one organism, to the most lovely, lilting waltz. I knew it was a waltz, even though the words inside my head didn't quite fit in with the tempo: If you want to be a big success, here's the way to instant happiness: stay young and beautiful, if you want to be loved . . . He said, 'Oh, my darling. Tomorrow, the coronation . . .'

I said, 'Roger, I knew perfectly well who you were; you could never pull the wool over *my* eyes. You're the Crown Prince Rudolph.'

'And you my own beloved Flavia.'

Next minute we sat together in our coach—it was daylight—acknowledging regally the cheering of the crowds; with a gracious inclination of the head, a dignified uplifting of the hand, now on this side of the route, now on the other. Roger, however (or Rudolph), only practised the first form of acknowledgement. While he bowed his head with solemn majesty, to left, to right, *his* hands began to do something rather wicked and very unexpected. They set out on a right royal procession, more a walkabout, of their own.

'Darling,' I said, gently, 'I don't think that you should. Not here. Not in the coach.'

'Give me one good reason why not.'

His head continued its solemn nods; my hand continued its gracious waves.

'Oh, that's unfair,' I answered. 'You know, of course, that I can't.' I smiled. 'All right. I've always been like putty in your hands.'

Well, as I say, it was very far from being a nightmare: the bells ringing, the populace cheering, the Archbishop waving us Godspeed from the cathedral steps—and all the while those naughty scampering happy fingers . . . oh mmm, just there, oh *yes*, that's it . . . Even when the coachman turned round to reveal the smiling face of Celia, it was still all right. 'Don't worry,' she said; 'Horatio wouldn't let you do it. He stopped you at the last moment—you only *dreamt* that bit about my fall.'

'Celia, I'm so glad. You must believe me. But do— please—please turn round.' She laughed. 'Oh, darling, what a naughty old daddy you have got!'—for one of the footmen turned out to be Thomas; a little older than the night before. 'So it's probably just as well—isn't it?— that Flavia can really be counted now as practically belonging to the family.'

Horatio, it transpired, was there as well. He was always there when he was needed. I nodded at him with sweetly serious gratitude. (I was still nodding at everyone, when I remembered.) 'Thank you,' I mouthed. 'Thank you for stopping me. I'm very glad you did.'

And yet he shook his head. 'Rachel, it really had very little to do with me. It was you who made the final choice.'

'You see?' crowed Celia. As one who had so nearly died she thought she could pontificate. 'In the last resort you are always alone.'

'What nonsense!' I cried. I looked quickly at Horatio. He and I knew much better than that.

His answering look was full of confirmation. Some-times, I find, there are few things more sexually arousing than sheer unhesitating kindness.

I have said I wasn't anxious to hurry through my book; and it's perfectly true—I wasn't. But in the May of 1885 Horatio became twenty-one, and although I in no way wanted to hasten the death of his poor father, it must be admitted that I *was* rather looking forward to the time when he and his mother and Nancy should move to Bristol. For although much of the next twelve years would inevitably be spent away from home—and usually in London—that first period of his life, in fact almost two-thirds of his entire allotment (at that time), still represented in some way little more than just a prologue to the main events. And the bright mid-September day on which the small family was eventually to move into *this* very residence, now No. 12 Rodney Street—a recently built dwelling in a recently developed area—that was what would truly signal for me, I believed, the proper start to the story.

By then he was a grown man, of course—with a lithe

and well-formed figure and an altogether striking appearance.

Exactly ten days after my coach-ride—at about nine o'clock on the evening of Wednesday 16th September, just as I was thinking of going downstairs to watch the news (dear Reverend Mr Morley, art thou listening down below?)—I had a further opportunity to judge something of this from my own firsthand experience; and—beyond any shadow of a doubt!—quite the best yet. He was again standing at the mantelpiece, now under his own portrait, with his back towards the room, staring down into the flames. I had had the chimney swept a few days earlier and had been lighting a fire up here each morning since. I wanted to get up and touch him; I wasn't sure I dared. I must have glanced away an instant (I was hardly aware of having done so), for when I looked again he stood there in that same position—always that identical position—but he was naked. It might have been quite shocking; somehow it wasn't. As I had known he would, he had a lovely, muscular back—broad shoulders tapering to a narrow waist—small buttocks, strong and graceful legs. Such handsome feet. I was right as well about his hair—because, of course, he wore no wig: it was dark brown, almost black (much the same colouring as my own), and short, with a natural healthy sheen. Yes, though his skin had a sort of marbled air, a little like a statue, it wasn't in any way a sickly pallor—no, not at all—Roger, by comparison, would perhaps have just seemed coarse. And I so much wanted to touch him.

I was suddenly aware of his eyes in the portrait—you know the way it is, when you feel that someone's particularly looking at you you immediately look up. There was no hint of embarrassment—nor of amusement. I couldn't have borne either. But was there—yes?—a deeper look of love?

He was always looking at me, of course, but there was something now a little different about the nature of his gaze. I felt quite sure there was.

While I returned his gaze, his other self disappeared.

154

But that was unimportant. I knew he would come back. (In fact I knew he hadn't even truly gone.) And the eyes remained the same.

39

Suddenly . . . I became so good. I had something to live up to, and I realized that my actions inside the house were no more important than my actions out of it. He could see me everywhere, knew just what I was doing. I distributed largesse. I did the one thing that I knew he would have really welcomed: I helped the poor. I was down to my very last twelve hundred at the bank, but even that didn't worry me: £10 here, £10 there: I felt quite convinced that somehow, in some totally miraculous but unsurprising way, he would provide. It was as though he'd actually told me that the more I gave away, the more difficult I should find it ever quite to run dry.

But it wasn't only money that I gave. I gave away my time as well: writing time, almost the hardest kind. I talked to old ladies in the street, and, more importantly, I listened. Sometimes I carried their shopping for them a short way, or helped them on to a bus. I had no fear. To think *now* about my nervousness as a younger woman could frequently amaze me. I would rush into any situation without even a shred of inhibition. When a man fell off his motorcycle I was the first to be beside him. Similarly, when some poor woman had an epileptic attack in the street. And it seemed I always knew what to do. In her case I hadn't got a pencil, so I used my parasol. Indeed, I almost welcomed such incidents.

I travelled specially—and often—into poorer areas of the city, with twenty or more pound notes neatly folded in my purse, each one carefully separate. And somehow

I seemed to attract people who said, 'Excuse me, lady, any chance you got the price of a cup o' tea on you?' and I was so glad. Even when I suspected it was more the price of a pint of beer that they were thinking of, that made no difference; I had no patience with people who said never give money to an alcoholic, they'll only drink it—they were as entitled to their moment of happiness, and of escape, as anyone. I almost advertised for hard luck stories; and from the young just as much as from the old—from students in snackbars, or dropouts and drifters, just as much as from hoboes lounging on corners not too far from the pub, or tired housewives standing at their front doors. The employment exchange and social security office each made an excellent venue.

Oh, often people gazed at me quite strangely—*very* strangely—but I didn't care. I always tried to look my best; my motives were only of the highest; I had no cause to feel embarrassed. Let them gaze, then. A cat may look at the Queen. I always stepped out with my head held high, my prettiest laugh and my gayest smile, whenever I believed I was the object of attention. They could only have admired me.

And felt envy.

Not that I wanted that. (Of course I wanted that.)

And of course, too, my writing did suffer; but even that was unimportant. Horatio was a man now—he was twenty-one—why should there be a rush? (In fact there was every reason why there shouldn't.) I had the strongest feeling that I was standing on the edge of something—some kind of frontier, perhaps, though none too well defined—like Alice adventurously following a path out of a garden to which someone had removed the gate and suddenly finding herself in rolling parkland: much less cultivated but—for that very reason—even more varied and more beautiful.

I had the strongest feeling—though I fully realized there just wasn't any logic in it—that I was standing almost at the foot of the rainbow.

Almost.

40

I made an appointment to see Mark Wymark. 'This *is* nice,' he said, as he walked into the waiting room to greet me. 'Come to ask me for a cup of coffee?'

'Yes, but first there's something slightly less important. I've come to make my will.'

We went through to his office. 'I take it, then, you haven't got one?'

I shook my head.

'In that case very wise,' he commented, 'even though it won't be needed for another fifty years.'

'You have a crystal ball?'

'The best in the business.'

It was a happy occasion; no, of course it would have been a happy occasion, anyway—I mean, it was a light-hearted one. 'In the past,' I said, 'I've never had anyone to leave anything to.' Though at one time, it was true, I'd vaguely thought of Sylvia. 'It wouldn't have worried me too much whatever might have happened. Some charity—a cats' home—even the government.' I shrugged.

'That sounds sad.'

'Does it? I suppose it does. But in some ways I don't much associate my present life with that of my past. Two different people—do you think that's rather odd?'

'No, not at all. Surely everyone's like that?'

'I've come into my own. It's the reverse of sad.'

'That sounds marvellous—though I'm not sure what it means.'

'Nor am I.' We both laughed.

'Whom have you got to leave it all to now—me?' As he spoke, he was looking out the appropriate documents.

'Well, in fact there's not going to be any money—unless I hit the jackpot; just the house and contents; and if you're going to have to wait the fifty years your crystal ball mentions, you may have a bit of difficulty with the stairs. Even you.'

That was a rather pretty compliment, I thought; but I almost wished I hadn't paid it. This was no reflection upon him, of course—it was simply that it sometimes didn't do to appear, however perkily, to be running yourself down, because people had a very disconcerting custom of believing you; and then you had to backpedal like mad—which was always undignified and often unavailing.

'That's an extremely lame excuse,' he smiled. 'Who won't, indeed, have bother with the stairs?'

'I'll tell you who won't. My godson, Thomas. He won't.'

The solicitor leaned back in his chair and regarded me approvingly.

'That's a kind thing to do, Rachel. It really is.'

'It's a natural one . . . I would say.'

'And since we're talking of wills and things—you know what they're going to write upon your tombstone?'

'Just so long as it isn't "Good!"'

We laughed.

On the other hand, I reflected, I'd really rather like it—provided that they put no exclamation mark!

'No; far from it,' he said. 'Something like: "She was a nice lady."'

'I'd rather they wrote: "She was resilient. And she looked about her."'

'All right,' he said. 'I'll take a note.' And he pretended to scribble it down.

How nice it was, sitting there with the sun coming through his window, feeling totally relaxed, talking eternal verities. I didn't yet take it for granted—my feeling so very much at home these days in so many different situations. I didn't wish to, either. It would be

158

good to remember.

'Do the Allsops know of your intentions?' he asked presently.

'No. Not yet. I'm planning a surprise. A sort of Mad Hatter's Tea-Party.'

'That sounds fun.'

'Perhaps you'd like to join us?'

'Yes, please.'

'Well—we'll see. I'm not sure. Maybe *not* on that occasion. Another time.' I laughed at his mock disappointment. 'Did you know that there's an old belief that crocodiles weep while luring and devouring their prey?'

'And I believe it to this very day!' he told me, solemnly. 'Spiders, as well,' he added.

This *was* a jolly conversation. 'Incidentally, how do you feel about *Alice*?' I asked.

'Who's Alice?' He looked up, smiling. He sounded preoccupied rather than perplexed.

'*Who's Alice*? Oh, you Philistine! Can even you be so unread?'

'Ah! You mean *Alice in Wonderland*?'

'How do you feel about her?'

'Great.'

I couldn't tell if he were being sincere.

'Personally,' I said, 'I much preferred *Through the Looking-Glass*. It's about the only other sequel that I know which improves on the original.'

'Other?'

I realized that *he* couldn't be expected to follow my every turn of thought—perhaps being spoilt at home was going to have its occupational hazards! I quickly cast around.

'Just think of *Anne of Green Gables*,' I said.

'Oh, yes! I am thinking.'

Deceitfulness dies hard. And insidious pride in one's own shameful cunning even harder. 'Rachel, my love, you will truly have to watch it. But all the same, you know . . .'

'What?'

'I only said: I am thinking.'

'. . . one really can't help smiling.'

'No, don't say that! That's positive encouragement!'

'Ah, but I didn't say of what I was thinking—now, did I?' It sounded rather coy.

'I'm sorry?'

'*Anne of Green Gables*,' he declared.

'No, surely not,' I said. 'Do you really mean that?'

He nodded. Yet I detected the slight trace of uncertainty.

'But why? Anne of Green Gables had red hair, as I remember. Quite candidly, it would never have struck me that there was any resemblance whatsoever to *her*. I don't know if she ever went to Vancouver, however. *I* should very much like to visit Vancouver. From all that they tell me about it, I mean.'

He said, 'Yes—well. A very lovely place, I should imagine—Vancouver.' He glanced at his watch—a little ostentatiously, I thought. Perhaps he was proud of his wrists. (He did have rather nice wrists, as it happened. Clean-cut. Lantern-jawed.) 'Now, then, reluctant though I am to say it—back to business, Miss Smith!'

'We were talking of my party.'

'Yes. Now, Rachel—'

'My surprise party! Or do you think it's really better not to tell them? Even the very *nicest* people, you know, might start to tick the days off. I mean, even despite themselves . . .'

But then I answered my own question. No. Roger and Celia wouldn't be like that.

41

And I did tell them. Of course. When you've got a rather wonderful present to give—indeed the best, materially, that it's within your power to make—and to someone whom you more than like; when you lie awake at night anticipating his pleasure and thinking how deeply, how *permanently* it's going to affect his attitude towards you, his already warm attitude; when you want so much to be a part of a family, almost any loving family, but especially one as exciting and attractive and magical as his is going to be; when, finally, following a lifetime's communication of less than total glamour, you feel drawn towards a way of holding nothing back; well, then it's well-nigh irresistible—the mounting urge you feel to tell.

I *could* have resisted it, of course. I could have gone on hugging myself with the knowledge of what a *glorious* surprise they would get when I was dead.

'If only we had known!'

'Life's going to be so changed without her!'

'When one just thinks of all the time we had her with us and of all the opportunities we missed . . .!'

'Where has all the magic gone . . .?'

Oh, yes, I thought. Some firm assurance that I'd be present at my own funeral (a gaily coloured butterfly, perhaps, prettily hovering at the graveside) might have been almost enough to make me plan a premature departure —despite my still being in my prime!

A joke—a pleasantry—of course! (I do believe in pleasantries.) An early death!—when nowadways there was so very much to live for! But, on the other hand, how *agonizing* if truly you should be able to hear the nice things people said about you at your funeral—to hear them, knowing both that they weren't justified and that if you could only have heard them in advance you'd have really done your utmost to make sure they were. Indeed, I wondered, mightn't that be one of the first real intimations of hell? A sad and painful snapshot from that undervalued holiday?

No, if I was really going to participate in my own funeral, I suddenly decided, I had no wish to be dependent on the impact of surprise legacies. Besides—the will wouldn't even have been read by then. One could hardly go round canvassing conviction: 'Just wait . . . you'll be so pleased . . . oh, yes, most certainly you can take my word for it . . .'

No, no! How soul-destroying!

I told them.

Of course.

Roger and Celia.

I had invited them to dinner—not just to tea. It was to be a very special evening, worthy of such a very special revelation. And Thomas was to be there, sleeping safely in his carry-cot, not left at home with some indifferent babysitter. It wouldn't have seemed right for Tommy not to be there. *This* was to be his home. He was the next in the succession.

I bought caviar and duck and we had *sauce à l'orange* and green salad and home-made meringues and cream. I bought two bottles of wine and also one of champagne. I already had some sherry in the house to give to them before their meal, and some Grand Marnier to offer with their coffee.

I decided I would tell them over the dessert. Roger had opened the champagne—and we had laughed as we'd hunted for the cork over on the other side of the room. 'Finders keepers!' we had cried, competitively.

It was Roger, of course, who found it.

'I'm going to take it home and treasure it,' he said. 'Darling, shall we put it in the place of honour on the mantelpiece—on a little stand, with an inscription?'

Celia laughed. 'I think we ought to give it to Rachel. She wanted it, too.'

'She doesn't need it, as a memory of her own loveliness.'

'Oh! Oh!' I said. I raised my hands. (We had resumed our seats at the table.) 'I don't think that *you* had better have any champagne.'

I felt my cheeks burning.

'Nor as a memory of a meal which—I really think—has been the most sumptuous I have ever eaten,' he continued unashamedly.

'It *is* only the wine, Celia. He really doesn't mean it.'

'Oh, that's all right,' she said, with a smile. 'Cooking was never *my* strong point. You'll see what I mean when you visit us. I don't enjoy it very much.'

But Roger ignored the pair of us. 'My one regret,' he said, 'is that we're not in evening dress.'

Perhaps that was my one regret, as well. I had been tempted . . . oh, I had been so strongly tempted . . . while I was spending all that money . . . while I was still in the mood for one final and extravagant fling . . .

Perversely, Roger wasn't even in a suit and tie. He was wearing jeans tonight—with an open-neck shirt and sweater. 'You see, I've taken you at your word, Rachel,' he had said, when they'd arrived. 'Tonight I'm at my most relaxed.'

And I had answered: 'You feel you don't have to impress me any more?'

'*Exactly!*'

Now he said, 'If only we had known . . .!' That made me smile a little. It was almost like getting your cake and eating it.

Celia said: 'I must say, you always do things so beautifully, Rachel. I rather envy you.'

Those last words would have been so funny and ironic, if they'd been true.

'And I *do* like this very sweet custom of yours of the extra place-setting. The unexpected guest. It's almost biblical.'

'Well . . .'

'It's certainly hospitable.'

'I'd like to propose a toast,' I said. I raised my glass. 'The first of several. To the unexpected guest!'

'To the unexpected guest!' We all drank, solemnly. Of course, to myself he was neither a guest nor unexpected, but one can't shed *all* one's habits overnight! Throughout life one's been so very steeped in shorthand.

'In any case,' said Roger, as though the question had not been put aside. 'I mean to keep this cork.' I think he *was* a little tipsy.

'But I insist on having it,' I said. 'I'll tell you why. I've got something else for you to have—something much bigger and better than a cork.'

I smiled at their air of mystification. 'I only wish that Thomas was awake.'

'Then wake him!' exclaimed Roger; and before either I or Celia could do more than very briefly, very half-heartedly, protest, Roger was beside the carry-cot and with the baby in his hands, lifting him above his head. It was almost as if he had some idea of what was coming.

'Oh, Roger!' cried Celia. 'He's not even properly awake. Think if it were you. It would be such a shock!'

And indeed he did look a little dazed, sitting a moment later on his father's lap. Dazed, but interested. Roger dipped his finger in champagne and let young Tommy taste it.

'Like father, like son,' sighed Celia.

'Come on, Rachel,' he said. 'We're all agog. What can it possibly be?'

'Don't be so impatient,' I said. 'Actually it isn't even for *you*. It's for Tom.'

'What is it?'

'This house.'

Well, you can imagine all the kissing and the hugging and the carrying on, and the 'Really, I don't believe it!' and the 'Pinch me, someone, am I dreaming?' and the further champagne-drinking and the further toasts and the tears. And the talk about fairy godmothers.

In short, it was all very lovely.

'I don't know what to say,' said Roger. 'There doesn't seem a single thing one *can* say after that.'

'He hasn't been doing so badly all the same,' I smiled at Celia. 'Then I can take it you're not *too* disappointed, Roger, that it turned out to be something for your son and not for you?'

'Rachel,' he said, his hand upon mine, 'life is full of disappointments. One must just be brave.'

'Yet far more easily said than done,' I answered lightly. 'So much depends upon your constitution—and upon the way you've slept the night before. But in any case there's a little something else which I have up my sleeve. A proposition—I could hardly say a consolation prize. Something I want you both to think about, very carefully, before replying to.'

'Something else?' they said. They said it both together. This time there could be no suspicion whatsoever that they had somehow guessed what lay in store.

'If it doesn't sound too curious of me—' I apologized—'what rent do you have to pay for that small flat of yours?'

'A hundred and twelve pounds a month,' answered Celia, slowly. 'Why?'

'Well—I don't know—I've been considering. This house is really too large, you know, for just one person. And when I think of you two having to pay out perfectly good money each week in rent—heaven knows, money that you can't afford—for a flat that you're not even very struck on in the first place . . . well, it just seemed sensible, that's all, for me at least to *mention* that you could all, very easily, fit in here if you wanted to. And you mustn't think that I'm just being unselfish about it: it would be rather nice for me, as well. Also, I feel that I could be a help—especially, Celia, if it's true that you don't enjoy the cooking very much . . . and I could babysit for you . . . and, well, I don't know . . . maybe many other things into the bargain.' I smiled and got up resolutely from the table. 'But, as I say, before either of you makes any comment whatever upon this subject, I

want you both to sleep on it and discuss it thoroughly
between yourselves. For one thing Celia mightn't really
like the idea of another woman in the house. Unless that
other woman were old, of course, or ugly—that would
be a different matter. Well, you must thresh out every
angle. Now—shall we go upstairs and have some
coffee?'

42

However, despite my every attempt to preach caution,
they gave me their answer almost as soon as we got
upstairs: if I had really meant what I had said, they were
both beside themselves with happiness. Their gratitude
would know no bounds.

'Roger,' I remarked, 'I think that you must have a spot
of French blood in you, somewhere.'

'Why?'

'Because the French exaggerate, too.'

'Then—not a drop! I swear it!'

We drank to it: to his protested lack of French
influence, to his innate abhorrence of exaggeration, to
our approaching *ménage à quatre*. ('Well, for the
moment, anyway,' I cried archly—delighted to find that
these days I could talk about such things so easily.) Oh, it
was going to be so much fun.

'A commune!' I said. '"One for all and all for one!" We
could call ourselves the Co-Optimists—like that old
concert party, many years before my time.'

'Why not the Musketeers?'

'We don't want to fight. We want to entertain; to sing
and dance beside the sea for ever. Besides—could there
ever have been a nicer name?'

'Naturally, we must pay you,' said Celia.

'Naturally,' I smiled. 'That means in laughter and in song.'

'Rachel,' declared Roger, 'you can have no idea of what you're letting yourself in for. The only place I dare to sing is in my bath.'

'Then you must bath often,' I cried gaily, 'and throw the casement wide.'

'We must obviously share all the bills,' continued Celia.

'I'll have to see,' I said. 'Besides—that isn't true. I heard you in the garden. I shall hear you in the garden again.'

'The whole thing about a commune,' pointed out Roger, severely, 'lies in the sharing.'

I felt so happy.

'I shall teach Tommy the dangers of electricity.'

'Yes.'

He had gone to sleep again.

'Rachel. Do you remember? You were going to tell us the story of that portrait.'

'Yes.' I smiled at her. 'I certainly hadn't forgotten.'

'Well, then . . .?'

There was a pause. I took a deep breath. 'I've often thought, you know, that in my next life I wouldn't mind coming back as a cat.'

'But is this telling us about the picture?' she persisted.

'Cats are such very comfortable creatures, aren't they? Wherever they are, they have such a talent for making themselves at home.'

'In that case—I'm surprised you haven't got one,' said Roger.

'Oh, I've thought about it. I imagine that they're quite companionable, as well. Mrs Pimm told me a grisly story.'

'We don't want to hear about it,' laughed Celia. 'We want to hear about the portrait.'

'Don't be so impatient! When I was a child I used to think I'd like to be a little red hen—imagine that! I had a picture on my wall of a sunlit garden on a drowsy hillside—half a dozen hens roaming entirely free; I could sometimes hear their peaceful clucking, catch the smell of the eggs in the straw. If I woke in the middle of the night I could even get back to sleep by imagining myself curled up on a shelf in the coop. And I remember saying to my father once, "I wish I were a chicken! I'd lay an egg and sit on it and keep it warm and be ever so happy!" And afterwards he called me his little Easter chick. I enjoyed that. Isn't it ridiculous?'

'It sounds idyllic,' said Roger.

'Yes, it was.'

We were quiet for a moment—they must have thought that I was lost in tender reminiscence. I played a little prank on them. I laughed. I said quickly, 'The cats—there were nine of them—turned out to be cannibalistic. *And* human-flesh eaters! There! I got that in, didn't I?' But they both looked slightly more startled, perhaps, than entertained. 'I warn you,' I explained. 'From now on there'll be lots of little japes like that. One thing you'll find, I hope, is that I'm not . . . particularly . . . predictable!'

'Oh, I think that we've discovered that already.'

'Thank you, Roger.' I inclined my head. (Which suddenly reminded me about my dream. I felt both amused and guilty.) 'Now then, Celia. What would *you* like to be, the next time round?'

'Well, honestly I don't think anything,' she answered, with a smile. 'This once is quite enough for me.'

'Oh—you poor thing!' We laughed—she, perhaps, a shade uneasily; I with a thrill of wonderful relief. I was so glad to be able, genuinely, to commiserate.

'What about you, Roger? What would you like to come back as?'

'Oh, I'm not fussy. Rockefeller—Vanderbilt—Onassis. King Midas, perhaps . . .'

'I don't think they led very happy lives; not the last two, at any rate.'

'I'd show them how.'

'I told you about Howard Hughes?'

'No.'

'Never mind. Perhaps it was the people in church. Yes, I think I told them. I preached a little sermon.'

'You did?'

'Yes. Did you know they have foxes in Bristol? At night they come right into the centre of the city. They scavenge from the rubbish bins. People sometimes feed them.'

'Yes,' said Roger, 'we did know that.'

'Don't you think that they're such a lovely colour— foxes? Such very beautiful animals.'

'But what on earth put foxes into your mind?'

'I don't know. Does there always have to be a reason? Perhaps God did. Perhaps . . .'

'Perhaps what?'

'Doesn't one sometimes just pick thoughts out of the ether?'

I paused.

'But you know, Celia,' I said with some urgency, 'you honestly should think about it before long. Though that's really a case of the pot calling the kettle black! I realize that I never did; not even after *Berkeley Square*. Except that I was a lot younger than you are. Anyway . . . You know the gentleman whose name is commemorated on the front of this very house, don't you?' I said.

'You mean, the plaque?' asked Roger.

I nodded; then made a gesture of presentation with my hand. 'Well, let me now introduce you properly. It is with very great pleasure that I present my good friends —Roger and Celia Allsop. It is with very great pride and pleasure that I present my good friend—Mr Horatio Gavin.' There! I had done it. I sat back tremblingly expectant—with just one silly, niggling regret. I didn't know why I hadn't introduced Roger and Celia with *pride* as well. I had certainly felt it. I could only hope that neither of them had noticed. I mustn't let that piffling worry, however—even slightly—mar this great occasion for us; I just mustn't.

'You mean . . . Horatio Gavin himself?' exclaimed Roger.

'Yes. Yes.'

169

'But how fascinating! How fantastic! Really, Rachel, that's tremendous.' This was everything I could have wished it would be; my little *faux pas* didn't matter one scrap. 'Was the picture painted, do you know, during his lifetime?'

'Oh, yes—certainly.'

'And it's an original—of course? I'm sorry. I know so little about art.'

I gave a small, forgiving shrug; and a smile of fond indulgence.

'Who's the painter?' he asked.

'Well, that, I'm afraid, I couldn't tell you.' Somehow it had never seemed important. Somehow I had never actually thought of it quite as a painting. That, perhaps, was strange.

'It's so very dark . . .,' said Roger. He was standing at the fireplace, with his fingertips upon the mantelshelf, gazing intently upwards. 'So hard to make out any signature . . .' After a moment, however, his heels came back to the floor and he turned his head to look at me. 'But where did you pick it up, Rachel? Or was it always here?' he asked, excitedly.

It was an excitement which I loved him for.

I laughed. 'What *are* you suggesting? "Pick up", indeed! Yes,' I said, 'he was always here.'

'May I take him down?'

'Oh, I . . . No, I'd really rather that you didn't.'

His hands were already halfway there; they continued on upwards, but Celia called to him sharply. 'Roger!'

He lowered them at once. 'I'm sorry,' he said. 'For a moment I just wasn't thinking.'

And almost as if rebuking himself—well, certainly as if preoccupied—he abruptly brought his head down and looked into the fire for a minute. One elbow was resting on the mantelshelf; he raised a foot and set it on the left andiron. Suddenly I felt that I was going to faint.

The instant passed. The worst of it, at least. And Celia hadn't noticed. I was sure of that.

Roger turned round. It *was* Roger. He was smiling

again with his usual sunny amiability. But, un-expectedly, I didn't like his smile. I felt almost as if something had been violated.

'Do you know,' he said, 'I really think this picture might be worth a small but tidy sum. Have you ever considered having it looked at?'

I stared at him—perhaps a little blankly. Celia said something. I was under the impression that she said it rather quickly. I suddenly became aware that she was asking me a question.

'What?' I turned my head slowly.

'I said you mentioned before that—if it hadn't been for him—you yourself wouldn't be here now.' Her tone was gentle again, relaxed, and warm with sympathetic interest. 'What did you mean by that?'

'Oh, I don't know—nothing—it doesn't matter for the moment.'

She was a tactful girl, sensitive; she didn't press the point. She gave a cheerful, understanding nod.

'I think it's high time that we made our way, Roger. Oh, incidentally—who's Mrs Pimm? That isn't idle curiosity.'

She smiled.

'No. The fact is, Rachel, we feel we want to get to know everything about you.'

43

I began to feel better. Later—after they'd gone and we had the house all to ourselves once more—I totally got over it. I truly did. Excitement reasserted itself, came flowing back just as it should have done. I *wasn't* like the child who knows what he wants while he wants it (they could hand you the moon—you'd grow tired of it soon). Oh, but I'd really started believing that I was. Just when I had almost everything I wanted, when I could see it all so nearly coming true . . . if I didn't feel a little happier about it, I'd said to myself, I must be quite impossible to please. Utterly spoilt! Incapable of ever being satisfied. What more truly horrifying thought?

But I quashed it. And as I say, thankfully, so thankfully, intoxication caught me up again. As I undressed, I sang. But of course. My theme tune. 'Oh, if you want to be a big success—pum, pum!—here's the way to instant happiness—pum, pum! . . .' I *was* young and beautiful. I must be. It couldn't have happened otherwise. None of this could have happened. They didn't *know* that I had varicose veins (even though mere children sometimes got them!)—they never would know—that was the great big glorious confidence trick. So what on earth did a few small silly little veins matter? Where was *their* importance in the scheme of things?

And then I stopped. I stopped singing. I stopped performing my little musical striptease. (So tantalizing to the gentlemen!)

I suddenly thought . . . how stupid I was. It came over me so strongly. Jesus had said, 'Pick up your bed and walk.' He had cured the blind, the paralytic, the mad. Just like that. Rise from the dead. Chase out those devils. Open your eyes. Walk. So easy. I really felt—I really did feel—the next time I ran my fingers down the back of my left leg they would encounter . . . only smooth flesh. I really did feel that.

Indeed, I tried it. No, not 'tried'—I just did it. And all that my fingers encountered was lovely, silky smooth flesh. No bumps, no blemishes, no blue. I was a whole person once again.

Really a whole person.
That night he came back.
And he came with love.
I'll tell you how it happened.
I hadn't been able to sleep again; and after what seemed

like hours of tossing and turning, half-dreaming and
then jerking awake, my mind still racing and delirious, I
decided to get up, go and make myself a sandwich and a
hot drink (it seemed ridiculous I should be hungry after
such a meal), then go and listen to some music. It was a
warm night, and with my young and lovely, firm, un-
blemished limbs I had no need of any nightdress. I threw
it off, luxuriously, so free, so unencumbered. I floated
down to the kitchen, and I remembered how we had
laughed and fooled about and sung over the washing up
and made it almost the loveliest part of the whole lovely
party. The kitchen seemed full of happy ghosts, my own
included. I then floated upstairs, to a room which
appeared equally alive, maybe even more so, and put on
a record and ate my sandwich and drank my milk and
stole such a pretty and delicate flower out of one of the
vases and threaded it joyfully through my maidenhair.
In fact I made a little wreath—no, not a wreath; it has such
doleful connotations. A garland, rather. It was so delightfully
gay, a small circlet of colour set against a background of dark,
shadowed fronds—in every respect (save that of actual
beauty, I suppose) exactly opposite to any mourner's wreath.
I may have fallen into a reverie; lulled by the Water Music I'd
put on. I saw myself searching for daisies in the moonlight,
feeling the dew-damp grass between my toes—I wanted to
run straight out and find some, had begun to leave my chair.
But then suddenly he was there again and even as I completed
the action—determined this time really to hold him if such a
thing were at all possible—he turned round and smiled and
extended his hands to me. And he said:
  'I've been waiting for you for so long.'

He admired the fine, upstanding quality of my breasts—even
before he started stroking them; the flatness of my stomach;
the smallness of my waist—'Surely my fingertips could
almost meet around it?' he laughed, longingly, in such a
tone of wonder. 'And oh my one true love . . . I can't
believe in so much excellence and grace. Tell me that
this isn't just a dream, that you won't fall to pieces in my

arms, some delicate fragment of a starved imagination, my endless years of waiting and desire.

> Then to Rachel let us sing,
> That Rachel is excelling;
> She excels each mortal thing
> Upon the dull earth dwelling . . .

All this outer loveliness *and* a heart that's filled with poetry, sweetness and delight,' he said; and clearly marvelled at it. 'My Rachel, my darling, my all. You have fresh flowers in your cunt.' He bent, and watered them with tears.

44

'Ah. I see that madam has come back. It is *so* lovely, isn't it?'

'I want to take it, please.'

'You do?'

'Yes, please.'

'I'm sure you won't regret it, madam.' Yet was it my imagination—or did she sound a little strained? 'Your daughter will be coming in?'

'No. That won't be necessary. Although I could say . . . that . . . in a manner of speaking . . .'

'But any small adjustments, madam, that might be thought desirable . . .?'

'We can see to those at home.'

This time I wasn't wearing gloves. It didn't matter; indeed, I'd left them off on purpose. She'd be able to see and admire the ring.

'In fact, I want to tell you something. My daughter and I very often get mistaken for sisters. Even for twins. We have precisely the same measurements.'

174

'You're fortunate, madam.' She began to gather up the dress. 'Very fortunate, indeed.'

'And, you know, I'd say with complete confidence that this gown is the correct size. Wouldn't you? And I don't really want to try it on. Not here. It wouldn't seem quite right.'

'I must admit,' she said, 'I should feel much happier if I could only see the young lady herself.'

I laughed. 'Oh, thou of little faith!'

'Madam?'

'And that remark applies very nearly as much to me as well.' I hastened to reassure her.

'Besides—I'd naturally be most interested to see her. We all would; it's a very special dress. We'd like to wish her luck.'

'Luck?' I said. 'Oh, no. You mustn't pin your hopes on luck. Nor on experiencing merely at second-hand. You just can't live your life vicariously.'

'I beg your pardon?'

'Poor woman—I *knew* that you were under stress. What can I do to help? You should learn to relax more, my dear; to let go; lean back; give way. That's the secret of it all.' I smiled, encouragingly.

Or was the trouble something else, I wondered—something a little less easy to prescribe for? In seeing me . . . was she perhaps seeing . . . herself? A younger self—a heart-rending image of what might once have seemed so possible? I remembered a snatch of poetry my mother had sometimes quoted (how typically!).

> I can endure my own despair,
> But not another's hope.

Oh, I didn't want to be a punishment to others—purely an object of envy—a knife-twisting reflection in some enchanted looking-glass. I wanted to be so much more than that. I wanted to be a glorious example: attractive, radiant, charismatic.

Irresistible.

'What is your name, my dear?'

175

She didn't answer. She seemed flustered. Oh dear, oh dear, oh dear! What *had* I done? She called through a curtained doorway, for another assistant to come and help her. Doreen. I couldn't believe that the *manageress* would be called Doreen!

Ah, but perhaps this woman was the manageress?

'Are you?' I asked. 'Or, indeed, why not the owner?' She didn't answer that one, either. I began to feel that I was talking to myself.

'I imagine, then, the wedding date's been fixed?' Her own attempt at conversation sounded chillingly un-natural, but I did my best to set her at her ease. 'Oh, yes. Any minute now.'

'How nice. The young man—is he local?'

I nodded. 'He was local long before most others that you'd see around today. He's thirty-three,' I added quickly, in case I might have given her a false impression. 'Naturally, he's a little older than I am.'

(She couldn't really have supposed that I had a daughter of marriageable age, anyway; she must have seen it was a jest—had probably put it down to shyness, however, rather than a sensitivity to the problems of others and a determination not to flaunt.)

The other assistant arrived: little more than a school-girl really, with a pale foxy face and anxious to please. I wished her a smiling good morning—merry, magnetic, inspirational; though of course it was not only her that I was thinking of as I did so.

The older woman laughed. (It was a harsh and none too pleasant sound.) 'Then you'll still be seeing a lot of them in that case. That's good.' At her mother's knee, I thought, she must have learned the Ten Command-ments: make conversation, keep up pretences, make more conversation, make a sale . . . 'Oh, please don't *strain*,' I wanted to tell her. 'If it doesn't *flow*, just fill your reservoir, in peace.' But I couldn't, of course; not in front of her subordinate.

'To whom do I make out the cheque?' I smiled. I hadn't really forgotten, though—that goes without saying.

She told me.

'Ah,' I complimented her. 'Much better! That honestly is . . . much better.'

Her little helper could have given her a lesson or two in *flow*.

'You live in Rodney Street, don't you? I've often seen you.'

'Yes, yes, I do. Next time make sure you wave hello.'

'My mum has the teashop just across the road. Sometimes I help out.'

'That makes us almost neighbours!

    Hey, neighbour, say, neighbour,
    How's the world with you?—
    Aren't you glad to be alive this sunny morning,
    Can't you see the sky above is showing blue . . .?'

Laughingly, I went back to their desk, to complete the writing of my cheque. 'How ridiculous! I ask you—where else would the sky be but above? But fun. It's foolish but it's fun. No, no—for heaven's sake—*don't* get me started again!' I concentrated on the cheque.

'Is that young man with the fair hair going to be the bridegroom? He's ever so handsome.'

'Yes, isn't he? Like some golden Scandinavian hero. He's got a really beautiful physique as well.'

'My.'

'You should see the muscles ripple in his back.'

'My boyfriend's got a back like that. He goes to weight-lifting.'

The other woman said, rather sharply: 'Thank you, Doreen. I can manage now. That will be all.'

'He just came in to buy some cakes, Mrs Pond,' the girl said, defensively and with a wobbly smile. I felt so sorry for her.

'Yes. Thank you, Doreen.' The woman almost shrieked. *Mrs* Pond. (I'd wondered whether it might just be her mother's wedding ring.) Undoubtedly divorced or separated or widowed—or else, worse, wanting to be. I felt so sorry for her, too.

I said to the departing Doreen: 'Why don't you pop in for a cup of tea? You know where I live. We can talk about your boyfriend.'

She nodded—and disappeared behind the curtain. 'Don't lose your spontaneity!' I called.

I would extend the same invitation to Mrs Pond, I thought, before leaving. She mustn't feel ostracized on any account, and the visit might do her a spot of good, poor thing, though I myself wouldn't be exactly looking forward to it.

'These school-leavers . . .!' she said, after a slight pause. 'I'm afraid she's still got a great deal to learn.'

'Haven't we all?' I laughed. '"And if it ever come to pass that I inherit wealth, I'll eat and drink, and drink and eat, until I wreck my health . . ." Those old songs can be remarkably comforting, can't they? They show that *other people* do it, too! There's nothing new, Mrs Pond, nothing new at all under the sun.'

'Oh, it's futile,' she said.

'What is? Dear lady, it doesn't *need* to be wrapped up quite as beautifully as that. You mustn't *worry* about the wrapping. The wrapping's not important.'

I didn't believe that, but—as I'd once pointed out to Tony (the recollection made me smile)—there had to be room in even the most truthful philosophy for a little white lie.

'Here—let me help you.'

'Madam, it's all *right*. Thank you.'

'No, Mrs Pond, it is obviously very far from being all right! Promise me, at least, that you will *try* to look for the silver lining, *try* to walk on the sunny side of the street. Remember, in thirty years' time you will look back and think—oh, if only I could have those sweet days back again! That morning, for instance, that I sold the wedding dress . . . if only I had *realized* just how happy I was then and appreciated every dear, God-given minute!' I smiled at her and spread my hands. 'How many minutes are there, Mrs Pond, in the course of thirty years? How many breakfasts, lunches, teas? How many opportunities for joy?'

She looked at me, and I saw her lips begin to quiver. I wasn't dismayed. A purification in tears. A baptism. A mulching for the young green shoots, new leaves, incredibly coloured, patterned, petalled flowers. I was ready to take her, welcomingly, into my arms, soothe her, tell her that she was not *inherently* rapacious, that all she needed was to reawaken love, or else to find it somewhere new.

'You're nobody till somebody loves you,' I would say, 'and, believe me, I do know. Love is the answer; someone to love is the answer . . .'

But then she was shaking—positively shaking—and staring at me in a fashion that really seemed half-crazed. 'Happy!' she said. 'Happiness! Oh, I'll tell you how. Care about nothing! Care about nothing! That's the only way.' And she was almost flailing her arms as she spoke; in one of her hands was a pair of scissors. I stepped back, rather than embraced her.

I said: 'That's certainly a point of view. Indeed, I believe it's the very basis of the Buddhist philosophy: sorrow is caused by desire, get rid of all desire. For those who could do it, I'm sure that it must work. But I couldn't. I wouldn't want to try. Oh, gracious—you're not a Buddhist, are you? I do hope I haven't offended you.'

She didn't answer; but at least she used the scissors just to cut the string—also her shaking had considerably lessened. I had managed to calm her, then, to that extent.

'Yes, I can certainly see how it would work,' I smiled. I wanted to consolidate the good that I'd done. 'Care about nothing! Perhaps you've found the very key. There was a programme recently about some Buddhist monks; no one could say that *they* didn't appear joyful.'

Before handing me the box, she scrutinized my cheque. She scrutinized the bank card, too.

I laughed. 'Then get thee to a nunnery.' I said it ever so gently, not at all in angry Hamlet's tone. (And she was no Ophelia!) But it suddenly seemed the one valid response to such a situation; a literally inspired piece of counsel.

179

In only very slightly different circumstances, I knew, I could well have been upon that road myself.

She still hadn't spoken.

At the door I shrugged.

'Of course, there is that all-important question, too. And here, one knows, you're all alone with your priorities and your scales and your god and your conscience. Is it so much funnery . . . in a nunnery?'

She probably thought I was being flippant. But if she really thought that—was there any point in telling her that it was just my way?

'Oh incidentally, you'll have seen I wrote my address on the cheque. It isn't far from here and any time you're passing I'd be awfully glad if you rang the bell. What I mean, of course, is—if you're ever in need of a cup of coffee and a *chat* . . . Well, you know where you can find a sympathetic ear.'

On my way home I was reminded of something; not by any of Mrs Pond's words, but by Doreen's.

Roger had never thanked me for those two pounds. It was most *odd*, when you came to think about it. It wasn't really that one so much wanted thanks, but—

Yes, it was.

And he had never even mentioned them.

I didn't like a person to be careless over small things.

45

He said everything I'd ever wanted to hear. I told him the things which I'd always wanted to say. It was bliss; it was sheer enchantment. I was twenty-five, and beautiful, and I moved through every day and every night in a kind of dream, a dream of heaven which I none the less took to be reality. I was happier than I would ever have supposed possible, as though I lived in Eden before the fall, and he was the only boy in the world and I were the only girl. Yes, he was Adam and I was Eve, and though we were not at all ashamed of our nakedness I at length covered mine with my white dress, to signify the purity that had always been his, that had always been waiting for him, and I floated through my days and through my nights in a dream of heaven which was here on earth. And I looked radiant in that white dress; my mirror told me so, but more especially did his eyes, as he stepped towards me and he held me close and we waltzed together on the gleaming ballroom floor, with the chandeliers reflected underneath my slippered feet and all the other dancers stepping back to clear an avenue for us, whisperingly, admiringly—'Who is she? Isn't she lovely?'—an avenue that led on to further enchantment, among rock pools and coloured lights, down narrow winding paths all tucked away from view. And I *was* radiant, I was a princess, with my lovely black ringlets and my rosebud mouth and the bloom of rouge and happiness upon my cheeks and the white satin slippers on my dainty feet which just would not stop dancing. (But that was a story which had ended tragically; this one was surely not the same.) And it was *all* a fairy tale: the large four-poster in the magic glade which lay at the end of that winding path down which we ran together in our wedding clothes (he had acquired his somewhere on the way). I shan't describe what happened in that bed—any more than I've described what happened in my own; but oh, the feel of him, the feel of him, the feel of him. Bursting stars upon a backdrop of black velvet.

That bed, indeed, was like Elijah's chariot (no—perhaps not—poor Elijah!) or some Arabian Nights carpet. It bore us high into the sky, while all the time the orchestra was playing, dreamily romantic, far below us, though we could still just make out the glittering barge on which it played, moored on an ornamental lake strung across with Chinese lanterns.

And I sang to him as we floated.

'Oh fuck me once, and fuck me twice, and fuck me once again; it's been a long, long time . . .'

Then I giggled.

That couldn't be right, surely.

Oh, yes, it could! As he willingly turned over and took me in his arms again—oh, those soft golden curls upon his well-developed chest!—the moonlight played such tricks upon the colour of his hair—he said, preparatory to carrying out all my demands:

'You're really quite a girl, Rachel!'

And I returned the compliment.

We were off upon a honeymoon that was going to last forever.

46

It was Celia who eventually turned up. She told me that she liked my dress; yet I could see she had her reservations. (I had of course removed the train—and I certainly wasn't wearing the veil!) But I saw things far more clearly these days: I saw them through *his* eyes, as much as through my own.

'Why didn't you come? I wrote to you a week ago.'

'Yes, so we noticed. The letter must have been delayed.'

'Where's Roger?'

'Well, he asked me to make his excuses. I'm to give you all his love. But he's got these important examinations coming up shortly.'

'Poor Roger. Yet I'm sure that he'll do well. How's Tommy?'

'Spending the day with my mother. Oh—he sends you a big kiss.'

She was speaking, I thought, a little absent-mindedly; as though it were in some way difficult. And she kept glancing at me—then looking hurriedly away if ever our eyes should meet. I realized what it was, of course: she was scared to see such certainty, such calm . . . such evidence of attainment. For all that's said, people still aren't comfortable in the face of complete liberation. They feel threatened. They affect cynicism: the only thing which partially conceals the size of their own failures.

'Well, about your all living here, Celia . . .' I wished to come directly to the point. 'I'm afraid I've had to change my mind. I see now that it wouldn't work. Yet I didn't want to put it in a letter—that might have seemed a little bare.'

She didn't say anything. I went on: 'But it makes absolutely no difference, of course, to Thomas's inheriting the house.'

She answered—and there was a hint of sharpness in her tone, certainly a coolness that I'd never encountered there before—'Why don't you think that it would work?'

'Because I am in love and—it was silly of me, I was confused, I really should have seen—of course we need our privacy.'

'Oh—yes—I . . . understand.' It was very plain she didn't. 'And he—this man that you're in love with—is going to . . . move in here?' she asked.

I nodded. 'He already has. Indeed, he was here long before I was. Long, long before I was. At least,' I amended, carefully, 'as far as I can yet be wholly sure. Up till now, you see, he hasn't said anything about it; and I haven't liked to ask. That's assuming that he even knows.' I shrugged, and smiled. 'Perhaps it's not important.'

She seemed uncertain what to comment. I held up my hand, to show her the lovely little band of gold that he had given me. (I noticed, impatiently, that the varnish was chipping off a couple of my nails. Happiness must not, I thought, just mustn't be allowed to make me

183

slovenly. When had I last washed?—I couldn't quite remember—life was so very full, with a man about the house, and every time I lifted up my skirt—oh, he was such a devil! And—let's be honest, too—one sometimes did forget things. 'With so much going on,' I said. 'I think that's understandable.')

She admired my ring.

'And this, of course, was my wedding dress.' I pirouetted for her, as I so often did for my husband. 'Though doctored a little, naturally.' I gave my usual gay and tinkly laughter. 'I can hardly bear to take it off.'

'So you're . . . married already?' she said.

'Yes, indeed I am. Oh, my—I would have to blush a great deal if I weren't!' Dimplingly, I covered my face, and feigned sweet girlish modesty. 'But aren't you going to congratulate me, then?'

'Oh, yes. Yes, of course. Congratulations, Rachel.'

'*Heartiest* congratulations, I hope.'

She nodded.

'You may kiss me, if you like.' Though I don't know at all why I said that; I really didn't care whether she kissed me or not.

But she did; it was a rather lacklustre performance.

'You know—it's just occurred to me—I don't think that you look at him in quite the same old way any longer, do you? Well, never mind. With you two it was always just a question of time; I saw that from the start. Now, my dear, which would you prefer: tea or coffee?'

'Oh . . . neither, thank you. I'm afraid I've got to go. I only popped in for the shortest moment.'

'I apologize for any inconvenience I may have caused you both.'

'We've already given in our notice. We did it just the other day.'

'Oh, dear. If you had only come to see me sooner.'

'We thought it all so settled.' She said, 'You've never spoken of this man.'

I laughed at that. 'Of course I have, you silly! You've even been introduced to him. What can you be thinking of?'

184

She looked so bewildered—suddenly so very unsure of herself or of the world around her (it was a little touching, unexpectedly pathetic, both of them had always seemed quite certain)—that I felt immediately constrained to add, 'You really *must* forgive me. I thought that it would all work out so nicely, in my simple unworldliness. It was he who made me see that it just wouldn't do at all.'

'He?'

'Yes, dear. Horatio.'

She still looked a bit dazed; it must sometimes be an awful strain for her, I thought, having always to live up to Roger.

'Perhaps you'd like to say good morning to Horatio? I'm sure that he'd appreciate that.'

It was almost a whisper. 'Is he here now?'

'Good gracious, no. Do you think that we'd ignore him? But he can hear you just the same, because he *is* here, in a manner of speaking. All you have to say is, "Good morning, Horatio—another lovely day!" Something like that. He won't mind you calling him Horatio; he's already getting used to the customs of the twentieth century.'

She said: 'Good morning, Horatio. Another lovely day.'

'Poor Celia,' I heard myself say. 'It *has* been something of a shock; I can see that. Listen, dear—surely you don't have to be back right away? You can spare ten minutes. There's a little coffee place across the road, where I could give you a cup of hot sweet tea and a bun and we could continue with our chat. Would you like that? Then spare me half a second and I'll just fetch my parasol and my hat.'

'Your hat?' She must have gathered from my tone that it was something rather special.

'Yes, it's new. Just wait until you see it.'

But obviously she must have felt that she couldn't. I was gone literally only three minutes—I hadn't even put it on—but when I returned she had let herself out of the house, and though I looked for her up and down the street, she was already out of sight.

People were sometimes rather strange.

It was a pity, I thought. Oh, not for the sake of the tea or the chat—they were immaterial—but she was evidently upset, and the sight of my new hat might have cheered her up a little. It was white and floppy and broad-brimmed: a picture hat such as I'd never had the opportunity to wear—until I realized that, quite simply, you have to make your own opportunities and that the day is all but spilling over with them. There was a full-blown, incredibly real-looking, soft red rose pinned to one side of it, that matched perfectly—picked out quite beautifully—the theme of tiny roses on the dress itself. And the long red ribbon which I tied under my chin made it a hat so very much like Scarlett's . . .

Yes, what a pity that she hadn't seen it.

47

But Roger—when he came on his own that evening—was more than just upset. He was extremely angry.

Not one moment of charm wasted upon either congratulation or compliment. His anger blazed in the hallway—I hadn't time even to take him into the breakfast room, where I had entertained Celia in the morning—like a great golden sunburst of volcanic energy.

'Look here, Rachel, what *is* all this? I can't believe what Celia told me.'

'Of my marriage?'

'Of your marriage—of your change of heart—of everything!'

'There's been no change of heart. Simply a change of mind.'

'Do you realize that in just over three weeks we shall have to be out of our flat—and that it's almost impossible to find rented accommodation in Bristol at a price we can afford?'

'Please, Roger—there's no need to shout. Can't you simply tell them that you're sorry but that you made a mistake?'

'Oh, don't be stupid. The flat was snapped up the day after we said that we'd be going.'

'Stupid', I felt, was not quite the word to use to somebody who had bought you caviar and duck and wine, had had silver christening gifts engraved, and made your only son her legatee. This house—together with its contents—was really all I had to leave.

And possibly, on reflection, Roger felt the same way. He was impulsive but he was not unfair. He had a passionate, mercurial nature, perhaps (and wasn't that at least a part of what I admired him for?), but there was no real meanness in it. He started to cool down.

'Look Rachel—I'm sorry, I didn't mean all that—I'm worried about my exams, as well as Celia and the baby. Couldn't we just talk about this thing?'

'Of course we could, my darling. First tell me that you like my dress.'

'Yes, I . . . I like your dress.'

'Now come and sit down, we'll have a glass of sherry, and you can tell me so with more conviction. For after all'—I now felt quite assured enough even to make a joke—'nobody in his right senses could possibly fail to like the *dress*, even if he didn't like it upon *me*!'

He gave a sickly smile but wasn't yet sufficiently recovered to join in with my laughter.

'I bet you lead that poor girl one fucking hell of a life,' I said companionably, as we sat down in the breakfast room—I quite forgot to fetch the decanter and the glasses. 'Do you flare up like that *very* often?'

He didn't answer. He looked disconcerted, and still

rather sullen. Of course, I had to remind myself, he was
extremely young. Men matured so much less quickly than
girls.

But he had a very lovely body.

'It was that that I first admired about you,' I said.

'What was?'

'The way you looked without your shirt. All those
muscles.'

'What?'

'In some ways I *do* prefer you in your jeans. I'm glad
you're wearing jeans. It would give me quite a thrill, you
know, if you were to take your shirt off now. I'd like to sit
and gaze—as on some splendid piece of statuary. Or do
you think I'm being too forward? I do hope not; why not
say what's in one's mind, when it's a compliment and can
surely just give pleasure? It's such a pity to be shy.'

He was staring at me but not replying. All my life, it
sometimes seemed, I had been carrying on one-sided
conversations.

'Of course, I don't care about Celia,' I said, 'or not so
much—at any rate she can look after herself. But I won't
have you giving my young godson hell.' I admonished
him with a forefinger that was only partly humorous. I
think he realized that. 'Otherwise, my good man, you
will have me to deal with.'

'Rachel,' he said. He appeared now to have lost all his
anger.

'Yes, my dear?'

'I . . .'

'Don't be afraid to say to me what's on your mind—even
if it *isn't* going to be wholly a compliment! For all my
present fierceness—not so *very* fierce, I think you must
agree—I'm still extremely fond of you, Roger. Why, you
should just have heard me stand up for you when . . . ! But no;
perhaps I shouldn't say that; I'm so much hoping that you're
going to be the very best of friends, you and Horatio.'

'Mr Gavin?'

Yet I recognized that this wasn't really a question. It
was more in the nature of a flat, tired statement; as

though a vain and incredulous lover were being forced, at last, to acknowledge the existence of a rival.

'Yes, sweet, you and my darling Mr Gavin.'

'Your husband.'

'Oh, such weary resignation,' I smiled. *Dear* Roger. He was just a disappointed little boy—who had never been designed to have his nose put out of joint; discovering now, for the first time, that life was sometimes hard. I so much wanted to comfort him.

Yet how ironic, I thought. Here were two people, friends, the very best of friends—chosen and favoured, gold like the sunshine and green like the spring leaves—who had started out along the same road at the same time, valiant pilgrims on a similar quest, looking for El Dorado, on the path to paradise. But one, so strangely, was still only at the beginning of *his* long journey; whilst the other had almost reached the end of hers.

One was very young in lifetimes; the other, perhaps, at last about to leave the wheel. But not alone. That was one of God's most precious, most affectionate of mercies. I would step off it, not unaided, but hand in hand with the one who had returned to claim me. To love me; lead me.

And therein, evidently, lay the germ of my great comfort for him; my little disappointed boy.

'Darling, this is the system. I feel sure that it's intended that one day—though perhaps not for hundreds of years yet—*I* shall come back for *you*.'

These were momentous words. Of course, he couldn't grasp them for the present.

I smiled. 'My real name—as far as I know—you don't have to call me by it—my *last* name, if you like—' I laughed—'*as far as I know!*—in this life, it seems, you can be sure of nothing . . . Well, let me put it this way. Anne Barnetby, meet Roger Allsop.' I held out my hand. He didn't take it. I was not offended. I understood what he was going through. I drew it back—and gave another laugh. 'Anne Barnetby, indeed,' I commanded, 'meet Rachel Waring!'

I sang.

> 'In my uncertain world—
> I am only certain of—
> How much I love you . . .
> My love.

It's all quite cockeyed, isn't it? The surer you are, the unsurer you get—to coin a phrase. Curiouser and curiouser!'

'Rachel . . .' He hadn't spoken for a long time. His voice was almost an intrusion.

'Yes, my love? Your Rachel is still here. So is your Anne. You know, I'm sorry in some ways it's not Penelope. I always liked the name Penelope—don't ask me why.'

Leaning forward suddenly, he placed his hand upon my knee. 'Rachel,' he said, 'I think that you're not well.' His charm had lost its normal hectoring quality, but it was, just the same, still very potent.

'Darling,' I said, 'I never felt better in my life. As if I'd just come back from a long sea voyage.' I giggled. 'Or as if, maybe, my husband had!'

'I think that you need . . . someone to look after you.'

'I've got someone to look after me. It's what I always wanted. All the time he was away . . .'

I lifted his hand off my knee and held it lovingly in mine. I kissed the back of it.

'But tell me—why are we talking about *me*? It's you and Celia and the baby: you're the ones we should be talking of. Where are you going to find a home?'

'Not here?'

'It wouldn't work, my darling. Horatio was absolutely right. At least . . . well, I just think he must be. He's had so much experience. And I trust him, implicitly.'

'We could look after you,' he said.

'That's very sweet, Roger, but as I've already told you . . . What about your parents? Or Celia's?'

He shook his head. 'They haven't got the room. Besides, we don't get on with them . . .'

'But, surely, just while you're looking for somewhere?'

'What about here, just while we're looking?'

'Oh, Roger, you do make it hard for me. What about, perhaps, a cheap hotel? Couldn't both sets of parents club together to help you with the cost of it?'

'I couldn't take it from them.'

'Darling, I do admire your spirit of independence, but . . .'

'It would only be for a week or two,' he said. 'A month at most. We wouldn't get in the way, I promise.'

'But you do know what honeymoon couples are like . . .' I was aware of sounding coy; it didn't really suit me. And he must have sensed that I was weakening.

'*Please*, Rachel. Anne. Penelope. Remember the Co-Optimists? "One for all and all for one"? Our commune? Our sharing? My singing to you from the bath?'

Oh, Roger the Bold. Roger the Fearless. How are the mighty fallen!

But perhaps only in tragedy sometimes—in apparent tragedy—did there truly lie some hope.

He stood up.

'You're not going?' I said. I felt a measure of relief; amidst my disappointment. He gently pulled away his hand.

'No fear,' he smiled. 'I haven't had my sherry!' He was himself again. 'It's just that it's quite hot in here. May I take off my jumper?'

'Of course you may.' I was preoccupied. 'I'll go and fetch the sherry. And while I'm gone I'll have a quick word with Horatio. Perhaps till now he hasn't fully understood the . . .'

'Situation', I was going to say; but Roger was unbuttoning his shirt.

When he'd removed it, he said, 'Rachel. Is that really all you want?'

There was a pause.

'No.' But I wasn't sure that he'd have heard that. I strained to make my answer reach him. 'No, Roger, it isn't.'

And when his jeans were off and underpants—and even socks—he held me closely to him, and how I could smell his deodorant and his after-shave (*had* I remembered to wash?—oh, dear) and how I could feel his erect, enormous winkle pressing right into me, hard against my wedding dress.

48

I don't know when the following conversation took place. I can hear it and see it and feel it—yet all the same it seems somehow cut adrift from time, like a rowboat abruptly freed from its moorings, while its occupant, entranced, lies whitely gleaming in her rose-embroidered silk, carolling, in no fit state to interlock each hill or field or willow tree upon her way. She knows them, yes—the shape and shade of them—but not their sequence.

It was a daring question that I put to him; and one I'd hesitated long to ask. But shyness keeps you always separate. 'What about Anne Barnetby?' I said.

For a long while I thought he wasn't going to answer. (Join the club of those who don't respond!) And I could not have asked a second time.

But then he did reply—and very simply (as I had surely known he would): 'Anne Barnetby? . . . I loved her.'

Now it was easy to go on. 'And she loved you?'

I prayed—practically—for an affirmative.

'I thought she did. I thought she almost did.' I held my breath. 'She toyed with me,' he said.

'Oh!'

But there seemed no resentment in what he had said. His tone had been (perhaps too carefully had been?) matter-of-fact.

No. There *was* no resentment.

He understood.

'What became of her?' I asked.

'She married. She married the man of her choice. That's all.'

'And regretted it, I know.'

'I've no idea. I never heard of her again. Or him, either. He'd been a friend of mine at school.'

His voice wasn't as casual as he no doubt hoped it would appear. But that was good. Yes, that was good. Even after all this time, he couldn't speak of her and totally conceal the fact that he still loved.

I wasn't jealous. It didn't matter (it was just as well) he didn't recognize me.

Or perhaps he did—and was simply wanting to spare me my embarrassment; since he didn't know, of course, that I already knew. He was waiting to break it to me gently—and when he thought the proper time had come. I was content: to let him feel that he was in control.

'A clean break,' I said, 'is always the best way, perhaps, in situations such as that.' (Oh, Rachel, Rachel, you should feel ashamed! But—loving—there is no such thing as being essentially underhand.) 'It must have made it that much easier getting over her.'

Silence.

'You did get over her?'

'I . . .'

'Never?' I asked. It was hard to find just the right expression of surprise and sympathy. I wasn't sure that mine was too convincing.

But it must have been all right. He said at last:

'When I began to think that I had done so, I soon found out that it was only self-deception.'

'My poor Horatio. My dear. I *know* she must have come to hate herself.'

I don't believe he heard me. In any case, he obviously missed the meaning of my words.

'It may sound fanciful,' he said, 'but later she returned to haunt me.'

'Her ghost?' I'm not sure what my feeelings were just then.

'No, no!' He laughed. 'My mother always said I was theatrical; that my rightful home was at Drury Lane with Mr Garrick. I was haunted, not by *her* exactly. By the *idea* of her. The idea of what I'd missed. Of the irrevocable mistake I'd made through having been so blind. Even when I could no longer—quite—visualize her face, the thought of all I'd lost still had the power—in fact at last it did . . .'

'What?'

I shouldn't have prompted him. My voice reminded him he had a listener; his eyes lost their intensity, regained their focus.

'Oh, nothing,' he answered, lightly, after a pause. 'It was enough to drive a person mad. That's all.'

I knew it wasn't what he'd been about to say, but never mind—I let him fob me off.

That wasn't the important thing.

'Her face,' I said. 'The face that you can't—quite—visualize . . . Are you never reminded of it at all?' (Leave well alone, my heart was urging me—it had even come into my throat to do so. Why can't you just leave well alone?)

'It's strange,' he said, 'that you should ask me that; because, not so very long ago—'

'Do *I* remind you of her?' I put my hand to my breast and looked at him wide-eyed, most charmingly a'flutter.

(You see, I told my heart, it doesn't matter what the answer is. Whatever it is, I can accept it, joyfully, and know that it is right. Acceptance. Not resignation. Submission and resilience. That is the key.)

'Oh, pardon, sir, I interrupted!'

'Perhaps,' he said, 'at odd times, you do remind me; a fleeting expression that . . . Well, what I was going to say was that just recently I did get a distinct picture of her. Suddenly. And recurrently. Though it kept on fading, unfortunately, as before.' He added, quietly: 'I had forgotten how very beautiful she was.'

194

I nodded, commiseratingly.

'Well, I certainly don't want to speak out of turn, of course. But I don't feel it can have been anyone other than I who reminded you.' I laughed. 'Well, after all, . . . it couldn't have been Celia. Oh, she's sweet, of course, and even almost pretty in a mousy sort of way—'

'No, it wasn't Celia.'

'And it certainly wasn't Sylvia.'

'No, no, not Sylvia.' We laughed together over that.

'And it just as certainly couldn't have been Roger; so it *must* have been—'

'I'll tell you when it was,' he said. My, my! Such manners. (Had I set a bad example?) But he *was* rather masterful. 'It was when you showed me that book.'

'Book?'

'Yes, you'd been to the library. Don't you remember? There were several pictures in it—of an actress that you wanted me to see. You showed me many times.'

'Because you asked me to.'

'Yes.'

It had been a little ceremony, a little act of adoration, that we'd silently enjoyed each day; for about a week.

The thing was, of course—as I had realized at the beginning—he *hadn't* recognized me yet; it wasn't at all a question of his wanting just to spare my feelings. And when he'd seen the book it was naturally *I* who had been holding it; no wonder, then, that he had got confused. He was my love—but he was not infallible. It was like when I'd seen him and Roger so very close together. I remembered how the room had almost spun. A kaleidoscope that someone had rotated—fragments of coloured glass—a mirror image shivered, shaken—a thousand shimmering reflections. Oh, such beauty, searing beauty, first in close-up, then in long shot, close-up, long shot, close-up, long shot . . . Ohohoh!

Ohohoh!

Ohoh!

Oh!

Oh . . . !

49

Rachel Anne,
Rachel Anne,
You will never be stuck for a man!

That was the chant the other children used to sing in the playground; not just the girls, either—the boys would join in as well, with equal affection, perhaps with even greater affection, since no matter how much the girls liked me, there was always, naturally, just the slightest dash of jealousy colouring their admiration. Indeed, as Eunice, my best friend and my successor for a term as Head Girl, once put it—'It's a good thing that no one can help loving you, Rachel, because otherwise we'd all be sticking pins in your effigy! We girls would. Do you realize that none of the rest of us ever gets a look-in with the boys if you're around? It's always *you* whose books they want to carry—always *you* they want to kiss and take to the pictures. Life isn't fair!'

Perhaps because I *did* realize this I was always extra nice to everyone, in an effort—I felt it was almost an obligation—to atone. I always shared out my sweets at school (and my mother's), for these of course were the post-war years, when sweets were still on ration. I lent my clothes, and I helped people with their homework when they asked, and willingly wrote some of their lines for them. ('*Manners maketh man* is the motto of Winchester College; so why don't I try to follow their example?' Sandra, who was always getting a hundred or so of these from Mrs Derry, on account of her high spirits, hesitated to ask *whose* example, in case this should add another half a paragraph!) I tried to have a cheerful word for everyone, and never a spiteful one

196

about anybody. When they made me a prefect I was renowned as the most lenient one in the school—yet I never received any cheek or had any problems over discipline. 'Oh, what it is to be beautiful *and* kind! And to excel at sports as well as classwork! No wonder all the younger girls have crushes on you!'

It was one of the teachers who said that. Another, on some later occasion, put it slightly differently. 'On top of everything else, Rachel Barnetby-Waring, I do believe that you're a saint, on leave from heaven! What's more,' she added, 'it must be rather *glum* for them up there while you're away!'

Yes, more than anything else, perhaps, there were three things I was proud of: that everybody seemed to think that I was evidently earmarked for heaven; that they all appeared to consider me such *fun*; that I was always such a triumph in the school play. (Though I repeatedly tried to emphasize in my curtain speech that the production was the result of months of hard work on the part of everybody concerned with it—a team effort of the most inspiring kind—no audience would allow me to quite get away with that.) I particularly, of course, remember the last play that we did. It was called *The Mask of Virtue* and Laurence Olivier happened to be in the audience. I say 'happened', but even if I had ever believed in such things as coincidence or luck I would have known his presence wasn't merely chance. Tipped off by some mysterious grapevine, he was there as talent scout—unassuming yet glamorous, silent, courteous, intent.

And, my word, was he glamorous! He and my mother came round to my 'dressing-room' immediately after the show. He congratulated me, but not fulsomely—with caution almost—and spoke to me unsmilingly about my performance. 'Darling, we're going to leave you to change now,' said my mother, laying her hand for a moment lovingly upon my shoulder. 'Make yourself look specially beautiful. Mr Olivier is taking us out to supper!'

197

'Larry,' corrected the young man. 'Larry to my friends.'

He took us to the Savoy Grill. I hardly knew what I ate. He was the most attractive man in the room—in the whole of the West End—in the whole of the country, or the world, I was almost willing to swear. As my mother said later, 'The eyes of everybody in that restaurant were upon you both—I don't suppose they'd ever seen another couple like you—no, never!' He was in his middle-to-late twenties; seven or eight years older than myself.

In the taxi to the High Street he wrote down our telephone number. 'May I ring you tomorrow?' he asked.

Then he suddenly exclaimed: 'No—dash it—I can't wait until tomorrow! I've already quite made up my mind! We're taking a production of *Hamlet* to Denmark in the summer. To Elsinore itself. Rachel—will you play Ophelia?'

We sat up, my mother and I, till nearly three o'clock, chatting in the kitchen in our night things, over hot drinks.

'Oh, darling, I'm so proud of you,' she said. '*What* an evening! *What* a triumph! If only Daddy could have been here to share it with us!'

'I'm sure, you know, that in a way he is.'

'I feel I want to cry. I don't mean because of that,' she added quickly, 'but because I can now see this is the final night of childhood for you, pet. You're going to leave me very soon—and it's only right and proper that you should, of course—you have your own exciting life to lead. But I can't pretend . . .' She smiled, and mimicked her own silliness, and took a sip of cocoa.

'Mummy, I shall never leave you. You know that. Not in spirit.'

'Yes, I do, my dearest.' She patted my hand. 'And I shall always be so grateful for the closeness we've enjoyed. Few other mothers and daughters, I think, can have had such a lovely relationship as ours. Sometimes I feel . . .'

'What?'

'As though I don't deserve it.' She laughed. 'Sometimes I feel I haven't been as good a mother as I'd have liked.'

I protested loudly and indignantly. 'You've been a perfect mother!'

'Shhh! Shhh! You'll wake the neighbours!'

'Then you mustn't talk such nonsense.'

'It's just that sometimes, you know—well, it hasn't always been too easy—I can tell you now that you're grown up—sometimes I've so terribly missed Daddy . . .'

'I know, Mummy, I know. Don't think I haven't understood.'

'. . . and if I ever have been less than I'd have wanted to be . . .'

'But you've been *perfect*—just perfect,' I told her again.

'Bless you for saying that, my love.'

'I *mean* it.'

'Yet all the same I want to ask your forgiveness for any little ways in which I may have failed you. Little and more especially, of course, large! No, please—this is important to me—don't say there's nothing to—'

'Then I forgive you *everything* with all my heart!' I interrupted, with a smile. 'There! Does that make you happy?'

'Yes; it sets my mind at rest.'

'But then you must do as much for me! Tell me that you forgive me for every way in which *I* have failed *you*— and for every way I ever shall.'

'Oh, there's—'

'Come on. You must play fair!'

'Very well. My forgiveness is absolute!'

'And mine, too. What a ridiculous conversation! Especially as I now believe, anyway, that even when we *think* we have something to forgive others for, we're really only blaming *them* for the faults which lie in ourselves.' I sipped my cocoa. 'For instance—just about the

199

last thing in this world I can imagine!—suppose that you became possessive . . . domineering? I would never be justified afterwards in saying that you ruined my life. (O misery me, she stole from me my birthright, my inheritance, my due!) For I could always have *broken away*! And if I wasn't up to doing so, the fault was in me and not in you!'

'You might say next, in that case, that even if I dropped a little arsenic in your bedtime drink . . . the fault would still lie in yourself!'

'Yes!'

'And the other way around. *Much* more likely—if I'm to become this creature you describe!'

'Yes!'

We roared with laughter. 'Oh, poor Mrs Fowler! Poor Mr Richards! Poor Neville and Joan!' I gasped.

'And what's more,' she said, 'the fault *would* be in me. And I forgive you unconditionally . . . ! But now I think we'd really better go to bed.'

We grew more serious for a moment. 'Besides,' I said, 'there's always a pattern. There would always be a purpose. God would be leading us ever on . . . to eventual sunshine. No matter what—through what form of hell. I firmly believe that.'

We stood up and left the saucepan and the cups in water and put away the biscuit tin. We hugged each other. 'I know what I believe,' said my mother. 'That *you* deserve to win through to success and happiness and glory as no one else I know!'

'Correction—as *everyone* else you know. Life is a vale of tears, life is a battleground—and who are we to judge the merits or demerits of a single travelling contestant?' I had my two hands to my breast as I declaimed this, and we both declared I was my Aunt Alicia!

In bed—despite the lateness of the hour and the silence of the pub across the way—I lay awake for a long time; but, strangely, not thinking so much about the future as about the past. This was indeed in a way the last night of my childhood; and it isn't everyone who can point to it so accurately, even as it's passing. I loved my room; I loved my bed; and in some ways I hated to think that they might now be slipping away from me. Home. Love. Safety. My bed was at the very root of home—my craft, my sanctuary, my dreamland; the place where I'd been tickled, healed, pampered most, comforted most, loved the most demonstratively; hung my Christmas stocking. Home.

Home was the place it was always so good to get back to—from your holiday. I loved our fortnights by the sea—especially, perhaps, when my father had been there to bury me in sand, build me castles, make me kites, give me pick-a-backs, teach me how to swim. 'You're my Sir Galahad,' I cried, 'Sir Galahad, Sir Galahad!' He answered: 'I think it's the first time I ever heard of the charger sitting astride the knight!' . . . but no matter, from then on, that's who he was. Yet even after he was gone, we still managed to have lots of fun, Queen Guinevere and I. (I myself, for some reason, never had an identity.) We would stroll out to fetch the papers before breakfast, filling our lungs with fresh sea air, and have an early cup of tea at a café on the front, watching the seagulls wheel above the prom. We would listen to the band and sometimes request particular pieces of music. (One year my mother rather fancied the band-leader—we laughed a lot about that.) We would go to the fol-de-rolles at the end of the pier. We would have a late-night cup of Ovaltine at Fortes, and we would sit up companionably in our twin beds reading our novels and eating a Crunchie—like Eunice and *her* mother sometimes used to do on holiday. (Sandra's, too, had once had a thing for a band-leader—but *he*, it appeared, hadn't responded in the least!) Oh, it was all such fun. Yet, just the same, it always felt extremely good to get home again. 'Back to our little grey home in Paradise Street!' I remember saying; though it wasn't at all grey and it wasn't really in Paradise Street—only *my* room and the bathroom over-looked it.

Home . . . I thought of how we used to sit together listening to the wireless, my mother perhaps doing some tapestry work, I, if it was music, getting on with my homework. (But if it was *Much-Binding-in-the-Marsh*, of course, or *Educating Archie* or a play that we were listening to, homework was out of the question.) On Sunday nights we used to eat hot toast with dripping and listen to *Grand Hotel*. That was generally after we'd got back from the first performance at the Classic.

Home . . . Saturday afternoons in summer by the lake in Regent's Park, having walked up a lazy, drowsing High Street, carrying our books and our deckchairs and licking our ice-creams . . . Visits to my great-aunt Alicia: always a Lyons cake on the table, with its coronet of yellow icing a good half-inch thick, which she swore had just been baked by Bridget. Always chocolate biscuits in profusion—*they*, perhaps, had come from a shop—and a scolding for my mother if she drew attention to how many I was eating. Always a song from *Bitter Sweet*. Luxury. Insulation. Permanence. Always the fascination of the loom . . . Songs around the piano at the pub. (The first time we went in, my mother was prepared to lie about my age, but it was never necessary.) She once sang a solo—after a great deal of persuasion: 'Other People's Babies'. She scored a tremendous hit with it—I felt so proud. It seemed she had an unexpected gift for merging comedy with pathos—so much so, that, as you listened, you almost thought here was a real nanny, old now, unwanted, just living on her memories—but rich and happy with the warmth of them. That song became her speciality, and I had one, too, though it never achieved quite the same success, which I was glad of (I must admit that I deliberately held back)—something by Cole Porter.

> Experiment—
> Make that your motto day and night;
> Experiment—
> And you will someday reach the light . . .

We used to spend at least one evening a week there—'our local'. We would sip sparingly at our sherries to make them last, though we were often treated to drinks, we found, because people were just so glad to have us there. They'd say, 'Oh, don't go home yet!'—not understanding, of course, that 'home' doesn't literally need to be bounded by one's own four walls . . .

So altogether—I realized it even then, lying in bed with a silly small-hours lump in my throat—it was something that would always be a part of me, and I was glad.

Even then, I knew that I should always miss it.

Despite the excitement of Elsinore—and Larry—and my career; and of all that lay ahead.

50

Sometimes, even towards the end of November, I went to sit in the park. Luckily the weather had continued mild—and sunny—so I was still able to wear my picture hat; and just a cardigan over my white dress was usually sufficient. I went to the park because I needed the exercise and fresh air and because I could no longer afford to go into cafés or to look for down-and-outs, into whose grubby palms I could press a clean pound note, and because when I searched for ordinary housewives or widows waiting by their garden gates for somebody (almost *anyone* would do, poor souls) to tell about their latest operation or the shameful way their daughter-in-law was treating them . . . well, maybe it was the approach of winter that sent them hurrying indoors. I don't know. But the ducks were made of hardier stuff and I could talk to them all right.

But, yes, poor souls. I felt compassionate to all the world. I had so much; I could afford a giant compassion. I had Larry—I had Horatio—I had Roger and Celia and Thomas (and that, despite my love's misgivings—Larry's—Horatio's?—really did seem to be working out extraordinarily well; we were all so very happy; even Mark was thinking of moving in as well: a real little commune)—and I had my health, my looks, and quantities of admiration. I was in my very prime; and, better still, was one of those rare fortunate people given the foresight to appreciate it while it was still mine and not just pine in retrospect for something that was gone—life's saddest situation.

And best of all, of course—and *very* best of all: I was *blooming*.

Yes.

At last.

Which was, naturally, the reason that I needed exercise. And fresh air. Every day, it seemed, the bulge became more noticeable. I was so glad I didn't have to wear a coat.

I was extra proud that I was blooming—exceptionally so, despite the usual morning sickness—for I had noticed that people couldn't help but gaze at me; small boys made wolf whistles. And this didn't embarrass me. I accepted it rather as a glamorous film star must—not as her due (that sounds oh—horridly presumptuous) but with grateful recognition and a lot of secret pleasure. Sometimes I even inclined my head, rather graciously, in acknowledgement.

I had also written a letter to a famous women's magazine. It was so important, I said, not to take your husband (or husbands) for granted, not to grow careless over your appearance simply because you were married, because your man (or men) was hooked and landed. A woman's appearance, I said, was such a very lovely thing, God-given and so precious, and of course she had a sacred duty towards it, *even after marriage*—oh, how I stressed that point. Wives, I said, *must* always be lovers, too—and I wrote out for them the whole lyric of the song, only putting in dots where I couldn't quite remember the words. I offered, indeed, to write them a series on marriage and beauty and its attendant responsibilities; on how to hold your man; my life with Larry; my brief, idyllic, poignant love-affair with James

Dean; and, above all, on some marvellous fucks I had had and on how to prepare yourself for motherhood.

It was kind of them. They seemed so pleased with the idea that they sent three of their most important editors to come and discuss it with me. Two men and a woman. They joined me one morning in the park.

'Hello,' they said, and sat down on the bench, on either side of me. I had expected to meet them in London, but had forgotten that the journalistic nose, having once scented a scoop, wouldn't just wait to let the hair grow out of its nostrils.

I introduced myself; though clearly this was quite unnecessary. 'It is so nice of you to come.' We shook hands; they seemed touchingly surprised at my politeness. That made me more than ever determined not to let them see my disappointment: I'd been imagining how it would feel to be welcomed into their Fleet Street office, a personality, someone of just a little consequence. 'You should have given me some warning, though.' I laughed; I felt perfectly at ease. 'If I'd known you were coming I'd have baked a cake!'

'No need for cakes,' said the lady. (I wasn't *sure* that she had seen my little joke.) 'Isn't it nice here?'

'Yes, it's a very lovely park.' (And really it didn't matter; it had only been a very *feeble* joke.)

'We hear you come quite often.'

'Oh, what it is to be famous!'

We all smiled at one another—the four of us already the best of pals. 'I always had this facility for making friends,' I told them.

'Would you like to come with us?' said the woman. 'We've got a car just over there.'

'I'd prefer to sit and talk for a moment. If that's all right.'

'Very well, then.' She looked at her wristwatch; it was a man's one, with a broad leather strap. 'Just five minutes.'

'You know—your watch rather reminds me of Sylvia's.'

205

'Who is Sylvia?'

' "Holy, fair, and wise is she"—and that's no exaggeration, either! She's an angel—the best woman friend I ever had; apart, perhaps, from my mother. When my mother died I was with E.N.S.A., delighting our boys in the Middle East. (And you know what they would say to me—oh, many a time? "Ma'am, you have given us back our reason for living—you alone, ma'am, single-handed." Indeed, it was sometimes difficult to know how to answer them, revealing all the gratitude that I felt in my heart, yet with becoming modesty. "Oh, fiddle-de-fuck, my dears," I'd laugh. I think I got that just right—don't you?) Well, Sylvia stood proxy for me at my mother's deathbed. She told me it was the sweetest thing that she ever witnessed. My mother said just before she went—Mummy, I mean, not Sylvia—that she saw friends coming along the road to greet her, with outstretched arms, and she heard music, the most beautiful music that ever was; and she passed, Sylvia told me, with a positive smile of joy upon her face. And I hope—and I believe—that when the time comes just such a thing can happen to all of us. The *big* adventure. Well, Sylvia herself was so affected by it that she periodically thinks about taking the veil. She's really earned herself that soubriquet, "holy". She watches *The Sound of Music* on her video recorder—oh, twenty times a week.'

I smiled.

'Such stories cheer one, don't they? Though I confess I do embroider. Seven times a week is more the truth.'

'Shall we go now?' said the woman.

'Oh, just a little longer . . . It's so very pleasant here.'

She complied; I wanted to reward her. What other preview should I give her?

'You know . . . He was always kissing me—holding my hand—he didn't mind who saw. He would say, "How's my pussycat?" "I'm fine, puss. How are you?" "What kind of a day did you have? Well, sit down and tell me about it." And he would say, "Happy Christmas, puss, my puss." We were the most popular couple in Hollywood—the most envied, the most glamorous. He told the press: "I don't suppose there ever was a couple so much in love." I said at the same time, "Our love affair has been simply the most divine fairy tale, hasn't it?" And they printed it, you know, in *Life* magazine. Glorious.'

I looked to the woman for comment. She said, 'Very nice.' I hoped that she didn't think I was belittling *Feminist* by mentioning *Life*. The men just smiled. They were the strong and silent type. I pressed my thigh close to that of the one who sat beside me on my right. I myself didn't actually get much of a thrill, but I was happy to think that I had brightened up *his* day a little further.

I smiled at him. 'Hey, genius. I'd like you to meet your Scarlett O'Hara.'

But those weren't *my* words; I may have opened my mouth—it was dear Myron's voice that issued. Before our very eyes Atlanta had risen from the water, a roaring furnace of flame and smoke and showering sparks, and I stood there in my broad-brimmed black hat, with the fire's reflection leaping in my eyes, and my complexion prettily aglow in the rosy, flickering light, and I heard him say, 'The end of years of searching. Nearly fifteen hundred interviews; over ninety actual tests. Every female star in Hollywood of even vaguely the right age; the most publicized hunt in screen history through all America. Now here she stands before you—the perfect choice, the perfect girl.'

'Well . . . fiddle-de-fuck!' I cried. 'And thank 'ee kindly, sir.'

The flames died down into the water. Little Lord Fauntleroy's drawing-room, temples from *The Garden of Allah*, forests from *The Last of the Mohicans*, skyscrapers from *King Kong*—all sank beneath the burning lake. The ducks returned. I stood up again—peered at them anxiously. Not a single feather singed in this awesome conflagration. Thank God. Thank God.

The editors had stood again, too. Fleet Street of course

might be a jungle, but *some* had learned from contact with politeness.

I sat once more. Uncertainly, they did the same. We were like a little row of jack-in-the-boxes, held down by the same lid. Togetherness. Well, that was nice.

'No roast duck *this* year for Christmas!' I joked.

And then I frowned. No more 'Happy Christmas, puss, my puss,' either. For he had aged so rapidly. He was an old man; while I was still a girl. Had it been wrong of me to take him? Yes. Should I have left him there, in Shangri-La? Yes. But could I really have done otherwise? We rode a streetcar named Desire, and few of us had the strength to clamber down.

So quite suddenly it came upon me—melancholy. There *were* clouds in the sky; I had sensed for some time they were gathering. Useless to try to close your eyes to them forever. It was so tiring. Resilience was so tiring. Awareness. Gaiety. These, too—they needed super-human strength.

And I felt so frail, all of a sudden; so far beyond being able to go on, day after day, making the effort. *I* hadn't got a superhuman strength. I sometimes prayed to God for strength; but I wondered now, abruptly, if God really listened.

This was my punishment, I thought. Life was a vale of tears; sorrow, the pervasive, inescapable experience of mankind. Retribution. Karma. Had I really believed that *I* could get away? I was no expert in escape.

No more 'What kind of a day did you have? Sit down and tell me about it.'?

And even Mrs Pond had never come to tea. Nor—more unhappily—had Doreen.

And he had thrown my Oscar out into the garden, because he had said that I was getting too high-handed.

But I couldn't really help it—hadn't he seen that? Not any more than he.

Oh, Larry.

And why, God, why, oh why—little Alfredo Rampi? Myself, I'd been so happy; I had had so very much. Was it not right to look for happiness—to think the world was good, or could be made so? Did anyone have the right to live in a fool's paradise—did millions, even—so long as just one person shrieked?

And was that all that it could ever be? At best? (Small comfort just to talk of the Millennium.)

A paradise for fools.

I stood up. (They all jumped up beside me.) I felt so very old: an invalid who needed three attendants. 'Shall we go?' I think I even smiled.

I had my baby to consider.

We walked along the tarmac path, a kind, attentive escort on either side of me, the woman walking close by on the grass. Those men in fact were gentlemen: each one had given me his arm. I said—and now I certainly put on a smile—'Who claims the age of chivalry is dead?' I felt that in a moment the three of us might all skip along together—

We're off to see the wizard,
The wonderful wizard of Oz.

It wasn't a tarmac path at all; how foolish of me—I should have seen: this was of course the yellowbrick road. 'Will he have a red enamel heart to give me, do you think?'

Suddenly I felt so *ungrateful*. The thin sunshine cast shadows on the ground in front of us. The sky was pale—but it was blue. People shrieked in the dark—little children amongst them—yet that was no reason for *me* not to try and sing in the daylight. What kind of series was I going to write for them, anyway? They didn't want something lugubrious. They wanted to hear about cheerful things; of course they did; everybody did.

'Shall we sing as we go?'

'You sing.'

'What shall it be?'

'There's the car.'

'I don't know that one . . . (That was a joke)' I said. 'It

209

ought to be, "We're busy doing nothing . . ."—you two as William Bendix and Sir Cedric Hardwicke, me as Bing Crosby. But what about "There's no business like show business", instead?'

In the car my gentlemen sat warmly pressed on either side of me; I felt so cosseted. We drove to a large grey house, not very far away, behind grey walls. It was an imposing place in which to have your offices—if not really a pretty one. 'Have you driven all the way from London this morning?' I asked, still trying to make some entertaining small talk to my nice but *slightly* unresponsive audience. 'You must have set out very early. Long day's journey into night, indeed! (Poetic licence: I know it's only noon!) Or rather—long night's journey into day—into soft yet blinding sunlight—that's the way I much prefer to look upon it, don't you? But then, of course, I *am* a believer—and an optimist—and what I enjoy more than anything else, I think, is a success story. In fact, my dears, I'm going to let you into a tiny secret. If I should ever write my autobiography— and I can see that that day could very shortly be upon us—the demands of my public, you know, so charming and so kind—that is precisely what I intend to call it: *Success Story*.' Unfortunately, though, I missed what was written on the board by the gates. I hadn't wanted to miss anything.

We went inside. It was by no means as luxurious as London must have been.

There was a long bare corridor and people in white overalls. They took me into a reception room with highly polished lino; and somebody brought me a cup of tea. It was very strong and sweet (I don't take sugar) in a thick white cup that had a great chip in its rim and, besides, was very grubby-looking. I didn't feel like a personality; a lady who had always been important and who always would be; and in addition someone of just a little consequence to *them*.

I took no more than a sip; having carefully wiped that part of the rim with my little lace-edged handkerchief.

'Please—I think that I should like to be driven home now.' I stood up and adjusted my gloves and my hat; even in retreat a lady had to look her best. Exits were always quite as important, of course, as entrances. I picked up my handbag and my parasol and smiled, as nice a smile as I could manage under the circumstances, as though I hadn't been affected by the chill of institution walls or disgusted by that brown and soupy tea. For nothing good, I knew, could ever grow within a setting such as that; our discussions must be held elsewhere. I smiled—to make it clear that I awaited their convenience.

But attitudes seemed to have changed. My three editors appeared totally to have abandoned me; I couldn't understand it. Instead, sitting squarely by the door, was the stout, overalled woman who had brought me my tea. Her face might once have been gentle, even pretty, but she had unfortunately thick ankles.

Perhaps it had not been very tactful, in her presence, to display my own. I should have kept them covered with my dress.

'I'd like to go now,' I repeated.

'The doctor will be here in a moment, dear. Just a little more patience; there's a good girl.'

'About the baby, do you mean?'

'To examine you, my love.'

'That's very thoughtful—very thoughtful indeed; an attention which I really hadn't expected. I can see that *Feminist* looks after its employees. But, between ourselves, I should so much rather see my own physician. I was planning to, anyway, in a day or two.' I gave a little laugh. 'I've got to find out all about ante-natal clinics and things. I'm quite a beginner, you know, but I didn't want to rush off, bothering people, the very instant that I first found out. I refuse to be a fusspot.'

'Doctor will be here in a moment,' she repeated. She was very kind, but it was as though she hadn't heard a thing. I began to feel quite angry.

I said, 'I know I shall be writing a series of articles for this magazine on motherhood and marriage and what to do if one breast hangs lower than the other, which I appreciate is quite a problem for the vast majority of women; but I'm afraid I don't quite see why *I* should have a check-up on account of it.

My own tits are perfectly symmetrical.'

(Untrue, untrue. It had always been a worry for me that one seemed smaller than the other. In fact—I was inclined to be neurotic over it. Sometimes it was the left, sometimes the right, that looked the less well-favoured.)

Besides, they hadn't given me sufficient warning. It was no easy matter—performing one's ablutions in a wedding dress. Perhaps they wouldn't realize all the difficulties.

I was not going to subject myself to such humiliation.

'May I get by, please?'

'Sorry, duck. You've got to stay here just a minute. Then, after the doctor's been, they'll take you up to bed. You can have a nice rest before you meet some of the others. We'll hold you back some lunch.'

'This isn't,' I said, 'a newspaper office.'

'No, dear.'

'You make it sound like some sort of hospital.'

'Well . . .'

I struck her with my reticule; there was my copy of *Pride and Prejudice* inside it, and the Reverend Lionel Wallace's *Life*, and the book about King David. I don't know which one of them got her; oh, of course—all three. I had swung the reticule with every bit of my strength and caught her, heavily, on the side of the chin. She only swayed for a second or two, but that was enough. I was through the door and running down the corridor.

All the other people in overalls had disappeared for the minute. There was no one in sight.

And as I ran I suddenly realized the truth. There had been a simply frightful error. It was a case of mistaken identity. This was a lunatic asylum.

It flashed upon me in all its dreadful clarity. Some poor soul must have been certified and her physical description had tallied, to some extent at least, with my own.

Which meant she must be young and probably rather nice looking. And I felt so desperately sorry for her. Despite the awfulness of my own situation at that moment, my thoughts were very largely with this unknown woman whom they had mistaken me for. How unimaginably terrible—at any age, at any age, but especially perhaps when you were young and beautiful and had such bright hopes for the future—to know that there were people, your own family maybe, your own so-called friends, people no doubt whom you had loved and trusted, who were willing to do this indescribably dreadful thing to you. How you must feel betrayed! Perplexed, wronged (so unutterably wronged)—betrayed. Poor bewildered creature. I would find out who she was and I would come to visit her. I would give her back something of her trust and her self-respect. If at present she was feeling frightened, I knew that she'd be thinking that she would always feel frightened. I would try to soothe away her fears.

It was not unimaginable, after all. I found that I could imagine it only too easily.

But I thought that I'd been wrong in one respect. It would be equally terrible if you were young or old—or middle-aged. There are no degrees of terror.

Yet in the meantime I still had my own predicament to consider. It was only a temporary embarrassment, of course, but it would no doubt be quite complicated, and degrading. Difficult, even, to pass off as a joke. 'Well, did you ever?—they actually carted me off to the loony bin; they thought that *I* had been committed! What a mad, mad world we live in!'

No, of course it would make a joke—almost anything would. Rather a splendid one, indeed. It was really very funny.

Oh, it was so *good* to have friends. I, if anyone, knew fully how to appreciate them. I, if anyone, could recognize their worth.

The asylum was situated on the top of a hill. This was good: out through the entrance hall, out through the open gates (I ducked past, at the side of a hearse then coming in), the descent adding momentum to my desperation and near-panic—I could already discern noises of pursuit. There was a bus going down the hill and people waiting for it at a bus stop. With both hands lifting my dress clear of the pavement—despite the reticule I clutched in one, and the parasol in the other—and with my lovely white picture hat, which had slipped down from my head, battering itself against my shoulders while it strained and fretted at my throat, I ran after that bus in my flying satin slippers. And as I ran I cried, 'Hold on, little one. Mama doesn't mean to harm you. It's a bumpy ride but it will soon be over.' I could imagine him standing there, scrabbling at the walls of my stomach, white-faced, wanting to climb into my arms for reassurance; and while I ran I did my best to bring him comfort.

I caught the bus. The conductor helped me on—a coloured man and such a gentleman. But the passengers at once moved further down inside, craning to stare at me—and some with nervous titters—as though even in so short a time something of those bare, stone-floored corridors had managed to rub off on me, making them afraid.

Some schoolboys from the upper deck jostled and gaped together on the bottom stairs.

And the bus would not set off.

'Please ring the bell,' I said to the conductor. 'There's no one left to come.' I could hardly get my breath.

'We're a few minutes early, madam,' he said to me politely; and I saw then that the driver was climbing down from his cab.

Oh God, I thought, oh God—please help me. You who understand everything. You who know how very scared I suddenly am beneath this brave exterior.

And as I watched the driver and conductor talking to each other earnestly on the pavement, glancing surreptitiously from time to time in my direction, and saw everyone bunched well away from me and holding out no straws, regarding me as they might something unfamiliar that had just escaped from the zoo, a totally unknown quantity, and saw too the men now running down the hill in their white coats, and one of them carrying a bulky wad of something which I instinct-ively recognized as a straitjacket (but a straitjacket might harm my baby; I wouldn't—I couldn't—let them use it)—I thought suddenly: This can't be happening.

It's a fantasy, a nightmare—it is quite unreal. I'll wake up soon and then there'll be a happy ending. This can't be happening. Not to me. Not *me*. Not the girl who once went to Paris and sat quietly eating Lyons cake at Neville Court. The

214

girl whose father had sung to her: 'Oh, the days of the Kerry dancing . . .': and rocked her gently on his knee, and buried her up to the chin in sand. The girl who had won two Academy Awards and gained the love of perhaps the most eminent actor of his time . . . a man, however, whom in the end she'd had to relinquish, since the one for whom she'd always been meant had been ready to claim her as his own. (But she had so *much* love to give—she still had so very much.) The girl who had taken Sylvia to one murder play after another and—just before leaving London—to the revival of *My Fair Lady*; and who had usually gone back to Sainsbury's in Marylebone High Street to do the Saturday morning shopping. No, this couldn't be happening. Not to me. Not to anyone. I was a person. We were all people. I had an identity, I had feelings, I didn't wish anybody any harm. Oh, didn't they see?

I was *me*. These days, I *did* have an identity. I knew who I was.

Only the violent had to be restrained. Was this other woman—the one I'd been mistaken for—was *she* a source of danger?

And I thought again, Oh please, God, help me. If I go down on my knees to you, unashamed, in full view of all these people, oh will you listen to me then?

And I did so. And I did so—although there were torn-off strips of ticket and a screwed-up chocolate wrapper and the dust and dirt off a thousand pairs of shoes, and my rose-embroidered silk was so very, very pretty. But what did it matter any more about this?

I said: 'It isn't me that I care about; it's my baby, my son, my small Horatio. And you must see that it's my duty to protect him. He's mine and I love him. I love him. It doesn't matter what he's like. He could be ugly. Deformed. Even—if such a thing were really part of your design—he could be mentally defective. Just so long as he isn't—yet he couldn't be—irredeemably—wicked. But whatever he is—I shall reverence him—because he's yours as much as he is mine, and therefore has a right to be reverenced—until he should show himself unworthy.'

And I tried to wipe away the tears on the back of my white gloves and I said:

'So—don't you *see*—we've just got to get home? Whatever happens—whatever happens—oh, listen, Lord—*somehow* we've just got to get home. You see . . . that's where I know we shall be happy. There are people there, good people, who'll always look after us—at home.'

But now the men in their white coats were there, and the passengers had started to inch forward: threatening, yet not unkind, and in their hearts, perhaps, no less afraid than I was.

Mrs Pimm was on the bus.

'Help us, Mrs Pimm.'

But she turned her rosy cheeks away, and as she did so a shiver of despair again went through me. It's so *hard* to be valiant against all disaster, I wanted to explain to her. Not long before I met you I turned over a new leaf. An immense new leaf, yet at first it seemed so light. Now—though I haven't yet supported it a year—I feel that it could crush me. I mustn't let it. Not *now*. Not just when new life is—almost literally—beginning. But I can't hold it up alone. Please help me.

Please.

Yet still she kept her gaze averted. And the men were pulling me up, quite gently, from my knees.

But suddenly it was all right. Incredibly all right. Suddenly I remembered the password: the password that would gain us entry into any group, open all gates to us. Oh, just in time, just in time. The password for which I had been searching all my life, miraculously re-revealed to me in this moment of extremity. 'The curse is come upon me,' I cried, laughing, tears of happiness running warmly down my cheeks. 'Listen, everyone. The curse is come upon me! Please let us in.'

A curse? Such irony—such charming irony! But sing it to the tune of 'Pretty Baby'—that would make it right.

The tears ran down unchecked; this time it didn't matter who should see. My joy was so intense I felt my heart must surely burst in ecstasy—could any mortal bear to be so happy? I smiled at the men who stood beside me. 'I have always,' I said, 'depended upon the kindness of strangers.' That seemed so right. And then, just a second or two before my legs finally folded under me and I sagged between the arms that held me, I looked around at everyone and beamed. All movement stilled and they appeared to freeze into a tableau—so gorgeously and yet so softly coloured. I had this picture of them standing in a garden, like the recreation garden of my childhood, only far more beautiful—and *they* were far more beautiful—and there was lovely music coming from the bandstand. I bestowed on all of them my blessing. Or, at least, I had intended to. I had wanted to let them know that it was all all right, that everything was fine. I had intended to say:

'Oh, fiddle-de-fuck, my dears! Just fiddle-de-fuck!'

ACKNOWLEDGEMENTS

Every effort has been made to trace the owners of copyright material, but in some cases this has not been possible.

'If Love Were All' from *Bitter Sweet*
Words and Music by Noel Coward
© 1929 Chappell & Co. Ltd.

'I'll See You Again' from *Bitter Sweet*
Words and Music by Noel Coward
© 1929 Chappell & Co. Ltd.

'The Boyfriend' from *The Boyfriend*
Words and Music by Sandy Wilson
© 1954 Chappell & Co. Ltd.

'It's Only a Paper Moon' from *Take a Chance*
Music by Harold Arlen
Words by Billy Rose and E. Y. Harburg
© 1933 Harms Inc. (Warner Bros.)
British Publisher Chappell Music Ltd.

'Ten Cents a Dance' from *Simple Simon*
Music by Richard Rodgers
Words by Lorenz Hart
© 1933 Harms Inc. (Warner Bros.)
British Publisher Chappell Music Ltd.

'September Song' from *Knickerbocker Holiday*
Music by Kurt Weill
Words by Maxwell Anderson
© 1938 De Sylva, Brown & Henderson Inc.
British Publisher Chappell Music Ltd.

'I Wonder Who's Kissing Her Now'
© 1909 Chas. K. Harris Music Publishing Co. (USA)
Reproduced by permission of EMI Music Publishing Ltd.,
138–140 Charing Cross Road, London WC2H OLD